THE SCARLET LILY

THE
SCARLET LILY

by

EDWARD F. MURPHY

THE BRUCE PUBLISHING COMPANY
Milwaukee

This book is printed in complete accord with the Government
rules and regulations for the conservation of paper and other
essential materials.

(Third Printing)

DEDICATED
TO
JOHN F. REILLY

FOREWORD

The Magdalene's vice, as Bourdaloue remarks, was that she had many lovers, and her virtue was that she loved much. From this observation, I have spun my story: necessarily weaving many a fancy into the fewness of known facts, and depending no little on the might-have-been.

"The Scarlet Lily" is not at all intended for Scripturalists or other exactors, but for such readers as have no objection to a fictional presentation of a Biblical character and are ready to sense in Mary of Magdala a type of our modern world — fallen from grace, groping in darkness, and at last finding the light, white with death and ruby with sacrifice, at the pierced feet of the Lover supreme.

THE AUTHOR

1

Herod could not sleep.

The little boat-shaped lamp of gold on a table beside his bed lapped the tomb-like darkness with the palest of tongues, and sent up wisps of bluish smoke which seemed to be molded slowly, slowly, by some invisible sculptor-hand, as unsubstantial as themselves, into a face. First, a forehead, distilling drops of sweat and waxen as in the last moments of life; then a pair of lids, languidly opening and revealing a lack-lustre stare; then a small proud nose, lips vague and almost lotus white, a soft-rounded chin, and a neck dripping with scarlet.

"Mariamne — Mariamne," the king begged, turning on his side and burying his face in the pillow, "do not come to me like this. I loved you —"

"Loved?" moaned a voice. And the great room was separated from the rest of the world by the sad and lonely sound. "Does love kill love?"

All atremble, the king forced himself to sit up. Flinging off the coverlets, he fixed his gaze on the face, only to find it dissolving back into the vapor from which it had taken shape. But other faces came to float in the darkness of the chamber, and soon it was alive with the very deadness of them. His three slain sons; the hundreds of chiefs whom he had caused to be stoned; murdered servants — friends —

"Why?" their awful silence questioned. "Why?"

Through dry cracked lips, his answer projected itself in almost a shriek. "Because you stood in my way! A crown can be held in place only by a strong hand. I had to be ruthless. I had either to wield the sword or become even as you. A weak king is no king at all."

The quiet of the dead, horrible in itself, again broke into speech which was more fearful. "Are you strong?" they taunted in maddening unison. "You are quivering, as the sere leaf on a barren tree quivers. You are smitten with disease: your flesh crawls with sores. This palace, though filled with food and drink, leaves your stomach empty and your throat afire with thirst. Your swollen feet can scarce support the vile structure that is your body, even as your greedy hands can hardly hold the poor power that, with the aid of the alien violators of this land, you have wrested to yourself."

"I am a king!" he defied.

The room shook with unhallowed mirth. "A king?" echoed the chorus. "Is he a king who cannot rule even himself and, therefore, renders his crown a mockery? Is he a king who, to the Romans, is a slave? What royal works have you ever accomplished?"

"I restored the ancient capital of this kingdom to glory —"

"And reduced the kingdom itself to tears and shame."

"I rebuilt the Temple of Solomon."

"And desecrated everything for which it stands."

Seizing the evil lamp from which these eerie accusers rose, Herod hurled it across the room; and it struck the opposite wall with a resounding thud, and the pale flame went out. Blackness filled the air and the spirit-faces vanished. But one reappeared — the one of her for whom Herod had protested his love.

"You shall know of a real king, my husband," her

blanched lips promised, "ere you come to join me. A king who will neither need nor carry a sword. A king of meekness, comeliness and sublime simplicity. Mark you, Herod: a real king — the kind with whom the vision of man has never been hitherto blessed."

"Mariamne, tell me more. Who can he be?"

"Come."

The spirit led him tottering from the bed to the single window in the room and motioned him to draw aside the heavy curtain that kept out the crisp air of the winter night; and when he had done this, letting in a wave of moonbeams, it drew a frail translucent finger out of space and pointed to the sky.

He blinked away the mist that marred his sight and looked up; and he could not believe what he saw, for lately the horrors of the grave had appeared more actual to him than the beauty of the heavens, and for years he had been looking down to earth rather than above and beyond it; and now he gasped. There, in a patina of silver, a star, so incomparably bright that all the others were as if they were not, was ruling the deepest recesses of the firmament; a mighty pearl, all agleam, in a foamy sea of innocent blue that blended into a limitless expanse of purple royal.

"It is the very sovereign of the sky!" he breathed. "Has all the light of the world grown old and died, only to be reborn, thrice as wondrous, in this unique shining? Mariamne, tell me, if you can, what it signifies?"

"Fair in itself, it announces a fairer."

"I — I don't understand."

"Time — the little of it that is left you — will be your teacher."

"I — I —"

But Herod, dropping the curtain and turning around,

[3]

found that he was again alone; and his sense of loneliness took the form of icy fingers clutching his heart until the throbbing almost ceased; and the darkness, fold on fold, smothered him.

"Mariamne," he called piteously, groping in the gloom. It was torture to have her here, and yet a greater torment to have her gone.

Weakly he tried to reach and raise the curtain once more, but the effort was too much for him, and he sank in complete exhaustion to the floor.

When the gray of dawn was creeping along the edges of the drapery of the window, Josue, a servant, entered the room and lifted up the wasted royalty of Israel; and he thought, with mingled pity and surprise, "This great man is no heavier than a child."

About the ninth hour, that day, Herod recovered from his stupor and presently ordered his slaves to carry him to the Temple. The feeling that he was a corpse and that this was a kind of funeral procession kept chilling his bones; for had not the night been peopled with the dead, and had he not been almost one of them? Mariamne had spoken of "the little time that was left him." But the star — that was a fresh and living thing; and every such thing must have a meaning. A new light had risen in the sky over Israel: might not a new life be stirring beneath it? Mariamne had said: "Fair in itself, it announces a fairer." Too, she had mentioned a new king. Did these two sayings make one? In order to know, he must consult the high priest.

His hand feebly thrust aside the curtains of the litter, made of sandalwood and lacquer and canopied with crimson, which six coal-black athletes from Abyssinia were carrying on their shoulders, though two would have been enough. "How one's needs dwindle with one's days!" he sighed to himself, thinking of the times when, on similar visits to the House of the Lord, he used to require a great number of attendants and a select band of trumpeters, whereas now the idea of an entourage sickened him. He had come to hate people, because he sensed how few were the faithful and dependable among them. The more of them that surrounded him, the more possibility there was of assassins; and so it had become his custom to let fewer and fewer approach him intimately, until now there was only one — the young man Josue — in whom he placed any real confidence. His rheumy eyes, scarcely holding a flicker of interest, took in the scenery drifting by. Zion, Bezetha, Acra and Moriah were lifting their whitened summits to the sun, with the homes of the poor and the rich perched on their sides in dreary tiers, so that the city resembled four huge collections of wintry tombs. True, there were many people in the narrow dirty streets, but nearly everyone seemed so touched with a degree of sadness or care that Herod could not help thinking of them all as candidates, like himself, for the grave. Here was a city yearning for life and nevertheless fated for death. The Roman eagles — vultures! — were poised above it as if to tear it apart at any time, and carry off long coils of entrails in their filthy beaks. The happiness of the people was gone, and only a stubborn hope for a Messianic deliverer lingered in its stead. Here was a city of shadows through which the citizens, almost lifeless in their humiliation and degradation, moved in a mechanical routine of daily acts, waiting, waiting for the proud era of David and Solomon to return and feeding their hearts on dust.

To shake off his gloom, Herod tried to fix his mind on the Temple ahead.

"Josue," he called; and the bronzed, firm-shouldered, slim-waisted youth walking beside him came close. "I wish to talk with you."

"What does your Majesty care to say?"

"Nothing. One talks mostly to relieve a mood. — Tell me, have I not out-Solomoned the son of David?"

"In what way, Sire?"

Herod frowned. "Stupid one, I have built more grandly for Jerusalem than Solomon ever dreamed. A thousand carts brought from the quarries the stones of my Temple —"

"Your Temple, Sire? Did you not intend it to be Jehovah's?"

"Of course, of course, fool. — Tens of thousands of hands cut those stones to measure and put them in place. Eight years have I spent already in lavishing choicest marble and metal on my project, and the labor still goes on. See how, even at a distance, the mass shines and glimmers."

"True!"

"Even the Romans, whose city on the Tiber abounds in splendid architecture, admire what I have done. Behold how immense are my columns. It would take three times the span of your out-stretched arms, boy, to encircle a single one of them. And the cornices shame Dionysius with their bunches of golden grapes."

"It is mighty. Yet have I seen more sparkling beauty —"

"Where?"

"In the face of the heavens by night, and in the faces of little children by day."

Herod lapsed into a testy silence, for he was quickly minded by this young fellow's sentimental words of the star which he himself had seen excelling all the grandeur of earth and, as a father, he had known the appeal of

[6]

small soft faces which all the art in the world could not compeer.

"You weary me," he yawned affectedly. "Move aside."

The litter was soon at the first terrace of the Temple, where pagans and aliens, along with the Jews, were privileged to foregather. Ready hands seized and held up the corners of the heavy tapestries between the two central pillars, to let the great guest pass within; and heads bowed low; but lips were curled in sardonic smiles when eyes caught glimpses, through the flapping curtains, of the ill and aged one who ranked first in Israel and looked too weak to raise a hand, much less hold a sceptre. And a shadow, cast by the litter, stained the polished tiles of the terrace as if some dark fluid were being poured out on them by a mischievous soul released from Sheol.

At the second court, reserved for the Israelites, the slaves put their royal burden down, and Josue rolled back all the curtains and arranged the pillows under the king's thin shoulders in order to enable him to sit up. The gold everywhere, blazing in the rays of the sun, blinded Herod's eyes and made his head ache. "Precious metal — perfect trash," he muttered, trying to shade his brows with a palsied hand on the back of which the veins were gathered in greenish blue knots. "Josue, stand between me and that confounded glare. No, keep away. Not too far, though. I'd as lief have the dazzle of the sun as the lustre of your honesty. They both irk me equally: the one, my eyes; the other, my understanding. I tolerate you, lad, only because — well, you're worth a legion of the rascals that lickspittle my every word and are impatiently awaiting my last gasp."

"I want only to serve you well in all things that are worthy."

"That sounds stiff, lad; but, I suppose, honesty is a sturdy tree and not a twisting vine. You convince me that goodness — divine dregs — can still be found at the bottom of life's cup. Where did you learn to be decent?"

"If there is any good in me, Sire, I must have acquired it when I lived with shepherds in Bethlehem."

"So? That makes the puzzle greater. Shepherds are ill-smelling creatures and their ways are mean."

With frank bewilderment, Josue regarded the monarch, who was known to have shed streams of blood and now was himself malodorous with sores that were dripping pus — as yellow as the gold that one saw everywhere in this structure — beneath his Tyrian purple garments. He could understand that royalty must be obeyed in all things that did not conflict with the law of Moses which was the word of Yahweh; but he was at a loss to understand how such as were able to command obedience could so far fail to express truth. "You are mistaken, Sire," he reproved, his clear blue eyes steady. "The shepherds of Bethlehem are as clean as the grass that nourishes their flocks. Their bodies give forth a breath as wholesome as the earth when the plow turns the sod in springtime, and their minds are stainless like the skies to which they are always looking up with reverence when they are not looking down on their sheep with tenderness. Two worlds meet and touch out there on the hilltops, and the shepherds live in both of them at the same time, and they love everybody and treasure all things, however small, as souvenirs of the God of creation. Mean ways, Sire? Can a simple mode of life be mean? They found me, those good shepherds, when, a wailing child, I was left alone in a field; and they brought me up as their own. I was more fortunate than most young ones. I had many dear fathers, and mothers too."

"Then why did you not stay with them?" snapped Herod.

"They advised me, when I got to be of age, to come to the city."

"Wanted to be rid of you, eh?"

"No. Their eyes were wet when I left. But they let me go because they thought there was work to be done here."

"I see. A job that paid better than shepherding would enable you to send money to them. Shrewed, filthy ways."

"They wanted no money. They hardly knew what it looked like. All they desired was that I do in Jerusalem what I had seen them doing in Bethlehem."

"Which was — what?"

"Living in the hope of God and tending sheep."

"Could an old goat like myself, by any chance, be one of the 'sheep' they expected you to tend?"

"Yes, Sire." The young man smiled the glistening white smile of perfect teeth. "But I'd not call you a goat."

"I should hope not," said Herod drily. "It would be unsafe."

"They said that you — the bell-wether — had gone astray and were leading Israel with you —"

"The wise idiots!"

"And were surrounded by wolves."

"The blind observers!"

"And that, the worse a man is, the more he needs a friend; and the stronger he is, the more he must have a protector."

Herod laughed unpleasantly. A protector! — this stripling? He had been called the scum of Hades, the first-born of Beelzebub, the jest of Jehovah, the vomitorium of the Romans, the Idumean serf, the crowned criminal, and the blood-soaked bat; but never, to his knowledge, had even the boldest men in the kingdom referred to him

[9]

as a lost sheep that needed a finder — a protector! Such an interpretation was a classic of its kind. He wished he could be amused, but his smile was forced.

"I'd never have suspected that even Bethlehem — the least of the towns of Juda — bred such numbskulls," he blinked. "However, those half-men didn't do so badly by you, Josue. I cherish you, even though your brains, like your shepherd foster-father's, could comfortably slip through the smallest of the rings upholding that Babylonian hanging over there. I'm not sorry that, when you came to me for employment, I accepted and put you in a soldier's uniform. A good heart is more serviceable to a king than a keen mind. Every sharp subject in my court would like to cut me to pieces; so I've done that same thing to not a few of them before they got a chance to do it to me. Ah yes, I've always needed a protector and long ago decided that nobody could supply the necessity better than myself."

"Your method of self-protection, Sire, has but increased the number of your enemies and the amount of your peril."

"I'm still capable of handling the situation. If needs be, I'll prove it to Israel in even a more spectacular manner than ever before. But I do need a friend. Once David, the shepherd boy, became a king; now a king comes to a shepherd boy. Yes, Josue, I am asking you to continue to be faithful to me."

"You do not have to ask, Your Majesty. You know I will."

"I think I do. But I warn you that your amazing directness, to which I am so indulgent that I surprise even myself, will be the death of one of us. Much as I like you, something tells me that it will not be possible to stand all this child-like quality of yours much longer. Face a king with magnificence, and you gird him for battle; but confront him with simplicity, and he is disarmed. I cannot deal harshly with either you, Josue, or with those bucolics to whom you and I owe what you are. But I demand that everybody — even you, my friend! — address me with propriety."

"Yes, Sire."

"Now go tell the high priest that I am waiting here for him. Have him bring his Scriptural scrolls."

"Instantly, Sire."

"Stay! — If you are so devoted to my interests, where were you last night, my young protector, during the long hours before you found me on the floor? Ere I swooned, I fancied that I saw and heard strange things, and I called out to you."

"I was in the little room that leads off yours, but did not hear. Your voice is weak of late —"

"Remember what I said! My voice is the most powerful in the land. I'll not have you blaming me for the fact that you were sound asleep."

"I was not asleep, Sire; but my mind was back among the hills with the shepherds. It often is, and never was it more so than last night. I was listening —"

"To what, dreamer?"

"To the singing of angels."

Herod sucked in his cheeks and shook his head. Could life be as morbid for the young as the old, with the only difference that the fancies of the one were as foul as those of the other were fair? Dead faces floating in the bilge-stream of the dark; menacing shades; horrible white lips that opened to accuse and warn: these were an old man's vision in the night, while a young one's over-charged brain yielded a waking dream of heaven. Suddenly, with envy, the king grew angry. "You weary me with your prattle as with everything else about you," he accused, his muscles tensing and his chin working with a twitch, for there was a pain-stab in his breast. "Angels! — singing! What have they to sing about in this stinking, suffocating, accursed cesspool of an existence called life?"

"Peace."

The king leaned back farther on the pillows, and a quiver ran from the taut cords of his neck to his knotted knees. "Peace?" he sniffed. "Your ideal angels sang a concrete lie. Life is pain. It flows into this world with blood and out of it with agony. To live is to be led by death, and door after door opens to deeper and yet deeper hell. And *your* chorus sang of peace! — What did you see while you imagined them singing?"

"What I saw was no imagination. Standing at my window, I looked up and beheld what might have been the very eye of God, though the name for it would have to be a star. Such a star! It must have come from another universe —"

Herod lay still. "I saw it too," he whispered. "You describe it well. It has caused me to wonder much and the wonder has brought me here."

"It sang, that star. Or rather it seemed to say, with its long sweet lashes of light, what the angels were singing. I have only to close my eyes to see it still — and hear them."

"Maybe, lad, the star was inside of us instead of without. Usually it is the mind that sheds its cold and meagre light down on the heart; but perhaps, last night, the process was reversed and the heart threw up a fountain-spray of its best and brightest hopes to the mind. The star might have been the shining of the Messianic trust that is in every Israelite bosom. But no, that could not be. I myself saw it, and my heart is cold and almost dead and incapable of filling my thoughts with aught but the things of darkness. No, as far as I am concerned, the light assuredly was not within. Yet it might well have risen, Josue, in such a soul as yours."

"It came to both of us. It shone for the city — perhaps the world. Today all Jerusalem is discussing the marvel of it."

"Did everyone see it?"

"Only the waking few among whom you and I, Sire, were fortunate enough to be numbered. But the news has spread."

"Hurry, son. Are you amazed that I call you that? I should be, too; but this mysterious happening which we have both experienced, draws us very close together. Hurry to the high priest, who will surely give us an explanation of the mystery. My curiosity is yet another sore added to the many of my afflicted body."

"Another David," Herod commented to himself as he watched the young man, so sincere and unspoiled, depart. "That military outfit is as unsuited to such a free and natural boy as Saul's armor on the shepherd king. I'll have a different dress prepared for him. Peace should have its uniform as well as war. This lad would be more at ease with a simple tunic and a shepherd's crook than with a breast-plate, tassels and a sword."

While he waited, his gaze wandered, until it was arrested by a curl of smoke above the draperies of the Holy of Holies; the smoke of the incense of seven plants. And again the faces of his dead victims seemed to be trying to form themselves in the rising rings, and he tore his eyes away. Was not the night enough for them, without their haunting him by day? Was there no escaping them? No, no. Even this sacred place was bloody — bloodier with the sacrificial knife than Herod's own soul with crime. Every year three hundred thousand sheep, many of which had grazed on the hillsides of Bethlehem and been given the tender care of which Josue spoke, were here slaughtered, and the priests waded in a dark viscous ooze. Could Jehovah be pleased? Had he not complained through the mouth of his prophet that all this killing was an offense to his nostrils? Did he not desire another — a clean — kind of oblation? This Temple, for all its activity, was stagnant and void. The very Holy of Holies which in Solomon's day was filled with the spirit of the Lord, now contained only a stone; the one on which the Ark of the Covenant had rested. Once bread had fallen from heaven to feed the hunger of the forefathers in the desert, and now the hunger of Israel in the desert of life was given only a stone. If this edifice had been reared by pure hands, would the spirit of God have fled it? David, with much blood upon him, had not been permitted to construct the first Temple. Why should a man like Herod have presumed to build the present one? No, Jehovah cared not for this empty amassment of honey-colored gold and blue-veined marble; and all the rarest incense of Araby could not disguise the foetor of the fact. And, as Herod pondered, he had a feeling that Israel's God had already chosen another place, as different from this elaborate structure as day from night; a simple place where simple truth could be fittingly cradled. And, further, he discovered himself thinking, to his own astonishment, of that abode of simplicity which Josue's unsullied spirit represented — Bethlehem.

Bethlehem. The word meant "house of bread." While here in this vast pile of metal-lined stone, only a stone was enshrined, out there on the hillside might not manna — the celestial bread that relieves the famine of the spirit — be found? Certainly those shepherds, if they were as good as Josue said, were near to God and worthier of his presence than this palatial and meaningless dwelling. And Herod, for the first time in his sombre life, longed for the privilege and favor of the poor.

"Pardon, Your Majesty." The high priest, parchments in hand, was standing by the litter and bending low. "Your soldier-servant has told me your wishes, but I knew them even before he spoke. You are concerned about the star."

"Did you see it?"

"Yes."

"Can you explain it?"

"Not I, but the prophets." The priest knelt and deposited the scrolls on the tiles beside him. Choosing and unrolling one of them, he said: "Here is the word of Isaias, the son of Amos. 'The people who walk in darkness —' "

" 'Who walk in darkness,' " repeated Herod slowly, thinking of the restless dead that thronged his room and lifted the veil of the tomb.

" 'Have seen a great light,' " continued the priest.

"With their sightless eyes — their worm-eaten sockets?" marvelled the king. "Yes, yes, even so. Mariamne pointed her misty finger to it."

"I know not of what Your Majesty speaks," confessed the reader patiently. He paused a moment before he resumed: " 'They that dwell in the land of the shadow of death —' "

"Therein every man dwells," interrupted the king. "This body of mine already belongs to corruption."

" 'Upon them has the light shone.' "

Herod lay back, limp and motionless, while the priest's soft yet rich voice almost chanted the rest of the text: " 'For unto us a child is born; unto us a son is given;

and the government shall be on his shoulder; and his name shall be called the Wonderful, Counsellor, the Mighty God, the Everlasting Father, the Prince of Peace.' "

Herod's lips were nearly as white as Mariamne's when at last he spoke. "You mean, priest, that last night's star marked the birth of a child that will one day take the throne of Israel and be honored by an abject people with such a collection of titles as was never bestowed on a ruler before? Why, to merit even a part of it, this creature would have either to be or become divine!"

"The prophecy, Your Majesty, speaks for itself. Last night a strange light appeared in the heavens. Last night, in Juda, a child of destiny was born."

"How do you know?"

"Moved by the wonder of the light, long ere the sun had risen, I sent the swiftest of my messengers to search."

"Surely in this city of seventy thousand souls, more children than one were born last night."

"It was beyond the city-gates I sent them."

"Why?"

For answer, the high priest took up and opened yet another scroll and read the saying of Micah: "Bethlehem Ephratah, though you be little among the thousand cities of Juda, out of you shall come the one that is to be ruler in Israel!"

Josue had been standing intently by. Now, with irrepressible enthusiasm, he broke into the scene. "Do you hear, Sire?" he exulted, his voice tremulous with awe. "In Bethlehem, where the kindliness of shepherds reigns, our king is born."

"Your king is here," frowned Herod, darkly, "and bids you contain yourself. What, priest, did your messengers find?"

"A cave in the hillside, silvered with the light of heaven

[16]

and surpassing all the splendor of this Temple. A shrine crowded with humble worshippers and entrusted with the beauty of another sphere. A child-mother pressing a little son, like a spray of lilies, to her bosom."

"Poverty — wretchedness — imagination," barked Herod in contempt.

"Goodness — glory — truth," cried Josue.

"Silence! So this is the infant spawn of prophecy who will grow up to seize what is mine? I am relieved, knowing well how to deal with — babies."

"It is my happiness that you feel relieved, Your Majesty," said the high priest. "But deep within me, I am disturbed. No harm should touch such a child, whose birth-place is revealed by heaven and over whose slumber the very angels of God keep watch and sing. Yes, sing. My messengers were told by the shepherds of melodies that rejoiced more than the ears — the very souls! — of listeners."

"Did your men hear those songs?"

"No; but —"

"I heard them, Sire," interrupted Josue. "I told you I heard them, coming from afar."

"There are songs that only the humble and the clean of heart can hear," said the priest. "The melodies above cannot communicate themselves to lives that are given to the clangor below."

"Pious tosh, not to be found in the Torah!" commented Herod. "And, pray, what is remarkable about a light falling on a cave? Have stars never been known to paint a hillside with silver before?"

"This star," reminded the priest with emphasis and evenness, "was different. It not only led shepherds to the cave, but it has also led you yourself, Your Majesty, here."

A faint flush seeped into the monarch's pallid cheek. "I'll have no more of this," he wrathfully ordered. "Who ever heard of a king born in a stable, and a special star being delivered out of the womb of nature along with him to illumine the puny event, and angels taking the trouble to hold choir over a cave in the barren rocks? All of a sudden, Israelites appear to have become demented. Under the bushes they bray and under the nettles are they gathered together."

"You yourself, Sire, declared that you saw and heard other-worldly things in your room last night," reminded Josue. "Is it not possible that strange things took place beyond it?"

Herod waved his hand feebly. "My patience with you, boy, is at an end," he groaned. "Did I not know that you mean well, I'd send you without delay in the same direction that I've sent many another who annoyed me less. I told you that my experiences were the froth of a tired, old brain, but you insist that yours were realities; and this wise chieftain of the Temple, turned idiot, supports you."

"Your lips are speaking, my Lord," said Josue boldly. "But that is not important. What does the throb in your bosom say?"

Herod averted his eyes and swallowed his bitterness, and signified that he wished to be on his way.

The high priest gestured to the waiting slaves and they came and lifted the litter with care.

Genuflecting, Josue kissed the hem of the holy man's garment and received two scrolls from his hand. "These," whispered the priest, "are the saying of Aggeus and Malachias. See that Herod, when he is in another frame of mind, reads them. I would that God might grant me further length and strength of days to witness the out-

[18]

come of last night's event, but already I am old like the king, and life's sands have run out for me. I fear that the child of Bethlehem will have few friends in Jerusalem to protect him. You, my son, must serve for many."

Exchanging looks that shone, the youth from Bethlehem and the servant of the Lord expressed a silent farewell, as the royal presence moved away.

At the vestibule of his palace, Herod once more addressed Josue. "The dead lips of Mariamne spoke to me last night," he confided. "They told me a real king had come. Am I not real? Is not — must not — this other be false?"

The limpid eyes of the boy who suggested David fixed themselves on the wreck of kingship before them and were large and frank with pity. And once again, as during the night before, Herod turned on his side and buried his face in the pillows.

Another night of terror.

Herod tried to blot out the faces that again, despite the light of the many candles with which he had commanded Josue to surround the royal bed, invaded the privacy of his room. Mariamne's was among them; a pale water-lily unpetalling itself in the stream of accusation. He begged her to speak, but she merely tightened her lips and shook her lovely — her ghastly — head.

The copies of the prophecies of Aggeus and Malachias, which Josue had brought from the high priest, lay unscrolled on the coverlets; and from them the king had taken some poor comfort. Did they not promise that the glory of the second Temple — *his* Temple — would exceed the first, for in it the Messias would appear? Hence his great work, after all, had not really been in vain; and the emptiness of the elaborate structure, of which he had

[19]

been so keenly conscious that afternoon, would be filled. Plainly, the child of Bethlehem was an impostor, else his birth would have occurred either in or near the Temple and not out on the bare hills. There was nothing to fear — at least yet; nothing but the ghostly beings that roamed the night —

Josue sat on a stool by the bed, holding the king's hand, but his curly dark head was bent in sleep. It meant much to the king to have him near, even though it was impossible for him to remain awake, after the sleeplessness of the night before. He was a kind of hostage against the powers of the dark and, in his own way, really a protector.

The dawn found Herod dozing from sheer exhaustion; and even from this mere touch of repose he was aroused by a loud knocking at the gates of his palace. Half-rising, he seized Josue's arm and shook him until the child-blue eyes, still dewy with a dream of Bethlehem, opened. "Go to the window," he ordered, "and find the cause of this disturbance. Those guards below, sleepier than yourself, will take their time."

The boy obeyed.

"What do you see?"

"Three kings."

"Kings? Three? Soon there will be as many kings in this insane land as there are sheep and asses. Come, come, describe them."

"One is not many years older than myself. His skin is as smooth as a plum and it gleams as if touched by the rays of the star. He and his stately camel are like a statue come to life in a dream."

"You and your fancy! Those shepherds emptied your brain and filled your skull with star-dust. The hills of Bethlehem are bewitched. — What of the second?"

"He is middle-aged and dark. His eyes blaze. His beard, streaked with gray, bristles from ear to ear."

"At least a man! The third?"

"Old and tired, as if a long journey had used him up."

"How do you know they are kings?"

"Their bearing proclaims it. Embroidered with jewels are their mantles, and their servants and camels and boxes of provisions are many."

"More folly is afoot. Hasten to them and bid them come here."

Presently the room was rich with royal presences.

"My name is Melchior," announced the eldest. "These others and I have come from the east where our scholars have long made a study of *Anu, the sky.*"

"I am Balthasar," said the second. "On the mighty scroll of the heavens, solemn truths are writ, which some of our wisest have learned to read."

"I am Gaspar," spoke the third. "We have seen a new star and, for four months, have been following it. The farther we came, the brighter it grew. The night before last, it was at its brightest; but last night, to our amazement, it appeared not at all. Our disappointment, however, gave way to joy when suddenly we realized that we must be at or near our journey's end. Such a wonder in the skies indicates that at least an equal wonder has come to earth. Here in Jerusalem or its vicinity this mystery lies, and we wish to see and worship."

"Not far from here lies Bethlehem," said Herod. "After you have partaken of my hospitality, go there, and perchance the object of your journey will be found. I, too, have seen the star and, like yourselves, am vitally interested. Word has reached me that, two dawns ago, a strange child was born in a cave on the hillside. I intended to send my representatives today to bring him gifts and offer my homage; but now I shall await your return and your impressions before I act. You will do me the honor of returning to this palace and telling me whatsoever you see in yonder town, will you not?"

The kings exchanged glances. They liked not the craftiness in Herod's bleary eye; so they merely bowed their heads and let him think what he would about their intent.

As soon as they had gone forth to another section of the palace for food and refreshment, preparatory to setting forth for Bethlehem, Herod sent Josue to summon his councillors so that he might deal with them about this growing nuisance of a little king of greatness in Israel. And when the grave men were assembled around the bed, he told them: "Beyond the Dead Sea, the desert, the Tigris and the Euphrates, a fantasy has already spread and it is high time that we squelch it. Before another sunrise, I would have the cause of this unrest removed from the land."

"What is the cause?" they asked.

"A child new-born in Bethlehem, whom even the high priest, misreading the Scriptures, believes to be the Messias. A child of poverty and weakness, surrounded by shepherds. If this were the answer to the sigh of the centuries, Israel would indeed have a right to despair. But this is *not* the answer, and there is only one way of dealing with impostors — the sword."

Josue, standing in the door-way unnoticed, shuddered.

"Has there not already been enough blood-shed in the land?" spoke up one of the men.

"There will never be enough while traitors live!" exclaimed Herod with a frown.

"Does the high priest know just where in Bethlehem the child can be found?" asked another.

"He does, but I expect that, because of his convictions, he would deceive us. Neither he nor his servants, whom he sent to the place of the nativity, can be relied on." Then Herod toyed with an idea: "Of course, I could torture the secret — if secret it be — out of them."

"Your Majesty," protested yet another, "the high priest and his household are untouchable. The wrath of Jehovah would strike Jerusalem, if violent hands were laid on them. Would it not be wiser to find out about the child from those shepherds you mentioned? Show one of them a piece of gold and he'll sell his soul for it."

"I doubt that these particular ones are at all venal," admitted Herod, recalling Josue's description of them. "No, they would shield the infant. But the visiting kings, who are now in our banquet hall and will shortly set forth for the city of David, will have no difficulty in locating the child and, on their return here, will tell us all."

There was much more speech before the meeting ended; but it got no farther than a general agreement to await the report of the royal trio.

Josue, having overheard enough, had slipped away in the midst of the discussion from the chamber to the banquet hall. Under pretext of bringing some choice pomegranates from a side-table to the young king Gaspar, he whispered in his ear about the danger that was being confected for the babe of Bethlehem; and Gaspar, believing the lad, whispered in turn to Balthasar, who passed on the information covertly to Melchior. All had to be careful, for the ears of Herod's servants were everywhere.

"This," remarked old Melchior to the other two, as they left the hall together to resume their journey, "confirms the evil of the glint that we beheld in King Herod's eyes when he spoke to us about the child. We shall be craftier in the right way than he is in the wrong."

"It is evident," observed Gaspar, "that he fears for his throne."

"He has reason to fear, even apart from the future powers and possibilities of this heaven-sent infant," remarked Balthasar. "His reputation is sinister, and any power dependent on blood cannot but be washed away by it. I have heard that the Emperor Augustus of Rome once said that he would rather be a swine than Herod's son."

"How shall we best elude his snare?" asked Gaspar.

"Our first problem," reminded Balthasar, "is to find the child. Strange that the new king of the Jews should have been born in a cave! This means dire want. It is well that we have brought rich gifts with us to enable him to have a good start in life; but it will be better for us to disguise both the gifts and ourselves, else the poor people of Bethlehem, in whose midst this wondrous one lies cradled, may suspect our motives and prevent us from seeing him."

"Let us, then, leave our servants and our camels beyond the gates of Jerusalem," suggested Melchior, "there to await our return. We shall not re-enter this city but, after seeing the child, join our caravan and return home the way we came. We'll come to the little king not in splendor but humility, as is fitting. We can turn our rich mantles inside out, so as not to affront his poverty, and leave the city-walls on foot."

"But what of our offerings?" interjected Gaspar. "Are they suitable for an infant, and especially for such a one, so different from our expectation! What could his baby fingers do with gold, frankincense and myrrh? Who would assume the burden of keeping this wealth in trust for him?"

"May I make a suggestion?" begged Josue, who had

been privileged to stand near and listen to the converse. The three kings nodded their assent. "Why not distribute the gold to the wretchedly poor of Jerusalem as you pass through the crooked streets toward the gates? Then you would be approaching the new-born king with an inner wealth akin to that which the plain folk in Bethlehem abundantly possess, and they would welcome you with open arms, recognizing you as friends; for charity is gold in the heart and shines in the face."

"This simple youth has a judgment like unto Daniel whose fame has been wafted to our distant realms," admired Gaspar. "He speaks well. Let us give our gold to the needy and our hearts, goldened with good deeds, to the child."

"And why not leave the frankincense at the Temple," further proposed Josue, "where it will be burned in thanksgiving to God for his great gift to man? You will be giving it to the child in the very best manner when you consecrate it to him who sent him. Assuredly this child from heaven, if he could speak, would bid you make tribute to the Most High."

"I like your mind — your spirit," said Melchior. "We will do as you say. But what of the myrrh?"

"When the poor close their eyes in the last sleep," answered Josue, "they are consigned to the tomb with little or no ceremony. Only the rich are properly embalmed. Why not donate the myrrh to those who have charge of pauper burials, so that the humble remains of such as have loved and served God equally with the wealthy may be shown a proper respect?"

"Rightly spoken," approved the kings. "Be it so. Our hands will be empty when we behold the child, but our souls will be filled, and the fullness thereof will be our gifts to him. The gold of love, the frankincense of grateful prayer, the myrrh of consideration for the dead in this land which, under a new leadership, will know newness of life. Come with us, gracious youth, to guide our way."

"King Herod desires me to be ever at his side," said Josue. "But it is clear to me that a Greater would have me briefly go. I will accompany you."

The following day, after a third sleepless night thrice-haunted with the dead, Herod's disposition was a seething cauldron. And when Josue returned from Bethlehem, starry-eyed with what he had seen, he immediately went to the royal chamber to beg forgiveness for having absented himself without permission; but a soldier with a spear was guarding the entrance.

"Stand where you are," commanded the latter, raising his weapon. "My orders are to run you through."

"I must see His Majesty!" cried Josue, unafraid. "Let me first pass and then do what you will."

Herod heard the voices and called out: "Tell the traitor that he will have the distinction of being the first to die for the new-born king. Tell him that the new-born king himself will close follow him into the realm of shade. Tell him that before this night gives way to another dawn, every male child in Bethlehem, and in all the borders thereof, under two years of age, shall be carved with a sword. Tell him that my spies have informed me of most of his movements and that I know how he cooperated with the orient kings against me. Tell him that, though they may escape me, he himself has walked back into his doom. Tell him that I would have heaped favors upon him, but he would not have it so. Tell him —"

"Hear me, Your Majesty," pleaded Josue through the open door. "I could have gone away with the monarchs of the east. They invited me to. But I preferred to come back here and be with you. My loyalty to the glorious child of Bethlehem has not made me disloyal to you. With all my soul, I wish to serve both him and you."

For a moment, silence fell. Then the outraged monarch again spoke: "Soldier, let him enter."

Josue hurried to the bed and dropped to his knees.

Looking not at him but beyond him, Herod declared: "It is not possible to serve two masters. You have offended me gravely, but I shall permit you to make your choice. Do you prefer this infant who will soon be dead, or me whose life, though far spent, will yet outlast his?"

"Oh, Sire," supplicated Josue, "force not this choice upon me. The heart is torn when claims are rival. I can serve both you and him, if you will but bend your pride to Jehovah's will; then there'll be one master for us both, and that will be the God who sent this child to earth to rule his people."

"Is this the way to speak to your king?"

"My king should be the humble servant of the Most High."

"My conscience is in my own keeping, fool."

"Oh, let me try to bring some of the goodness of this holy one of Bethlehem, my king, into your unhappy life. Simplicity and honesty — are they not virtues that befit a palace as well as a cave in the rocks?"

"Was it honest and simple of you to deceive and betray me?"

"I was but striving to save the child from your evil design, and you, Sire, from yourself."

"I need not the kind of care that thwarts me." King Herod's voice turned low and almost wheedled. "Josue, you can undo your mischief and restore yourself to my good graces. Will you?"

"How?"

"Mine is a score to settle with the trio of orientals for partaking of my hospitality and then eluding me. Tell me which way they went, that my soldiers may follow and overtake them."

"I must refuse. They but followed the star and found and worshipped the new-born king. What offense is theirs? To depart in peace is their right."

"And has the king of Israel no right to be respected?"

"The evil that is unworthy of a king is not to be honored even by his inferiors, much less by his equals."

"How did they know that I intended harm to the child, unless you overheard me and my councillors and warned them?"

"I did warn them, Sire. Again I tell you that I was thinking not only of the safety of this son of heaven, but also of your own good. Would you add new torment to your anguish in the night?"

"My torment in the night will come, what ere betide. What is one face more or less to the ghostly crew? — I am abject when the shadows fall, but at least by day I am king."

"The day is dying, Sire. See through the window. The west is ruddy with sun-set."

"Note it well yourself, Josue. If you refuse my next and last demand —"

"What is it, Sire?"

"That you lead my men, as you did the Magi, to the child."

"I will not."

"Where, then, is all your shepherd kindliness? What is it but illusion? Would you have the innocent infants of Israel, including the one you think divine, die? I swear that my sword is ready."

"He shall not die!" exulted Josue. "He is beyond the reach of your hand. You can never find him."

And the happiness of a secret of secrets flowed like a streamlet of milk and honey through his being. What a tale he could, but would never tell! A tale of how an angel of the Lord had come to Joseph by night and commanded that the child be borne into Egypt and safety; how the three orient kings, as a guard of honor, had accompanied the holy family from Bethlehem to the walls of Jerusalem; how, enwrapped in Gaspar's mantle, turned inside out, so that it looked ordinary enough to casual eyes but touched the infant with appropriate splendor, the most precious of burdens was carried; how the little company paused in their flight briefly to visit the Temple and give thanks; how there the high priest received the little one and, illumined from above, prevailed on the parents to let both themselves and the babe be concealed in the Lord's house — the most hallowed and inviolate enclosure in all Israel — until the eight days might be accomplished in which the child's circumcision and his mother's purification could be quietly performed, and the journey to Egypt resumed. All these things were locked in Josue's grateful heart, and Herod would never know. And the boy merely added to what he had already said: "Heaven is guarding its own. And as for the others, Sire, your sword can but open the gates of paradise to their innocence."

"And the gates of Sheol to such a false friend as you!" shrieked Herod, a frenzy upon him. Seizing a jewelled dagger which he always kept under his pillow, he plunged it deep between the neck and the breast-bone of the youth.

"Let this be our link," he panted, still holding the hilt. "Go to your king — your real king. To this — this! — has your choice of him brought you."

The boy's head fell back as his blood covered his tunic and crimsoned the coverlets of the royal bed. His moist eyes, wide open, shone with twin rays of the gentle glory of Bethlehem. His forgiving hand groped for Herod's. His lips, still red and plastic, formed the words: "I thank you, Sire."

"For what?" asked the king, already limp and melancholy at the sight of what he had done.

"For letting me be the first."

2

THERE was among the servants of Herod a certain woman, Zora by name, whose husband had been among the chieftains whom the king caused to be stoned to death. With no means of support for her young daughter, Mary, and her infant son, Joas, she had constrained herself to accept employment in the palace of him who had stricken her family with grief.

To Zora fell the task of preparing the body of Josue for burial; and while she was removing it from the royal chamber, with the assistance of some other servants, she could not but hear the king telling his councillors, hastily assembled: "Thus I act with all who oppose my will. This boy Josue was high in my esteem until he crossed my interest. He could have facilitated tonight's business for us, knowing the exact place of the Bethlehem infant pretender who, by now, has probably been spirited away. Blood begets blood. Tonight this land shall reel with misery equal to that which, in the long black hours, is mine. Prepare groups of soldiers and issue my edict. The child must not escape. Every male infant in arms, without exception, is to be destroyed!"

Zora, weak with the sight of the slaughtered youth and the news of the forthcoming massacre, almost swooned at her task. What would become of her own little Joas, now that the same hand which had been raised against his sire was ready to strike the very flower of this unhappy country's future? Her heart was leaden within her as, back in the servants' quarters, she washed the body of the dead and studied the livid wound of Herod's dagger in the throat. "I could bathe you, poor motherless boy, in my tears," she murmured, "save that your face is lovely with peace and your lips are parted with a smile of pearl and your eyes have the very hue of heaven. It was not so when my husband lay slain. His face, gashed beyond recognition by Herod's stones, bespoke the deepest agony of Israel. And while our cruel king lives, the guiltless can only die. This night, alas, another Jordan will flow, and its torrent will be the tears of mothers. I shall save my sorrow for my son and mingle it with theirs and commend the soul of this youth, blameless and fair, to his fathers."

But many of the poor of the city had already gathered at the gates of the palace, for the sad tidings of the untimely end of the boy whose kindness had brightened more lives than one, were trickling through Jerusalem. And a soldier, who loved Josue because of the latter's having once pleaded well with Herod for him in a case of an unwitting breach of military discipline, came to Zora and whispered: "Such a noble youth shall not be consigned to an ordinary grave. Of myself, I have nothing but the life that he saved from the king's wrath; but three of the paupers at the gates have been able to bring much help. See what they gave me for him?" And Zora was startled to behold sparkling gold pieces, rarest incense, and precious myrrh.

"How comes this wealth from the poor?" she asked.

" 'Tis said that generous men passed through the city streets yesterday, distributing treasure. This gold must be part of it. The incense, I understand, is from the high priest, who personally tendered it to a beggar in the

Temple with an order that he bring it here. How he foresaw what would happen to Josue, I know not. It would appear that an angel spoke to him, or that he ascertained the will of the Lord by means of the *urim* and *thummin* in his sacred breast-plate. As for the myrrh, it was offered me by a man in rags who said that his father, one of those in whose care is the burial of the forgotten, charged him to hasten here with it."

"God has remembered Josue," rejoiced Zora in the midst of her sadness. "He shall be laid to rest like a prince."

But night had fallen, sombre and starless, and well she knew that before dawn the king's mercenaries would have worked his murderous will through the land. There was not a moment to lose. She must save her child, if it were humanly possible, even as Josue had sought to save the babe of Bethlehem.

Leaving directions with the other servants to purchase a tomb and a pure linen winding sheet and a rich coverlet with the gold, and to embalm the body of Josue with the aromatic gum resin, and prayerfully to burn the incense in a brazier at his head, she hurried to her private room, where she found her daughter holding the infant Joas and singing him to sleep.

"You love your little brother, Mary?" she smiled, her eyes blinking away a salty rush of tears.

"More than anything else in the world, my mother," said the girl, puzzled at the question, tossing her rich auburn curls and pressing the warm bundle of humanity closer to her bosom. "And he loves me, too. When I have him in my arms, his eyes light up; and when I leave him on the bed for a moment, they brim with tiny diamonds of tears. With my father gone, Joas is all that's left us. He is our very life."

"And tonight, Mary, he must die."

[33]

"No, no. What are you saying?"

"Because of a child, new-born in Bethlehem, the king has decreed the death of all infants."

"What manner of child can the Bethlehemite be?"

"All I know is that, to be assured of his destruction, Herod would destroy all."

"He shall not kill our Joas!" The girl stood erect with flashing eyes, a small maenad of anger, determination and protectiveness. "As young as I am, I have strength. I'll steal into his chamber and thrust a knife into his heart. I'll —"

"I myself, daughter, have already thought — could not but think — of doing such a thing. Jehovah forgive me! But that would only be the end of all of us. And, besides, the decree has gone forth. Nothing can stay it now."

"Could we live on, my mother, if Joas died?" The girl's voice broke on the last word.

"No, Mary." Zora's tone was low and decisive. "But we can at least strive to keep our loved one living and save our own lives in saving his. Hurry. Give him to me. Throw that long dark blue veil over my head and I'll conceal him in the folds. Keep at my elbow, dear. I need your fresh young strength to bolster up my own. Together we'll cheat Herod of a morsel."

Out of the room, down a corridor, and into a corner of the royal gardens, the mother cautiously picked her way. The darkness of the night would have been a shield to her purpose, only that soldiers with torches and swords were on guard at every gate, and still more of them were stationed along all the pathways to the palace. Evidently Herod was wary about the possible outcome of his measure, when mothers would be turned to tigresses and fathers to raging lions by the loss of their offsprings and bear down in snarling and howling packs on their ogre of a master. Already, off in the night, the stridulous wail of women's voices was beginning to swell, in evidence that the carnage had started. Already there was the murmur, deepening into a rumble, of a throng at the gates. If it was thus in Jerusalem, where the King's sentence would probably be less heavily carried out, because the city lay the distance of a two hour journey from the main seat of the disturbance, what would the scene be, before the night ended, in Bethlehem? And Zora's heart, wrenched with fear for the child in her arms, could not but ache, too, for the mother of the infant whose birth was occasioning this horrible issue of blood in which its own would certainly be shed. There was still, despite everything, a possibility of Joas being saved, but not any at all for that other ill-starred babe on whose cradle, according to empty rumors in Jerusalem, a heavenly light had shone.

Since it was out of the question to get beyond the royal estate, Zora stole back into the palace. "What shall we do now, Mother?" asked Mary.

"I am thinking so hard — so desperately — that I can scarce think at all," said Zora piteously. "Help me, my daughter, if you can."

"Are you not in charge of preparing Josue's body for burial?"

"Yes; but in order to be with you, Mary, and have Joas with me, I relinquished my duty to other servants of the king."

"Are the remains to be removed from here this night?"

"I think so. King Herod told me to use dispatch. My idea was to have the body taken to the home of a friend tonight—the K'far Jonah—to await sepulture tomorrow."

"Joas is very little and — quiet. He makes no more noise than a birdling in a nest."

"What are you suggesting?"

"That, when Josue is about to be taken away, we slip

[35]

our baby under the funeral coverings. You can contrive to be alone with the corpse for a few moments, and this will give us the opportunity we need."

"My daughter is wiser than her years," exhaled Zora, with the first breath of relief that she had experienced since hearing Herod's awful word. "This could be a way, and it sounds as if it may succeed. Once we are out of the palace confines and a little distance off, our chances will increase. There are friends of your father in Jerusalem who will assist us to reach my sister in Galilee."

And so it happened that, next to the dead youth swathed with bandages, a warm and palpitating mite of humanity was placed; and, if the servants suspected what had been done, they mercifully gave no sign, for they all esteemed the widowed mother and knew that another loss, in addition to that of her beloved spouse, would be beyond her endurance. And the two bodies — the dead and the living — were borne as one from the palace of the king; and Mary and her mother were among the mourners whom the guards let pass without question or interference of any kind.

All might have gone well only that, just outside the gates, a mob, now large and menaceful, had formed; and it was difficult — almost impossible — for the funeral procession to break through. The thunder of many voices awakened the sleeping child, who immediately began to cry; a fact which would have been unnoticed in the din, save that scruffling feet tread on an overlapping side of the long velvet coverlet on the bier and caused it to glide off. With a cry of anguish, Zora plunged forward and seized her son, hastily enfolding him again in her dark blue veil. Too late. One of Herod's soldiers saw what she had done and, springing at her, tried to grapple the precious burden away. Mary's fingers, turned claws, tore at the military dress and person. The mob, distracted by the incident, ceased their imprecations of Herod, lowered their clenched fists, and muttered their pity. It seemed as if Joas might yet be saved, for the maternal arms were of steel, and the soldier could plainly see that the crowd was against him and would yield to extremes if he harmed either the infant or the mother.

"Let them go!" a man's voice rang out, and it was immediately reinforced with the demand of many another; but the soldier, disliking to appear weak before so many people, did not withdraw his hand. A stone whizzed through the air and gashed his cheek so painfully that he threw all hesitancy aside, whipped out his sword, flourished its flashing length above his head, and cried: "The king shall be obeyed!" Another stone, hurled by the same hand, concealed in the crowd, hit the up-raised steel with a sharp sound, and a jeer of utter defiance swept the crowd. Humiliated and infuriated, the soldier struck Zora so forcibly in the face with his free fist that she reeled back and her arms loosened. Grasping the child from her, he ran his sword through the soft body, and, to the screams of women and the curses of men, held up the writhing, dripping trophy impaled on his weapon.

Welded into an intense unit by the inhumanity of the scene, the mob was utterly beyond control. Moving on the murderer, it trampled the fallen mother and milled and swirled with the single motivation of death.

Mary stood fascinated with such horror as the eyes of youth have rarely seen. Her brother's little corpse disappeared in the macabre setting; her mother was likewise gone; her whole world turned black and red and was crashing around her. She wanted to scream, but no sound came from her throat. She wanted to dash into the maniac mass of people and be part of it, but could not move. A trunkless arm — the soldier's — sprang up, torn from its socket, in the sea of bobbing skulls; then another; next, bits of armor and, most terrible of all, a gore-spurting head. And all the while the clangor of pandemonium filled the night not only with the suggestion but the very actuality of the abyss.

It was hours before Herod's militia were able to subdue and disperse the rabble. And then Mary found her mother, a thing of gaping wounds, her face bashed into the dust, and her fingers clutched to the final ache of a breast that would hold the throb of life no more. Of little Joas, there was not a recognizable trace. His flower-like body, too frail in the churning vortex of human passions, had been broken to nothingness and left hardly more than a crimson smear on the sodden earth.

The girl would have died from the anguish of the night only that her icy horror was yielding to a flame. Stretched too far, her nerves had now snapped back and she vibrated with an emotion that she had only once, but not nearly so vividly, experienced before. When her father perished, her good mother had not let her see his battered remains and therefore spared her eyes an unforgettable sight; so that her memory of him, though sad, was sweet; but here, in all this naked evidence of man's savagery to man and the depths to which evil can drag life, there could be only a searing and lasting bitterness. Still a child, the girl had become, in a single night, a woman; yet one without a woman's trust and faith; one without love and with an abiding hate. Hate for Herod who, like a great foul spider in his palace, had spun out this excess of crime; hate for his soldiers, so pliant to his diabolic will; and hate, most of all, for that child in Bethlehem whose birth was the immediate cause, however innocent, of the loss of her loved ones, and of a flow of the purest blood in Israel. Had this disturber never come into the world, Joas would be alive and cooing. And Mary's arms, filled with the pain of loss, folded themselves on her breast as if to hold back the torrent of futile rage within it.

She looked at the calm face of Josue, from which the winding sheet, together with most of the bandages, had been pushed away. Through the turmoil, the youth had lain in the dignity of death, while the indignity of life raged all around his remains. His silent lips, partly open and emitting a sheen, seemed to speak to her of peace and patience; a message that she would carry in her sub-consciousness through life but from which, at this time, she could take no meaning. Peace? Life laughed at the idea of it in a world built on a volcano of men's emotions. Patience? How could she think of it when her spirit was as mangled as her mother's form and as ground into extinction as her brother's meek flesh? Let the dead and the living have their dreams; all that remained for the afflicted girl was the reality of pain and wretchedness.

And yet she could not take her gaze from Josue; so like a young king asleep, his long velvet mantle of a shroud half-covering him, half-trailing the dust, and a scent of burnt blossoms wafting itself about him. He was fair enough to be the elder brother of little Joas. His countenance would remain with her through the years as the sole endurable detail of a stark visitation of woe.

Dawn was breaking when Herod's servants came to carry the body to the K'far Jonah — the house that Zora had designated — and to clear away the grisley relics of a night that Jerusalem should long remember.

In a daze, Mary followed the pallbearers. There was nothing else to do. Her plans, if any, were vague. Somehow she would manage to put this city of tombs far behind her. Somehow she would get to Galilee — to Magdala.

3

In the town of Magdala by the Sea of Genezareth, Mary
found shelter. Her mother's sister, Rebecca, received the
weary one with sympathy and did her best to woo her from
such memories as no child should ever have. But the
woman's best left much to be desired, for, like Rahab of
old, she conducted an inn and busied herself with more
than the regular duties of such an occupation.

A striking person with olive complexion, quicksilver
eyes, pursed red lips, and sea-shell ears from which loops
of gold dangled, Rebecca moved about even her most
ordinary tasks with a voluptuous grace that succeeded in
glorifying them. Scorning to conceal her long raven hair
under the veil which Hebrew modesty prescribed for her
sex, she took pride in combing it over and over again in
the presence of her male guests; and when heliotrope
twilight filled the square courtyard of the inn and the
young moon was sabering the sky with silver, she would
sit on the raised platform in the centre, like her to whom
Solomon offered his royal bounty, and strum such dulcet
music on a mahalath, as delicately curved as the crescent
in the heavens, that tears always glittered in young Mary's
eyes; for the very voice of Joas seemed to rise from the
touch of the singing strings. At times, too, Rebecca would
lend her own voice, honeyed and warm, to the instrument, and the blending was so mellow that Mary usually

slipped away through the gate and let herself be lost in the falling shadows. With her heart still in woe, the sweetness was more than she could bear.

At first, the lonely little maiden felt less at home with Rebecca than away from her, for the difference between her mother and this woman was marked; so she would wander through the fields that circled Magdala and make friends with the things of nature, even the least of which reminded her in some way of those she loved. The almug tree, with its fine-grained garnet wood and its heavy clusters of blossoms, was to her a union of springtime and tragedy. The peach-pink of almond buds gave the exact tint of Joas' baby flesh. Lilies, scarlet as the night of nights, grew everywhere, bending their heads, curling their petals upward and pointing their stamens and pistils down, as if offering their blood to God and their beauty to earth. Indeed it was these gorgeous blooms that largely wooed Mary from her depression with their fair suggestion. Surely the blood of the innocent — her mother's, her brother's — was dear to heaven; and, if so, it could not have been shed in vain. Surely the charm of their goodness, apart from the evil of the night of their sacrifice, would remain floral and fragrant with her. Those lilies were as so many lips, silently eloquent of truths beyond time and space; lips breathing a lesson that could make life seem even lovelier, for all its malign aspects, than themselves. And Mary longed to have their language interpreted to her.

The sea, too, meant much to her reveries. She would stand for hours, letting her gaze trail the great scimitar of the shore; and she thought that all the world's tears were gathered there, and wondered how the stars and the sun could smile down on such concentrated sorrow. Yet, if these were really tears, the glory from above, which they caught and reflected, turned them, when the wind was calm, into a vast smooth mirror; and, when it was high, into jewel-tossing waves. Could it be that a celestial touch changed anything — everything — into a semblance of itself? Could it be that even such horror as Herod's massacre, since heaven looked down on it with tolerance and permission, was transformed to holiness? It must be so, or God would have shattered the earth for its outrages long ago; but He had not, and night serenely followed day, and birds sang, and all the tyrants that ever lived could not prevent the coming of a single spring. No matter how much blood was shed, beauty still abounded — the more sublime by contrast with the ugliness that men, refusing to imitate their Lord, created.

The sea and the meadows might well have healed the bruises of the young soul and purged it, only that the influence of Rebecca and her establishment had its way. For Rebecca was, to all outward appearance, a practical woman who believed that, since life had to go on, no matter what happened, it was senseless for anybody to languish in grief. "One must either move about or clutter up the way," she used to say. There was work to be done, if food and drink were to be earned. And more and more she plied Mary with tasks and little responsibilities around the inn, which helped to give the girl an active interest in living. But there was one door, deep down in Mary's being, that the woman's efforts did not and could not touch; a portal to a sub-cellar of dark and fierce recollection in which unspeakable things propagated their kind and crawled. And the atmosphere of the murky depth, with its admixture of thwarted peace and hopeless patience, was hate.

Guests at the inn found this girl very attractive, with her wide eager eyes from which the pupils sprang out like large beads, only to sink back into the sombre blue rounds of the irises, and with her flowing wealth of auburn tresses vividly framing her milk-white face and reaching her slender waist. They liked to have her serve them, and often they sent for her when they wanted nothing more than a glimpse of her rock-rose appeal. They praised her much and were happy to spoil her, and Rebecca looked on with pride and approval.

One man, a merchant from Tyre, went so far as to place a string of pearls over her head, letting it fall around her snowy neck and rest on her soft swell of bosom. And that night, Mary, who had never before possessed anything so fine, did not slip off into solitude when Rebecca sang, but remained in the group of admirers and smiled and applauded with them for more.

"The bud is rich with promise," Rebecca nudged the merchant when Mary's glance happened to be averted. "Wait till it unfolds!"

"I have no doubt," he laughed, "that she will one day be worth all the necklaces in Galilee. You had better not let the Roman soldiers see her, woman, or you may lose her forever. They have a roving eye for the choice and rare."

"Which, of course, you haven't," twitted Rebecca. "I have noticed your generosity to my maids before this, Phares, but never such a frank display of it. Those pearls —they have already coiled around young Mary's heart and will do more to make her forget the loss of her family in Jerusalem than anything I could do or say."

"You are mistaken, Rebecca. I have read the child. There is something in her that no earthly power will ever be able to change. Many men will love her, when she comes into her full dower of beauty; and they will love her all the more because she can never return their passion. I noted a gleam less of appreciation than of triumph in her eye when I gave her my gift, and had the feeling that she was merely accepting the first of many favors which she will demand from life for the pain it has caused her. It was good of you to tell me her story, since otherwise she would have remained a complete puzzle to me." He smirked. "As it is, I can see into her, from a not inconsiderable experience with the sex; but only so far as she will ever let any man peer. Men — my sort — appreciate the pursuit of a maiden more than the capture, and Mary will be as uncapturable as captivating. Why, she has scarcely looked at me since I gave her the pearls, and therefore I'm already thinking about offering her a ring. You see what I mean."

"Tell me, Phares, were those pearls real?"

"Well, no. But they will serve a very real purpose of readying your nymph for her future life in Magdala."

"You never gave me even an imitation jewel."

"Why should I? You'd only have snickered at it. And I'm not a wealthy man. But I owe you not a little for many a light hour; so I've at last presented you with a true jewel which will render your inn famous. I have started Mary on a career that must enrich your own. A river of gems — real ones — is what I see, in the not too distant future, pouring into her life, even as the present bauble encircles her pretty neck this night. When either jewelry or tragedy touches a girl, she becomes a woman. And Mary has been doubly awakened, having been touched by both. Thank me for my half of the good work. As I recall, the girl herself scarcely took the trouble to do so at all."

"Why should she?" laughed Rebecca archly. "The child indeed has plenty of glamor ahead of her, but that is a poor substitute for love."

"I repeat — she'll have lovers no end."

"The love to which one cannot respond does not relieve the soul of a woman but only increases its sadness."

"*You* seem happy."

"Yes — seem." And Rebecca returned her attention to her mahalath and, strumming the three silver strings, sang a little song that could have come from the throat of a nightingale whose breast was pierced.

When Phares came back to Magdala, a few years later, he found Mary in possession and charge of the inn. He was pleased, until on inquiry he learned what had happened to Rebecca. Mary told him — her jaw trembling ever so slightly, but her eyes cold and hard. The story came in snatches, with long pauses in between . . .

Rebecca's moods were many, and her cheerfulness only a mask. One moonless night, when the air was singularly chill and all the flowers of Galilee had withered and gone, she went off by herself without a word to anyone. Some days later, her body was washed ashore by the restless waves of Genezareth. A parchment, found among her effects, left all her possessions — "dross" she called them — to Mary, with a hope that the girl would "eventually barter them for better things."

"She always seemed a sensible woman," remarked Phares, understanding and yet perplexed.

"She was very sensible," asserted Mary harshly. "There's small difference between an empty life and an ended one."

"But her life was complete. It brimmed over into her songs. I never saw a woman more alive."

"How little you knew her!" sighed Mary. "Men see the surface and think it all."

Phares stared. The girl had acquired a cool and cynical

expressiveness much faster than he had expected she would. To have ideas about men in general meant to have had experience with many of them in particular. He would have smiled at the development, only that changes had been occurring in himself, too, and now he was inclined to fear for Mary. Would Rebecca's fate be one day — one night — hers? She was too young, too fresh, to be bitter; yet he could see that her bitterness was so mingled with sweetness that it could not lessen but increase her appeal for the type of admirer who preferred piquancy. A blossom yielded more perfume when crushed in the palm.

"Your cheeks are too pale," he observed. "A holiday away from this place would bring the color back to them. Let me take you to a dreamy village I know."

"I prefer to remain here."

"Do accompany me," he urged. "I promise not to annoy you with such attentions as rightly come from younger men. The foolish fire of yesteryear has left me. It was dying when I last saw Rebecca. She knew it, even better than I. And now, with her, it is dead. We can travel as father and daughter, and the relation will be a balm to the sore that is in the spirits of both of us. You see, Mary, I do look beneath the surface and do not consider it all; though I admit that, in the past, I have been blind."

"Where is this village?" she asked without enthusiasm.

"Among the hills of Lebanon. The people there are very humble and kind. They have a way with them which makes one forget how acrid life can be."

"I'll never forget."

"Yet memory, like everything else, can be eased. I know a family there that, out of nothing, have made a little heaven for themselves. Yes, the wings of angels seemed to enfold me all the while I was with them. There is a young wife and mother who could have glided down into this world on a star-beam — so gentle and gracious is her nature. Her son is the most unusual little boy I have ever seen: beautiful beyond belief, and with eyes that are windows to another world. And the father has the unconscious bearing of a king, though he makes a living by sawing wood. Oh, I realize that this must all sound flat and unpromising to one whose taste is for a showy existence. But I do want to try to make amends to you, Mary; for it was I who helped to awaken you to the world with a tawdry gift some years ago. Now I am offering you, if it is not too late, something real."

"Nothing is real but heartache."

"Come and see."

"I am weary of each day's duties in this busy house where everything speaks of unhappy Rebecca. It would doubtless do me good briefly to slip away. Already I am amused at the family that you so over-enthusiastically describe. One who gives false pearls to little girls can himself be readily deceived about many things."

"I am not deceived," insisted Phares. "You will love the spot and the people, especially the family of Joseph. There is no other place quite like Nazareth."

4

I<small>T WAS</small> April, and Nazareth, a hollow plateau thousands of feet above the level of the sea, had the appearance of a huge bowl of blossoms — the warm snow of spring — as Mary, perched on a camel, gazed down from a hill. "I've never beheld so many flowers at once," she exclaimed, deep-inhaling the perfume. "The whole town seems to be made of them."

"That's how it gets its name," explained Phares. "Nazareth means 'flower.' Here is the heart of Israel. In Jerusalem, one finds the pomp and the vestments. If I were Jehovah, I'd live here, and appear in the city only on great feast-days."

"But it is not all beauty," sighed Mary. "Over toward the west I see tombs — so many of them!"

"Look rather to the east," invited Phares. "You'll find a spring of clearest waters which fill a deep well with such refreshment that therefrom Nazareth had drawn its very life."

"Life and death," pondered Mary. "What a strange association of them our Maker has wrought! They are mixed together into one, like the darkness and the light; and, because of the one, the other is spoiled."

"Not so, Mary. Because of the one, the other is enhanced. But think not of death. This land is alive, doubly alive, since its people walk with the Lord of all living. The tombs are but symbols of their final union with him. Down in that cluster of white houses yonder, in the bright green setting of trees, is the home of Joseph."

"Forgive me, Phares, but I have decided not to go there." ..

"What! Why? We have come so far — " Phares' voice was deep and tremulous with disappointment. "That home is an abode of such pure happiness as earth has seldom, if ever, seen."

"I believe you — now. That is why I refuse to go. My eyes have looked on pure happiness for the last time." Mary's voice softened to a murmur. "I, too, had such a home once, and it can never be mine again. Never, I tell you. The sight of another, belonging to strangers, would tear open a depth within me that is best kept closed."

"It is for this very reason, Mary, that I brought you. Such a depth should be opened."

"The key is lost."

"Here in this verdant valley — in Joseph's humble house — it can be found. I swear to you that my own soul, dark as mandrake leaves, was bathed in sunlight when I spent a day with him and his loved ones, and I came away a changed man."

"It's no use, Phares. My mind is made up. For a woman, the past is everything; to a man, nothing."

"Mary, you are still very young, and far from being a woman. The soul should have its springtime, even as the cycle of the year."

"I am old within. It seemed to me, when I first saw Galilee, that I might find childhood's gleam again — "

"It's there in yonder house. The eyes of Joseph's boy are as bright as the light that is said to have shone a few years ago in Bethlehem."

"But in Rebecca's inn, I lost the last of youth. I belong to the night — the only groom I'll ever know. Not even one day in Nazareth can be for me. My presence would cast a stain on the holy household you cherish, and therefore add another shame to my account."

"It will take away all stain. It will renew you. I swear — "

"You perhaps noticed, my friend, that I used to slip off by myself when Rebecca played and sang so touchingly. I could hear my brother's voice in her music and feel all the happiness of other days, which would never return, in her songs; and a dagger in my bosom, already wounded beyond healing, would have been more kind. Think you that I could endure the sight and sound of the heavenly boy, who might have been my own innocent brother? Or of that gracious mother, who likewise might have been my own? Or of that father whose dignity echoes the worth of him whom Herod stoned?"

"I understand, Mary," said Phares sadly. "Yet had I hoped — "

"Had I first come here to Nazareth instead of to Magdala, my life might have been changed. Now it is given to things that lie as far apart from this placid village as the Dead Sea from the living waters."

"I would it were not so. I'd give everything I possess, not to have offered you that string of pearls."

"Blame not yourself, Phares. Had you not offered it me, another would; and the effect could not but be the same. The spirit is gone, and only the flesh remains, and it is by means of what I have that I must go on living."

"Was not Rebecca's end a warning?"

Mary smiled twistedly. "Rather a suggestion. She did not wait for the end. Having made her own manner of life, she chose her own way of finishing it; and this was her revenge on existence. When I feel ready to follow her, I'll hesitate no more than she did."

"What of the hereafter?"

"For such as me, can it be any emptier than the here?"

Mary's eyelids, for a moment, locked tight, and two or three drops distilled on the edges. But she flung back her head; riffled her long flaming hair, unveiled as Rebecca's had always been, with the whitest of hands; and let a snatch of song rise not from any depth within her but only from her throat. At last, she said earnestly, "I thank you, Phares, for bringing me; and I'll thank you more for taking me away. Be not downcast. I am meant for life's falsities. You knew it well when you placed those foolish — fitting — pearls around my neck."

5

From Magdala, Mary made many journeys to Jerusalem during the ensuing years. The vividness and restlessness of the great centre matched the turmoil within her, for her nature demanded a constant change of scene. She became well known in the upper city where an admirer had given her a little jewel-box of a palace surrounded by a garden which owed its extraordinary blooms, it was said, to the fact that blood, drained off from the sacrifices of the Temple, enriched the soil. But she accepted luxury, for the most part, with an innate disdain and preferred to wander in the lower districts where the massed wretchedness of human existence made her own unhappiness seem less and she could be more herself.

One day she took a particularly long stroll, visiting first the teeming marketplace in which the fishermen of Genezareth displayed their catch — strange creatures of the depths with bulbous eyes and scaly skins, like an arrangement of old gold and silver coins, and forked tails with trails of ghostly substance, grotesque as the dreams of mortals; and she thought of life's great sea that yielded up so many poor victims for a feast of regal power or sheer human lust. Would the time ever or never come when men would toil to satisfy something other than the bodily, the noble rather than the brute, hunger of the race?

She noted the abundance of food in the shops: figs

luscious and bursting with juices; clusters of grapes such as only the mother-hills of Sharon could produce; thick dates from Jericho; wheat of fabulous quality from Ephraim; wines of distant Cyprus, smoother than air to the throat but heady with power; pyramids of cruses of oil and jars of honey; everything for the stomach — nothing for the soul. Would there ever or never be the kind of bread and wine that could sate the famine and the thirst that lay under life like a dungeon in a desert?

She was impressed with the bolts on bolts of fine materials for raiment in the booths along on the street of the dyers: oriental silks that caught the sunlight and threw it back in rainbow shimmers to the eye; Tyrian purple apparently ripped from the midnight sky; wool as soft and white as the blankets of blossoms that covered the Lebanon hills in spring. Everything to enfold the mortal flesh; nothing for the nakedness of the eternal spirit.

The air was inexpressibly sweet with the aroma of spices of every kind; yes, but equally foul with the stenches of life.

Goldsmiths spread out an endless array of rings, anklets, and bracelets, cunning in design, fiery with jewels, shrieking to the vanity that every woman knows. Everything to ornament the limbs of the purchasers; nothing to offset the shabby innerness of their lives.

Finally Mary's steps led her to the Temple. Surely the answer to her yearning should be there. Was not this the house of the Lord and must it not have what the worldly marts utterly lacked? She looked around and was disappointed, for the world had invaded Jehovah's own home with its wares and ways. Here was hardly more than a forum and market combined, where people excused their love for dispute and harangue by tying it up with divine interest, and bought and sold as freely as in any place else. There were sober scholars and interpreters of the law, and groups of silent listeners; and she knew there were ceremonies, elaborate and impressive; but the would-be holy edifice seethed with an unrest as real as that which obtained in Mary's bosom. In fact, the Temple seemed an enlargement of herself. Its walls were beauteous, as were her form and face. They were highly adorned, like her arms and neck and fingers. Here men sought to buy forgiveness and atonement with fruit and flesh and gold, even as she tried to buy a portion of pleasure, if not happiness, by the sacrifice of herself to men's desires. The heart of this edifice was a stone, and a stone was Mary's heart.

Her full attention was at length attracted by a number of venerable men gathered around a boy and listening with close attention; and wonder, like a sunbeam, was playing on their withered visages. And as she drew near, her hand flew to her throat. She could not believe her eyes. It was as if the years had rolled back to the night of Herod's slaughter and Josue had come back to life and risen from his bier. The countenance of this boy in the Temple was almost exactly the same as that of him who had died at the king's hand. Could it be that Josue was living in him? Could it be that the dead entered the body of the living and endued it with their semblance? Was this the meaning of immortality?

And Mary listened as raptly as the rest.

"You have feared God," the boy was saying, "because you have not known him. You know only the works of his fingers: stars molded by them and flung into space; the blazing sun set in the firmament; the waters thrust back from the earth; life poured from an inexhaustible vial into the deep and the dust; man emerging from the

[54]

womb. And you have been smitten with the greatness of creation rather than with the goodness of the Creator. Ah, you have known God's fingers and not his heart. Had your knowledge been deeper, your fear would have been surpassed by your love."

Sonorous words from the lips of a mere youth. His eyes recalled to Mary Phares' description of those of the boy in Nazareth: windows to another sphere. His face was the kind that eluded any word-picture, because its features seemed to fade away in the warmth of his earnestness as wax melts in a flame, and one presently focused on what he said more than on how he looked. Too, his body was pellucid to his soul, just as purest crystal almost loses its outlines when a light shines through. As Mary gazed, he suggested less the individual Josue than all the Josues that ever withstood pride and power with the dignity of simple worth. This was not a youth but a generation. More — a regeneration. But his message — love — was mistaken; yes, mistaken — however earnestly, Mary knew.

"Why," a bearded doctor of the law was asking, "should we not fear the hand that delivered the tables of stone midst the thunder and lightning of Sinai, strewed the land of Pharoah with ten plagues, divided the waters of the Red Sea, struck and shattered the walls of Jericho, and tore open the earth and cast down into perdition, body and soul, Core, Dathan and Abiron?"

"You speak but half the story," answered the youth steadily, his countenance aglow. "That same hand put the warm stream of life in your veins and wrote the divine word on the fleshly tablets of your hearts. It fills the earth with spring's awakening. It unites your lives with its own. It rears the towers of reason. It repairs the ravages of men's mistakes. It raises up the faithful to the bosom of Abraham."

"But fear is necessary," contended another doctor. "It prevents evil."

"Love is better," asserted the youth. "It inspires good."

"But are not both vital to the complete worship of our God?"

"Yes," agreed the astonishing boy with heavenly calm. "But they must not be kept apart. By itself, fear terrifies, and love presumes. Blended, they make a third virtue which contains the merits of both without the defects of either."

"What is this third virtue?"

Mary rubbed her eyes. Whether it was an effect of the sun or the radiance that came from within the lad, she could not tell; but a soft light surrounded the shapeliness of his head, as he bowed and murmured, "Reverence."

She would most certainly have remained to hear more, if there were more to hear. But at that moment, a slight disturbance occurred. Two people — a man and a woman — thrust their way through the circle of listeners and fell upon the speaker with embraces and expostulations. She could not see their faces, for their backs were turned to her; but she studied their gesticulations and evident emotion. Then a friend, who had espied her standing there, came to her side and slipped a possessive arm around her waist, drawing her away. "Since when has our Magdalene taken to lending her shell-shaped ear, which nature intended only for love's lyrics, to boy-orators?" he teased.

"He was speaking, Phanuel, of love," she explained tersely. "Of love and — reverence — "

"Reverence?" laughed the friend. "It would put love in chains. Birds were never meant for cages. Like life, love is free."

"I wouldn't know — "

"Well, you know freedom, if not love. And it's just as good."

[56]

"Good?" echoed Mary, and the sound of the word trailed off into a sigh.

"Come away," Phanuel invited. "The day is advanced and, this night, a special revel is planned. A prince from Babylon is honoring Jerusalem with a visit and I am arranging an informal reception, of which you shall be the hostess. Gold drips from his fingers like water through a sieve, and his ketonets are so sparkling with jewels as to turn even Herod Antipater sea green with jealousy, and his appearance is as stately as a Roman's god's. He has heard of your charms and insists on meeting you. I've been searching everywhere, but might have realized, right at the start, that I'd find such an unusual darling as you only in the most unusual of places. How can you waste your time attending open-mouthed to a callow youth, when fortune is eager to empty a cornucopia of favors at your feet? Hasten home and bedeck yourself like the queen of Saba, for tonight you must out-gleam the moon."

As she left the Temple, Mary was paying almost no attention to Phanuel's fluency, for her quick ear was given to the conversation of two old men who were walking near by.

"The boy is probably no more than twelve years old," one was remarking, "and yet the truth of the ages is in his eyes."

It was Mary's intention to inquire about the mysterious young person who dared address the doctors of the law and, in an atmosphere reeking with smoky blood which no amount of incense could perfume, speak of love and reverence. But the next weeks passed like an oriental dream; a medley of mantles of silver thread, the sparkle of priceless gems, olive leaves wreathed into crowns, spraying fountains, violet marble turrets and emerald al-

[57]

coves, delicate and exotic viands served on dishes of gold, pillows stuffed with herons' down, coverlets as light as sea-foam, oils scented with cinnamon and rush, ribbons of song twirled around hours of dallying, swans arching their slender necks over crystal waters, stars pouring down a pearly lustre on naked flesh, couches of Jordan sycamore, sweet lanquor of wine, eyes veiled yet frank with desire, words that in their very meaninglessness made music, and sighs as soft as spring's awakening.

It was not that she cared too much for any or all of these things as such; but they served as a necessary curtain to what she would forget, and she dreaded to have the tapestry removed. But when the dream ended with the departure of the prince for his native land, there proved to be something still left to veil the appalling things of the past. It was itself a memory. A memory of a boy speaking in the Temple and interpreting life as the love of God, and the art of living as a course in reverence.

Again, with deep regret for the delay, she betook herself to the Temple. Perhaps he would be there and she could unbosom herself to him. It was not unusual, after all, for one to find direction from youth, as yet untouched by life and clean from the hand of the Maker. Had not a prophet spoken of a child leading Israel? Had not Josue, the youngest soldier of his time in Herod's palace, been the confidant of the king? Had not learned old men in the house of the Lord listened with respect, if incredulousness, to one whose age was infancy in comparison with their own? Could she — Mary of Magdala, harlot — do less?

But that day the Temple was more restless than she had ever seen it before. Caravans of camels, humped by nature and superhumped with gifts for the holy place, were lined up outside the Corinthian bronze gate which led to the

Court of the Women. Females of every description were pouring in from all directions, and their babbling was as the waves of the Sea of Galilee when a storm is about to unleash its fury. A blast tore the air to shreds; the sound of the great rams' horns through which the sentinels on the look-out towers always blew a warning or a summons. And the crowd quickened its pace — a mass of leaves thrust forward by a gale of excitement.

Mary could not but contrast the present commotion with the calm and serenity that reigned on the day when the boy spoke.

"What is the matter?" she asked of a creature in tatters beside her, holding a pair of doves to her heart with tight yet caressing fingers.

"A great one comes," answered the woman abstractedly, scarcely looking up from the gentle birds which, offered to Jehovah out of her poverty, would render her tired soul as fresh and unblemished as themselves. "A Roman. I think his name is Pilate. Pontius Pilate, the new procurator of Jerusalem."

"What is great about an enslaver of our people?" muttered Mary with indignation.

"I know not," said the poor woman, raising her eyes which Mary saw to be two dim slits in what seemed like sores. "His power, perhaps. He and his people have taken our bread and almost our existence, but they have left us our Temple and our God. Jehovah is still Jehovah. The time is nigh when the Messias will appear and all poverty will be changed to wealth, and all wealth to worthiness, and all sorrow to joy."

Mary gazed pityingly on the disease-ridden body beside her and marvelled how it could encase such a vision — more enchanting by far than the luxurious one that had been her existence for the last few days and nights.

"Tell me," she spoke, "does the boy give utterance in the Temple today?"

"What boy?"

"The one who astounded the doctors a fortnight ago."

"I did not hear him. Nor have I heard anybody mention aught about him. And my roofless life leads me from one end of Jerusalem to the other."

Impatiently Mary turned away.

Within the first court of the Temple enclosure, she espied a white-robed priest standing apart from the crowd. She approached him, asking, "Is the boy present this day, whose tongue spoke heaven?"

"What boy?" exclaimed the holy man. "I have never seen nor heard any such."

Within the next hour, she put the same question to ten doctors, and only one — the last — had any recollection of the youth she sought. "Ah yes," he smiled. "A clean-cut youngster with considerable possibility. I've been told that his parents very sensibly took him home where he belongs. He should make a good rabbi some day. But I am not sure. Figs that ripen too quick are tasteless. As I remember, he said something about love superseding fear. He has not lived long enough to know life's pangs. He will learn."

A quick pain came to Mary's bosom; a keen sense of the utter fickleness of human opinion; for suddenly she recalled that this man was one of the two whose conversation she had overheard while leaving the Temple with Phanuel on the day of the boy's discourse. The very one who said: "The truth of the ages is in his eyes."

From the window of her room, that evening, she looked down on Jerusalem. The city was dotted with flames, since this was a time of celebration and, according to custom, old clothes were dipped in oil and fed to the great purify-ing element of fire. Hardly a roof-top lacked a ruddy glow, and the Temple itself blazed not only with the largest illumination of all but with a dazzling reflection of the conflagration in its innumerable golden panels. As if this were not enough, the setting sun was heaping its glowing embers high in the west. And Mary thought: Would this city, one day, like a worn-out garment, sodden with its excesses of wealth and poverty, be ignited by the wrath of Jehovah and as completely destroyed as the shabby tunics and vestments that were now so cheerfully flung to the demands of a ritual?

She could hear the music of harp, sackbut, flute and cymbal wafted on the hot breezes. She could see the people dancing in the streets, consigning their cares as well as their useless bits of raiment to the nothingness that de-struction creates. And she thought of another night when no joy but a throbbing agony was the pulse of this strange city, and the only flash was Herod's sword, and the only sounds were wails and anguish. What right did Jerusalem have to rejoice? Had it no memory? Or were its moods like Mary's own — a futile attempt to forget the funda-mental horror of life in spasmodic bursts of living?

Her mind went back to the radiant boy in the Temple. It was part of the forgetfulness of Jerusalem, alas, that he should be forgotten. Maybe it was better so. His mes-sage, too fair for a mad world, would shrivel like silk in a furnace. The doctor was probably right in shifting his opinion about him. The boy said that men feared rather than loved God because they knew mostly the might of his hand. What else was there to know but nature, if the author of it kept invisible? And nature, with all its wonders, was harsh. Had not Mary seen it in the starkness of Herod's night of hell? Had she not experienced it when she dared to stroll through the lanes beyond the Dung Gate, in the Valley of Hinnom, where lepers threw their vile mantles over faces swollen and eaten with hideousness, and crouched in the mud like swine, devoid of all human semblance, let alone the shining touch of a good God's finger? Had she not felt it in Rebecca driven to a watery grave by a lash of loneliness in the very midst of what men called life? That Jehovah was great, and that his visitations were as awful as himself, Mary thought she could plainly see. But that he was lovable, notwithstanding that he had permitted a child to be born in Bethlehem over a decade ago, whose coming meant the murder of many little ones, did not appear at all clear. Every gift of his, however fine in one phase, was fearful in another. Life itself, his greatest, was shadowed by death. Youth and beauty were so brief that they amounted to little more than a withering and a decay. Light sombered into darkness. Stars fell. The earth yielded thistles and thorns as well as wheat and roses. The heart, so suited to hold joy, regularly brimmed with sorrow. The jubilee of today was the sackcloth and ashes of tomorrow. What did it profit to have the warm stream of health in one's veins when the chill of certain dissolution blew steadily over it? What was spring's awakening in comparison with winter's terrible sleep? As for the towers of reason, they enthroned the rulership of fools, for kings and high priests had alike committed Israel to suffering and shame. And the bosom of Abraham — hope of the faithful! — had it not been barbaric, even as Herod's own, with a willingness to slay the innocent boy Isaac? Love, as an inspiration to good, was better than fear, as a prevention of evil; but how could love grow and bloom in a winter-world? Reverence was ideal; but how could it be the soul-expression of a people whose lambs were led to the slaughter and whose God, to whom sacrifices were continually made, had let the land be stripped of dignity and left it to languish under the Roman heel?

Mary finished her reflection by telling herself: "It is true that the lad with a message of love has not yet known life's pangs. Like all of us, he must learn. And then the light will be dimmed in him — he will no longer be radiant."

A parchment from the Babylonian prince lay on a tabouret by the window where she had thrown it. Scarcely a day's journey from Jerusalem had the magnificent one gone, when a renewal of his desire for her had geysered up again within him and flowed over into a torridly worded plea that she rejoin him. His messenger, with a rich caravan, was waiting at the gates to convey her. The parchment promised everything — everything but love, and only love's shameless travesty, passion. But what more could Mary wish for or expect? Should she not be grateful for so much — so little?

With a sigh, she called to a servant, "Make ready; we are setting forth. It will be a long, long time ere we return. Perhaps never. There is nothing in Jerusalem for me. And, for a moment, I had thought there might be everything — "

6

THE years passed, and a new city, Roman in design and named Tiberias in honor of the dishonorable Emperor, had risen not far from Magdala on the Sea of Galilee. Herod Antipater, who inherited the position but not the royal title of him who massacred the innocents, had built and made it his capital and, urged on by his wife Herodias, so out-did himself in currying the favor of the Romans that he won not their esteem but aroused their suspicion. To offset this effect, he ground still more taxes out of his wretched subjects for the expensive entertainment of the wise conquerors who well knew that what he wanted was to be not a tetrarch but a king, and appreciated the profitability of keeping him hoping and guessing. "Surely the time is at hand for a real king," the people concluded among themselves, "for the throne of Israel holds less than a shade."

Mary's home in Magdala was no longer an inn. Out of regard for Rebecca, she kept it intact, but in a way characteristically her own. She covered the exterior with marble and lined the interior with gold-leaf, and placed a fountain in the midst of the court-yard where the raised platform formerly stood, on which the unhappy woman sang to the skies. And when the waters sprayed upward in the moonlight, Mary felt that they gave to her eyes what the music of the mahalath had once given to her ears.

Time had touched her lightly, as if to compensate for the depth of early tragedy. In a land where maturity comes fast and the transition from beauty to plainness is a breath, she kept blooming like some rare plant in dankest soil, and the number of her admirers increased rather than diminished, for now she appealed not only to the emotions but also to the minds of those who surrounded her. She had learned how to hold their desires in leash by eliciting their confidences; and men found a soothing in her presence that was at times preferable to a wild excitation of the flesh.

Tullus, a rich chiliarch, especially fond of her, always insisted that she attend the major games and banquets in Tiberias; and there, in time, she attracted the roving eye of Herod Antipater himself who, right under the smoldering gaze of Herodias, paid her court and favor. He listened to her as to a kind of goddess and, much as she pleased his eye, never laid a lustful hand on her. Herodias was lenient to her husband's many bursts of debauchery, since they usually reacted into a quickening of his appreciation for the Roman-bred culture and quality which lay like a fine veneer on her stormy nature, and they swept him nearer to her; but his contacts with this singularly alluring Mary of Magdala, more maternal than romantic, and all the more perilous for that very fact, drew him farther away and heightened her fear. There was nothing much, however, that Herodias could do — as yet — to prevent the flourishing intimacy, and she had to endure the frequent sight of Mary in the halls and gardens of the palace of Tiberias, and even to accept her as one of the guests in the fortress of Macherus beyond the Dead Sea, to which her husband, when he wished to doff ceremony and be most free, would repair with his family and favorites.

Mary relished neither Herod Antipater's regard nor Herodias' resentment, and earnestly wished that she had never met either of these personages; but having long ago released herself fatalistically to life's tide, like the piece of flotsam that she held herself to be, she felt helpless. The situation must work itself out in its own way. If the end were to be the usual one of fickleness on the male˙part, she would be glad; or a poniard or a cup of poison on the part of Herodias, she little cared. Without hope, what was there to live for? And Mary's life was so constituted that she seldom or never looked into the future, but only back at the indelible images of the distant past which, somehow, had not grown dim but kept the awful clarity of their birth. Her method was to drift unquestioningly into the years ahead and face always the evil of her early days, except when in sheer self-mercy she let the tinselled veil of sense-pleasure fall between her and the remembrance. She knew that it would be healthy and normal firmly to dismiss what was by-gone and to exist in a trustful light of better things to come. She had tried. But the monstrous fascination of King Herod's night of blood twisted her psychology to itself and would not let her go. Only a still more violent shock could turn her around and away; and neither Rebecca's death nor any other occurrence had been nearly enough.

In Macherus, a weird experience awaited her. Her morbid urge to look on misery greater than her own, and thus to lessen her inner hurt, led her to the prison-cells in the bowels of the fortress, and there she beheld human specimens as woeful as the lepers that grovelled in the mud beyond the Dung Gate in the Valley of Hinnom: living dead men cast into a hell of darkness, hunger and hopelessness because of their inability to pay their debts or because of treasonable words that they were alleged to have uttered against either the tetrarch or the Romans. Fettered shadows of men whose chains clattered on stones. And there was one among them with the physical aspect of a long-buried corpse but the eyes of a seraph. His body was a great skeleton covered with a sun-dried skin through which every bone traced itself; and yet an awesome beauty shone in his countenance from his cheek-bones up and from his matted tangles of jet-black hair down. His voice could have come from a sepulchre, and yet it was resonant with the notes of a high and holy sphere. His fingers were talons, and yet Mary surprised him lifting the head of a dying fellow-prisoner with those same forbidding hands as feelingly as a mother presses her child to her bosom. Who could he be?

On two occasions she saw him through the bars of his cell, fascinated by the unique wretchedness of his body and the glow of his spirit, not wishing to draw near him but still incapable of remaining away. The third day, she asked the jailor about him, and he told her that this was merely a simpleton called John, who had come out of the desert, after years of subsistence on a diet of locusts and wild honey, to announce his crazed notions about a new king to the people, and the necessity of being purified by submersion in the waters of the Jordan rather than by sacrifices in the Temple. "And," finished the jailor, "he aroused the whole court by denouncing the sinfulness of Herodias in the role of Herod Antipater's wife, since she belonged to the tetrarch's brother Philip."

"I would have speech with him," Mary said.

The keeper, with a shrug of the shoulders, took a large key from the pocket of his tunic and opened the iron-grill.

"I am of Magdala," she announced to the prisoner, not knowing what else to say. The latter's vision was fixed on space and he gave no motion nor sign.

[67]

"My name is Mary."

At the word "Mary," the man's amazing eyes lit up with love. "It is the name of his mother," he breathed.

"Whose mother?"

"The mother of one whose sandals I am not worthy to loose."

"Is he a holy man — a prophet?"

The prisoner regarded her pityingly for having put such a question, and he replied with fervor, "He is holiness itself. He is the fulfillment of all prophecy."

"How do you know?" demanded the Magdalene boldly.

"The heavens opened when I poured water on his head, and the spirit of God descended on him in the form of a dove, and the voice of the Most High was heard by me, lady, more clearly than your own, saying, 'This is my beloved son in whom I am well pleased.'"

"Is not this the kind of imagination that stirs in the brain of a body that has long been starved?"

"Starved? Fasting is food for the soul, and a sound soul sees the truth even as a healthy eye the light."

For a moment Mary was silent under the unintended sting of the remark. But she had to speak on and found herself asking, "Who is this man whom you believe to be what the voice said?"

"Jesus of Nazareth, son of Joseph."

"'Nazareth — Joseph.'" Mary's thoughts immediately reverted to the day when she and Phares almost entered the blossomed little Galilean town together, and she could still hear in her memory Phares' ardent words: "The eyes of Joseph's boy are as bright as the light that is said to have shone on Bethlehem." Her heart throbbed fast. "Tell me, is this Joseph a laborer who earns his living by sawing wood?"

"He formerly did so," answered John. "He used to be a

carpenter. But now the carpenter is gathered to his fathers, and his son has set forth on a mission of rebuilding Israel."

"But how can a son of God be the son of flesh and blood?"

"Joseph was only the foster-father. A virgin-mother conceived and delivered Jesus."

"But this could not be. Never have I heard the like before!" Mary looked away in affected scorn.

"All things are possible to the Holy Spirit."

"Even the impossible?" The note of sarcasm rendered her voice harsh. "Was it in — Nazareth — that Jesus was born?" she suddenly asked.

"No, in Bethlehem of Juda."

"How long ago?" she further questioned, holding her breath.

"A score and a half of years."

"Did a star — a special star — shine down on his birthplace?"

"Yes. The most wondrous that ever pierced the sky."

"Was it because of this — this Jesus — that King Herod caused so many little ones to be slain?"

"Even so."

Abruptly Mary turned away and requested the jailor to lead her to the upper region of the fortress. In the ascent, she had to keep one hand on his arm to steady herself, and she threw the other before her as if against the on-rush of an intolerable realization.

The child of Bethlehem — the source of all her sorrow! But for him, a loving mother and a manly brother would now be here. Her life would have been spared the sickly strain that had expelled true happiness, and the dread fixation of Herod's night could never have been the cancer of her soul. All her misery had stemmed from the city of David and the coming of one whose crafty parents

[69]

— simple folk, Phares called them! — must have contrived to bear him away to safety while so many other infants were butchered for his sake. And all the old animosity, buried in her heart, stirred to life, darkening her mind, as Herod's own chamber had been dark, and arousing in her the same sadistic sense that had moved the king to infernal action.

In the quiet of an alcove overlooking the courtyard, she stood and mused. How could she revenge herself on this child, now become a man and still posing as a king? She had never acted consciously unkind to anyone, though a well-concealed revulsion had been her attitude toward most of her followers. It must have been that she was saving her spleen for one — one. And now circumstance was sending him her way.

Rebuilder of Israel — son of God — fulfillment of all prophecy. Mary laughed almost insanely to herself at the reasonless faith of the man in the dungeon. Would a restorer of Israel have begun by destroying, or permitting to be destroyed, such a valuable part of the kingdom's future as the lives of harmless babes? Could this author of devastation be the son of God? If such a demon were the completion of promise, then the prophets themselves had been as witless as this John the Baptist, and their words were worse than a lie, a frank mockery. And born of a virgin! — this well-spring of agony! — as if the ordinary course of nature were not good enough for his wretched advent! As if the prostitution of Israel were to be at all relieved by the cruelty and shame that his nativity had wrought on a people already beaten to the dust!

And Mary's emotion, overflowing its confines, poured out its searing acid on the Baptist to whom this Jesus was clearly divine. Might she not begin to revenge herself on the master by striking him through the servant? With a disciple less, Jesus would be the less influential. To be sure, John, in prison, seemed already lost to him; but prisoners were frequently released. She must see that this particular one would never go forth, never.

Glancing down from the window, she became conscious of Herodias' daughter Salome disporting herself in the courtyard; and somehow this wild flower of a child fitted into her sombre preoccupation. Dark in body, Salome had a disposition to match; a nature that rejoiced in making others suffer. Just now she was holding a pigeon with her two hands and stretching the wings so far apart that the creature fluttered in pain; and her eyes were glittering like bits of phosphorus. Mary had more than once seen Herod Antipater's eyes glitter like that when they were fastened on this singularly alluring and premature girl who wore her brief red garment as naturally as a young tigress wears its skin, and needed no bracelets nor anklets to render her appearance vivid. Perhaps — perhaps — But Mary quickly abjured the notion that entered her fevered brain.

Herodias happened to be strolling in the yard. She paused at the sight of her daughter torturing the bird, and merely smiled. It was plain that she approved of this show of spirit, so harmonious with that which throbbed beneath the thin and polished surface of her own alien training. On sudden impulse, Mary hastened down to join the mother and child. But Herodias turned disdainfully away at her approach and would have had no word with her, only that Mary placed herself squarely in her path and spoke:

"I know, my lady, that my presence here is unwelcome, and I want you to know, too, that I'd far rather be at my home in Magdala. The moment you can arrange to have me depart, I shall be most happy to do so."

These words had a softening effect on Herodias and the intense dislike in her countenance lessened, though she swept a haughty glance over her rival's person. As a woman, she understood her kind. "I perceive," she shrugged, "that what you really want to say is something further. Be quick, for I have no time to waste."

"I have nothing further to say. My mind is still filled with impressions of a prisoner in yonder dungeon whom I have just seen."

"You mean the man John?"

"Yes."

"He fills my mind, too; and with loathing. It was I who had my husband apprehend him for his insolence. But why are you interested?"

"Because I also have reason to abhor him."

"Has he slandered you likewise?"

"No. He scarcely knows me. And the worst he could say about me, anyhow, would be all too true. It is simply that he is the announcer and champion of one whom I have the best of reasons to execrate. With him gone, I'd be nearer to the other."

"You mean the Nazarene whom the rabble are proclaiming to be the Messias?"

"I do."

The two women locked glances and, for the first time, felt themselves to be close.

"What would you suggest?" asked Herodias.

"It is not for me but only for you, my lady, to make suggestions."

"My husband is reluctant to act, because of this criminal's great appeal to the people, who are murmuring at the taxes they must pay."

Impatiently Mary made a gesture with her hand as if to wave away the obstacle.

"I have tried to make my husband see differently," gloomed Herodias, "and thus far failed. Recently, though, a certain thought has come repeatedly to me." Her eyes, shadowed by her long dark lashes, turned slowly toward Salome who was standing by, intently listening.

Mary followed the gaze. Her breathing almost ceased.

Herodias drew her aside and, avid to share a secret, especially with a safe inferior, she let the excess of her hate for John find outlet in a whisper. "Tonight the tetrarch makes a feast. Much wine will be drunk. At such a time a man is most responsive to a request — if the right person makes it."

"You mean — "

The answer was a nod.

The banquet hall was not the less like the interior of an enormous death vault, for being illumined with torches set in serpentine holders that jutted from the high marble walls and threw a pale gleam fitfully on the face of each guest. The window drapes were flung wide, but hardly a breath of air was blowing in from the salty expanse of the Dead Sea, and the two huge bouquets of red roses with which Herodias had decorated the long table were wilting in their crystal bowls and dropping their petals like splotches of blood on the fine linen cloth.

Herod Antipater's gaze was glassy with wine, and he paid not the slightest attention to the melodies of the harpists behind the heavy green curtains that hung between a pair of Doric columns at the farther end of the hall. The blur within him, together with the encircling smoke from the censers which slaves were swinging to purify the air, rendered everything unreal to him except the little dark-eyed daughter Salome who had placed herself on his knees and was fingering his beard with one hand while she kept time to the notes of the music with the other. Herodias and Mary, seated near on gilded stools, were watching every movement with mounting approval and expectation.

"You love your father, do you not?" gruffed the tetrarch with drunken sentiment.

"Does my father love me," tinkled Salome, bobbing her perfumed black head up and down so that her necklace of many coins and her earrings flashed challengingly in his face.

"You know well that I do."

"But will my father prove it?"

"He will — if you will."

"How?"

"I'll grant you anything you wish."

"Anything?"

"Anything." And Herod sealed his promise with a great gulp from the goblet which the master of the feast, in accordance with Herodias' prearrangement, kept replenishing.

"Then what would my father have me do?" cooed Salome, linking her arm around his neck and rubbing her soft chin against his hairy chest. "Shall I show him my newest dance — the one the Arabian slave-women taught me?"

"Why not?" grinned Herod. "The Emperor Tiberias has a fond eye for the charm of little girl performers. I dare say my Salome can out-glitter them all. Show me!"

"But don't forget, my father, you've promised me anything I ask." The child's voice dripped with sweetness as she tweaked the tetrarch's ear, and her eyes laughed up into his bleary vision.

"I won't. But mind you, minx, you must please me with your best."

[74]

Herodias whispered to the feast-master to have the musicians play a certain sultry tune. And Salome slithered down from the tetrarch's lap, stood apart from the table, and struck a pose. With her hands — a pair of lotus blossoms — held high above her unruly tumble of curls, and her little bosom thrusting itself through its thin silk half-jacket, and her lissome body as erect as a young sapling, and her bare feet fluttering like two brown birds, she was visible music. As the strains grew wilder, so her muscles rippled the more sensuously to them. Now a quiver ran from the hollow in her neck to the soles of her feet; then from the twinkling toes up to her twilight countenance in which her eyes glistened like live beryls. Her hips swayed with the most insinuating of rhythms while her diaphanous skirt threw out its folds in the shape of a bell. She tore a flower from her hair, bit its beauty with her sharp white teeth, and threw it to the tetrarch who strained forward and muttered beneath his breath.

Louder the harps sounded, twanging the passion of hot desert nights and singing flesh, twirling their many-colored ribbons of melody around the verveful form; and the child matched the crescendo with such abandon that Mary wondered whether this was indeed the offspring of Herod or a sprite released from the brain of Beelzebub himself.

Turning her back to the tetrarch, Salome let him see the fluid fire of the dance move up and down her spine. She edged nearer and nearer to the ruler and ended by flinging herself — a moist palpitating mass — into his arms.

"You are all the blossoms of Israel crushed into one," his thick lips told her as he held her closely. "Tiberias in Rome has never seen the like of my own perfect daughter. What a woman, Herodias, she will make! And now, child, what can I give you for pleasing me so much?"

Salome's hands drew down his shaggy head and her lips pressed themselves to his rough ear, breathing rather than speaking the demand that her mother had prompted her to make.

"No, no," cried Herod, startled. "A severed head? — his! Has the very devil entered you, girl, to make you even think of such a thing? Are you possessed?" And his arms, loosening, tried to release her; but she clung as tight as a suckling cub to a brute breast.

"You said 'anything', my father," she reminded, pouting. "Everybody heard you. A king keeps his word."

"I am only a tetrarch and, unless I keep my people fairly satisfied, I'll be less than that," growled Herod.

"To me," lisped Salome, "my father is always a king."

"But, child, how can I do this thing? How — "

Salome silenced him with a kiss.

For several moments he held her, while a tumultuous debate raged within him. Instead of humoring this tiger-lily of the pit, he should be plucking her from evil with a severe reprimand; but her fragrant and insistent personality, as strong as the sweet Cypriot liquor with which he was sated, and her arch reminder about the honor of a kingly word, left him helpless in her shapely hands.

Shuddering, and as pale as one of old Herod's midnight visitors from the grave, he murmured, "Go to your mother, child. Your dismal wish shall be granted — Jehovah deliver me!"

"Will it be granted right away, my father?"

"Your haste is as accursed as your soul. — Well, so be it." And he signalled to his soldier-guards standing at the entrance of the hall to approach him. "Go to the depths of the fortress," he commanded, "and bring me the head of the prophet."

"Fetch it in this," ordered Salome, thrusting aside the

[76]

heap of roses in one of the crystal dishes and scattering their blood-tinted beauty over the table.

Herodias, flushed with excitement, had the master of the feast introduce some special singers to fill in the interlude of waiting. And as Salome came and cuddled at her side, the mother's lips were wreathed in a triumphant smile; but there was terror in her heart, too, now that the hour of vengeance on the hated Baptist had come. And Mary, from beneath drooped eyelids, watched the sordid actors in the unfolding drama, satisfied that, though Jesus of Nazareth was somewhere far off in the night, this scene was the first blow at his career.

Herodias desired the singers to be gay, but the song of their choosing was as doleful as a wind lost in the forlorn branches of December's trees; for these chanters knew and cherished John, and their spirits were heavy with the consciousness of his doom. Tears trembled in their eyes, and the cords of their throats were tautened.

Suddenly their voices ceased and a hush enveloped the hall. The soldiers, with a funereal tread that echoed through the silence, were returning. In the unsteady grasp of the foremost one of them lay the crystal bowl half-filled with dark fluid from which the upper portion of a gristly head appeared.

The soldier placed the object on the table and, covering his face with his palms, moved mournfully away, leaving the sight to such as had ordered it. Now let them gorge to their foul hearts' content and burst with the horror of the vision!

Up from the miniature pool of ooze that the hacked arteries had made, the eyes of John, wide open, stared the lustreless stare of the dead. All the guests averted their glances and swallowed hard against a surge of disgust and nausea. In an age of violent deeds, it was not unusual for delicate women to look unflinchingly on the unspeakable; but the spectacle of this poor head, turning the nameless color of a decayed blue and weltering in its own gore in a glass dish on a banquet table, was too much for even the strongest nerves, especially when the baleful flickering of the torches on the wall caught the surface of the eyeballs and silvered them with a flash of seeming life and denunciation.

"Remove that — thing!" shrieked Herod Antipater. "Let the imbecile that put it there be flogged!"

Another soldier stepped to the table and lifted the awful crystal; but his quivering hands could not hold it and it slipped with a crash to the hard mosaic floor, breaking into a hundred pieces, spattering blood in every direction, and causing the head to roll to the very foot of the tetrarch's chair.

Herodias threw her mantle over Salome who was frenziedly clutching at the maternal lap and burying her face in the abdomen.

Mary alone looked calmly on, giving the dead man's eyes stare for stare. "Thus perishes," she silently exulted, "the mouthpiece of him whose coming took my loved ones away." And she was glad — glad! — that, without any effort of her own, the first installment of her debt of hatred for the Nazarene had been paid.

Glad? Rising from her chair, she dropped to her knees to inspect the terrible face close up and gloat over it. But suddenly a weakness seized her as the smell of blood smote her nostrils, and an icy sweat seeped though her garments, and the marble walls of the hall melted into a swirling blur. For near to the eyes, without the lying flicker of the torches upon them, she saw that they were livingly agleam with a blend of such patience and peace as had dignified the countenance of young Josue, slain by Herod years

[78]

ago; and, again, they sparkled with the soft radiance of the wonderful lad whom she had heard speaking of divine love to the doctors in the Temple, and with the same light that she sensed when she said to the prisoner in the dungeon, "My name is Mary," and he remarked with emotion, "It is the name of his mother."

7

THE following morning, Mary asked the servants in
Herod Antipater's household about the Nazarene. At first,
they were loath to speak, for they suspected that her mind
was against him whom John the Baptist had loved unto
death; but when they saw the unhappiness in her eyes,
they felt her to be a sister to their own deep yearnings,
and they told her that, far beyond the range of the fortress, Jesus had gone; away into the desert to fast and pray.
And an impulse possessed her to go forth and find him
and upbraid him for the woe that followed his name.
What kind of person could he be, to have occasioned
great bloodshed at his birth and to inspire a faithful
herald like John to suffer prison and a hideous ending
with patience and consecration for his sake? Of a cer-
tainty, he was cruelty incarnate. Yet how could that be?
The servants described him as one who cared for the
poorest in Israel and walked among them with consola-
tion and without stain. They compared his personality to
the first breath of spring in a wintry land, and declared
that his passing left a trail of blessedness behind. But was
not this the very acme of vileness? — to capture men's
souls and, under the guise of befriending them, let their
grateful lives be crushed out without mercy? For surely
more blood would flow because of this man. Had she not
heard Herod Antipater thunder, in his terror, that blood

begets blood and that the fate of John the Baptist would now be that of many another? Had she not heard Herodias warning him that only in a wholesale extermination of such disturbers as these followers of the false one, could peace be restored to the state? "A tumor must be cut to its root," Herodias had stormed, seeking to conquer her own fear with truculence, "and the root is the Nazarene."

Arraying herself in her plainest dress and placing a ringlet of coins around her neck, Mary dismissed her maid-servant to Magdala and left the fortress, without informing either the tetrarch or his wife of her intent. A dagger, as sharp as the pain in her bosom, lay between her flesh and her robe. She would serve Israel, if she could, like Judith who slew Holofernes with her own hand. Yes, the hand of a harlot would be ennobled with a deed of deliverance. She must not wait for the slower and uncertain procedure of the tetrarch and his spouse. John, betrayed, must be avenged, even as she herself had been avenged in the fact of his decapitation.

The thought of the woman, the mother of Jesus, whose name had meant so much to John and was the same as her own, gave Mary pause; but she remembered her own mother, trampled to death by a mob, and convinced herself that this other woman, no matter how reverently the prophet had referred to her, was unworthy of regard. Had not the Baptist been mistaken in his loyalty to the Nazarene? Could he not have been equally deluded by one who bore such a son? And Mary resolved that nothing would be permitted to withhold her weapon when she was ready to strike.

Along the way, she made further inquiries of the poorest-looking people she met in the arid fields. Evidently it was this type that the Nazarene most favored and impressed. And, sure enough, two were able to tell her just what direction he had taken in seeking solitude. For fasting and prayer? Mary bit her lip cynically at the idea. Rather for laying fresh plans to mislead the simple!

The *jeshimon*, or desert, was not a stretch of sand but a waste land on both sides of the Dead Sea. Gnarled tree-limbs reached up from the ashy soil like the contorted arms of half-buried and beckoning corpses. Tufts of cacti, like green-moldy heads or ears with gray hairs standing out straight from the surface, lay all around. The scenery became more desolate, as Mary plunged deeper and deeper into the region of malediction, and she kept pondering that, of all places, this was the most appropriate not for a god but for a ghoul. Here lay the withering curse of Jehovah on what had been an abode of sin. Here the shafts of the sun smote the earth even as once fire and brimstone had fallen on Sodom and Gomorrah. Here only the bewildered and monstrous of soul — Mary herself an example of the one, and the Nazarene of the other — would penetrate far. The cracks of the roof of Sheol ran in long crooked lines beneath the feet, and a scent of sulphur poisoned the air and choked the throat. But now that she had come so far, Mary would not turn back; though, from fatigue and weariness, she could scarcely lift her head, and her eyes saw only the lonely rocks and the patches of brown grass and the scraggly florets that dotted the bleak and saline expanse.

When at last she lifted her veil and looked up, a mountain rose in a serrated mass before her, sufficiently distant for one to view the peak. A dark cloud enshadowed it. A shining white figure stood with out-stretched arms beneath the frown of the heavens and above the hardness of the tower of rocks. Could this be the Nazarene? He indeed it must be, for there the two poor strangers on the way had told Mary that she would find him. As she gazed, another figure, black as the womb of night, crawled up the sere summit and silhouetted itself like the outflung wings of a bat in the gleam of the moon. Round and round the shining one, the evil thing wove its way, gesticulating, pleading, wheedling, commanding, crouching, defying, trembling, and pointing to the four corners of the world. But the shining one stood firm and serene. And Mary, believing that the whole spectacle was an effect of eye-strain and an imagination superheated by the experiences of the previous night, and yet knowing that she had never been more awake and in possession of her senses before, watched as in a trance. The immemorial drama of light and darkness — Ormuzd embattled with Ahriman, as the bits of philosophy that floated into Palestine from Persia and Arabia phrased it — was unfolding before her very eyes.

Time stood still. Moments or ages might have passed. How long she remained motionless, with riveted vision, Mary would never know. Her heart pounded against the steel in her bosom, and her knees liquefied, and her gullet was as dry as the desert grass.

Slowly the clouds drifted away and the sun sent down a myriad of beams on the mount, and the summit seemed encircled with a crown of seraphs, and the white figure in the centre grew tall and taller, and the dark being — its mantle spread wide again in the semblance of a bat's hooked wings — swooped dejectedly down the middle of the mountain-side, leaving a streaming shadow as of blackest blood.

With a cry of terror from the core of her soul, as the thing came nearer and nearer, Mary threw her veil over her eyes and sank in a heap to the earth. Breathlessly, she waited, and every nerve in her body was tightened to the point of snapping. A stench as putrid as the essence of the tomb spread through the air. A presence, lead-heavy, pressed down upon her, smothering her lungs, rolling clammily over her flesh like an obscene tangle of serpents, freezing her skin to the bone, and cracking her lungs and heart with horror. Her fingertips and teeth dug the soil. To be buried alive were better than to be embraced by this spirit of uncleanliness, ferocity and doom.

The thing lingered, and all the voices of the damned, pressed into a single prolonged wail, accompanied its writhing.

But presently, when every sense was violated and flesh and blood could endure no more, it passed. And Mary lay more dead than living.

Some time after, she was revived as if by the passing of another presence, wholly different. The fragrance of springtime flowers — the same kind of perfume that had wafted itself on the mild April breeze when Phares led a girl to the hills over-hanging Nazareth — blessed the atmosphere. A hand, as soft as that of a mother soothing the brow of a sick child, moved over Mary's head, hardly touching the veil and yet dispensing a wealth of feeling. But when she dared look up again, there was nobody to be seen.

The mountain, as ordinary as any height of nature had ever been, loomed tenantless before her.

The dagger, which had fallen from her breast, glistened harmlessly, futilely, on the ground.

Mary now had one abiding thought — the Nazarene and Nazareth. She dragged herself from the desert and, having shekels in the ringlet on her neck, she was able, without returning to Macherus, to command assistance on the way up through the long valley of the Jordan, past the city of Tiberias, and over to the town that nestled in the hills of the west.

'It had been in the glory of springtime that she first glimpsed Nazareth; but now the place no longer resembled a bowl of blossoms. Rather, with its autumnal tints of russet and scarlet, it suggested a huge replica of the crystal, half-filled with blood, that lay on the table of Herod Antipater's feast; and Mary shuddered as she descended the hills, with a feeling that John's head, enlarged a hundred times beyond its natural size, might rise up out of the level of the scene.

She arrived on the morning of the sabbath day. The town was stirring, for the people were setting forth from their homes for the synagogue; and she joined a group of them.

"May Yahweh's light shine upon you!" greeted a woman in the group, whose wrinkled face contrasted with the smooth veil that fully covered her head and was caught up in a neat fold under her chin. "You are a stranger to Nazareth, I see. You come to us on a day of days. One of our men — the son of Joseph and Mary — has attained the rank of a rabbi and honors us this morn with speech. It is said that his power is great, and his good deeds many."

"Do the people know that the man John was slain in prison because of this rabbi?" asked Mary.

"Yes," answered the woman with sudden glumness. "The news came to us with the first frosty breath of winter. Soon all the leaves will have fallen in Israel. But Jesus is said to bring a message of an eternal spring."

Mary smiled wanly and spoke no more.

Near the door of the synagogue, some men with brown, weathered faces were gathered around a person who was pointing a finger to the skies. She would have paused, for something within her seemed to say, "This is he!" But the good old woman took her arm and suggested, "Let us hasten in. We are not too early."

The place was almost filled when the two entered and took chairs in the section reserved for females, which double lines of pillars separated from the rest of the building. Here the women could listen without seeing or being seen. The sin of Mother Eve lay dark on all her daughters, and Israel would not forget, and this segregation in worship was one of the many ways of remembering. Mary sighed to herself at the recollection that, through a woman, evil had first entered the race; and she wondered whether, through a woman, the order of decency and dignity would some day be restored. Must the female be ever disprized as the weaker vessel? Could not even one be found, in all the land, whose soul was a pearl? Even as Mary reflected, she noticed a blue-mantled figure kneeling meekly beside one of the windows, absorbed in prayer. She could not see the face, but was much moved by the grace and beauty of the outline. A white veil dropped its pure folds from the queenly head, and a hand, shining like a piece of alabaster in the morning light, clasped the front of the cloak and rested on the bosom.

The companion, noticing where Mary's glance was turning, whispered, "That is the mother of Jesus."

Just then, the voice of a man — the master of the congregation — sounded: "There stands at our portals a native of Nazareth who has become a rabbi in Israel. It is fitting that we call on him to read the Torah and expound its meaning this sabbath day. Jesus ben Joseph, come forth."

Mary strained forward to catch a glimpse of the Nazarene; but the pillars so obstructed the view that the effort was fruitless. She would have to be content, for the time being, with his words.

He began with a prayer. Wonder spread over Mary's countenance as a realization came to her that she was listening to a voice that she had heard before, years before, when she visited the Temple at Jerusalem and found a boy discoursing with bearded men. It was fuller and richer now, but essentially the same in its earnest unearthliness and calm authority. And she felt that, if a star-beam from heaven could speak, it would sound like this and say what the rabbi was saying —

"O Father, who did make all things good, behold how sin has spread its devastation beneath your throne. The sheep of Israel have strayed, and night hangs heavy o'er the land, and lives that should reflect your splendor yield only the deeds of darkness. But you have sent to the race a new day and yielded them a fresh start according to your holy plan. Your house is being repaired on the top of mountains, and is being exalted above the hills, and all nations shall flow into it. Your hand is upon the tall and lofty cedars of Libanus, and upon all the oaks of Basan — "

A new day. A fresh start. These were notes that sang into Mary's soul, relieving her sense of deepest guilt with hope.

And now the rabbi began to read from the sacred scroll: "The spirit of the Lord is upon me, wherefore he has anointed me to preach the gospel to the poor, he has sent me to heal the contrite of heart — "

The contrite. Alas, this gospel of forgiveness and healing, after all, was not for a refugee from Magdala. As yet there was no compunction in Mary's bosom for the past. There was no gift of tears for her eyes. Her experience in the desert had shaken her to the depths of her being but left many questions unanswered; and now these queries returned with all their painful insistency. If this man were as compassionate as his words proclaimed him to be, and if the spirit of the Lord were really upon him, why had so much unhappiness trailed his path? Could a text restore a dead brother and a mother and undo the wretched course of a life? If the Nazarene were powerful, would he not have prevented the fate of John as well as of Joas and Josue? His voice was as the honey-comb; but did not deceit drip from his lips? His hand, as she had seemed to feel it passing over her head when she lay in horror on the ground, was gentle; but the sword of the tetrarch was strong, as King Herod's had been strong before it. What were phrases, however exalted, when outweighed by facts? How could he forgive who himself had so much to be forgiven? His birth had brought disaster to the innocent. The day of which he spoke, was a fantasy; for Mary, it had meant but a long and shameful night. Her vision in the desert, of light wrestling with darkness, could have been only a mirage, however actual it appeared at the time.

No, no. The allure and appeal of the Nazarene's tones were but a seeming. The land had had many magnetic deceivers before. Here was yet another.

Faint with hunger, for she had eaten only a few morsels of bread during her long journey, and depressed by her thoughts, Mary rose and groped her way out of the synagogue. The old woman followed here. "Is there not something that I can do for you?" she sympathetically asked.

"No," Mary answered listlessly. "I know not why I came, and only know that I should depart. The rabbi's ideas are too winged for me, and I cannot harmonize them with life as I have known and lived it. He speaks of a contrite heart, but mine still knows no contrition — only hate. Hate and — confusion."

"Why not hear him out?"

"I have heard enough."

"Let me bring you to the home of his mother, there to await the end of the service."

"It is best that I be gone. Farewell."

The woman looked wistfully after the retreating form and mumbled to herself. "There is the weight of a rock on that poor soul," she puzzled. "Why has not Jesus lifted it?"

8

THE dying rays of the sun spread a vermilion canopy over the home in Magdala by the sea. Surrounded by other structures, it nevertheless seemed to be set apart and lonely.

"I am not displeased," confessed Mary to her maid-servant, Rhea, as she sat waiting, "that tonight Tullus with his friends will be visiting me. Too long have I tarried here since my return from Nazareth, mulling over my cares and shunning company. With all the guest rooms empty, this house must be dismal for you, too, child. I should have thought of that. But I have so much to forget!"

"Forget, my mistress?" Rhea's young face was warm with earnestness and interest.

"Yes, but I cannot. The past . . ." She stopped abruptly.

"Is it so powerful," asked the girl, "that it robs you of trust in the future?"

"For me and my kind, there is no future."

"There is the present. Let me adorn you with your rarest jewels and your richest robe."

"Do so, child," Mary rallied herself. "Make me fair. As fair as she who is Tullus' favorite goddess. Cynthia. Cynthia of the moon-beams. Tullus says that men are slaves to the night because of her. With her graceful bow, she shoots a gem-tipped arrow into the heart and leads her victim in keenest ecstasy to her realm of shadows blue. A pretty conceit, is it not?"

The girl placed on an ivory in-laid table a salver with rose water and lifted Mary's finger-tips into the vessel. Then she stroked the long auburn hair with a gold comb which flashed through the fine texture as sun-light in autumn leaves. Next she garlanded the fragrant head with pearls.

"You have not answered me," remarked Mary. "Did you not hear?"

"I did, my mistress. But I was thinking."

"Now it is my turn," smiled Mary faintly, "to be solicitous."

"I was thinking how much fairer than the myth of Cynthia are the truths that I have heard."

"You, child? What are such truths?"

"Beautiful ones. Beautiful enough to be true."

"There are no such things. All too soon you will learn, as I have learned, that beauty and truth are but words — words."

"And love?" breathed Rhea, lowering her eyes and dropping a transparent garment of amethyst silk, trimmed with silver, over her lady's shoulders.

"Love is the emptiest word of all. It lives only in a maiden's fancy."

"But, mistress mine, I have *seen* love."

"No. Into this mad world of ours, love is not yet born. Or, if born, it is strangled at birth. Men prate of it, and women sigh for it, but nobody lives it. The evil of life is more honest than the good, for it is usually selfishness with frankness and without pretense, though at times it does wrap itself in lofty speech so as the better to work its wrong. Men, Rhea, have always shown me much regard. Here in this very house, when almost as young as

[91]

you, I was given my first string of jewels by Phares. But it was as false a gift as the affection that he offered with it. Since then I have received numberless tokens of genuine value and yet as worthless. Whatever my so-called lovers offered was not for me but themselves. They were adorning their property." Her lips curled. "Alas, child, life is as far from love as the Dead Sea from the stars that shine above it."

"Stars, my mistress," offered Rhea softly, "can shine on the black surface of the sea as in the heights of heaven."

"How precious it is to have youth and pictures!" Mary turned her head away and gazed through the open curtains at the fountain in the court-yard throwing its sparklets into the gathering gloom, and at two doves mistily preening their wings in the gossamer spray.

"Did you not promise me and yourself, my mistress," chided Rhea, "that you would cast aside all brooding and not be sad tonight?"

"It is easier promised than fulfilled. While sunset makes my fellow-fools forget what they should remember, it reminds me of what I would forget. See how the court-yard is turning red in the after-glow, like blood —"

"Rather is the twilight spreading it with the flush of roses."

"No, Rhea. Blood — blood."

"You mean —"

"Another night. A night of death that lives on and must live on within me, casting its spell over my every day and year. A night when Juda suckled the breasts of anguish. You have often heard of the deed of King Herod: that, over a score and a half of years ago, at the bringing forth of a babe called Jesus, whom kings, led by a star, came from the east to adore, he was consumed with fear for his throne and decreed the end of little ones."

"The tale is whispered at fire-sides, and children quiver when it is told."

"But never have I told you — and I know not why I tell you now — that, the time Herod's sword fell, my happiness was slain. I had a baby brother, a golden-curled boy with a face like a rose bathed in star light. They called me his little mother. How I loved him!"

Rhea leaned over Mary's shoulder to adjust around her neck a delicate chain from which dangled a vial of subtle perfume. "Loved?" she echoed, with mild emphasis. "But you have said, my mistress, there is no such thing as love."

"For me and such as I, there assuredly is not. But once it seemed to be mine; yet so briefly that it rather seems never to have been at all. I must have dreamed. Such a love! The devotion of child for child, as clean and pure as April's breath. Oh, he was so small, so dear, Rhea! He fitted right into my arms. His eyes would laugh when I romped with him and fill with tears when I went away. There was a dimple in his cheek, and Mother and I always said, 'That's where his angel kissed him.' Strange how the sight of him is as vivid to me, after all the years, as it was in my girlhood; yet not so strange, for it was the last thing of living beauty I ever saw before the darkness fell."

Rhea slipped a pair of sandals on Mary's feet, smoothed the folds of the robe, and then seated herself on a low stool beside her. Thinking to woo her from melancholy, she reached for a lute, Rebecca's mahalath, behind her mistress' chair, and began to play; little knowing that music of this kind could not but open wider the doors that were best kept closed.

Mary's head drooped, and her fingers lay entwined in her lap, while the dulcet notes wove around her. Her lips kept moving, though her words were hardly audible, for they were more of a soliloquy than a disclosure. "It was

[93]

an evening in winter," she was saying, "and the gray old year had almost turned into the new, and a too early promise of warmth and sunshine was creeping into the air. False promise, Rhea. Spring never came for me again."

"It will be here when winter has passed and the rain is over and gone," sang the girl, still stroking the strings. "Poppies will toss their heads in the meadows. Irises will dance around the fountain. Lilies of the valley —"

Mary did not heed. "We were alone, my mother and I. Of what avail were a woman and a girl against destiny? — Oh, Rhea, we tried. How we tried! We used all the ability of our poor shaken reason. We concealed the infant. We —"

Her lips were a twist of pain. For a moment, she could not go on; but the handmaid continued softly to play, still hopeful that her effort would at least lessen the harsh discord of recollection.

"When Herod's soldier roughly seized the boy from my mother's arms," Mary mourned, "the little one opened his eyes — a smile slowly came to his lips. That smile, like a pale light, has often shone in my memory when life was loneliest."

"Please, dear lady, do not renew the heartbreak of it all."

"I could do nothing, Rhea. I turned to stone, even as Lot's wife was changed to a pillar of salt when she looked on evil. I could not move, but I could see my mother trampled, my brother engulfed in a wave of men's passions, my world come to an end. When the dawn filled the east, I was still alive after a dozen deaths. Only for the holy face of a young man, Josue, murdered by Herod but slumbering peacefully on his funeral bier, I'd have gone stark mad. I was alone."

Rhea laid aside the lute and, rising, lit some tapers, for the dusk had deepened into night and the shadows in the room were as dark as the gall of the mussel fish, called *hiluzon*, which was found in the waters of Genezareth and from which Magdala distilled a deep purple dye.

The emotion of Mary's countenance hardened into a marble mask, sinisterly beauteous in the candle beams. Her tones now came forth harsh: "That is why I am here, living the way I live, disbelieving in love, pandering to the selfishness of men, profiting from it, hating them and — myself. Yes, child, that is how I learned to hate. King Herod who feared little children — I hated him so much that my breast was a nest of vipers. And above all, I hated the child, Jesus, out of whose life had gushed death. Moses struck a rock and brought forth water to slake the thirst of our forefathers. Jesus struck our very flesh and the issue was blood."

"But why blame him, my mistress, for Herod's wickedness? As a babe, was he not as helpless as your own little brother?"

"Often have I put the same question to myself, Rhea, but a full answer has never come. Can you suggest one?"

"Who am I to answer the questions that trouble my mistress? I only know that a cruel king, and not a small child, was the cause of Israel's sorrow and yours. But you are over-wrought. Have a little rest before your guests appear."

With much effort, Mary again restrained herself. "Your advice is good," she said. "To speak of the past is to re-live and not relieve it. It is folly. Did you not say, Rhea, that you have seen love? What meant you?"

Rising slowly, Mary walked to the doorway with the fluid ease of limb which, whatever her inner tension, she could always command, and gazed beyond the fountain, off into the night. The risen moon's reflection in the sea was broken by ripples into a shimmer like the wings of a flock of the doves that Magdala bred for the sacrifices in the Temple, and the heavens were hung with purple as sombre and royal as the dye for which the town was famed. Among the many houses that adjoined Mary's estate, there rose one, more spacious than the rest, that afforded a meeting place for local thinkers; and tonight there were torches blazing on the roof of it because men stood listening to someone — doubtless an itinerant scholar — who was addressing them. For a moment, Mary, taken with her own thoughts, gave no ear to the snatches of the discourse that a breeze lifted her way. Her mind was on the contrast of the two industries of the town: dove-raising and purple dyeing; symbols of innocence and pride, light and shade, good and evil, side by side, forming the life of a community. Would it be ever thus? Birds could fly aloft into the realm of night, temporarily conquering it; but knives awaited their spotless bosoms, and the purple of death in the Temple of the living God was their appointed ending. Poor Rhea. Dove-like. Joas —

Of a sudden, Mary turned fully in the direction of the illuminated roof. Her chin tilted, her lips parted, and a spark swam in her eye. The voice. Could it be? Yes, yes, his — his. Was it everywhere? — in Jerusalem, Magdala, one's very soul?

"Listen, Rhea," she called. "Do you, too, hear it?"

And the words on the mild night-breeze were a bidding: "Love your enemies."

Rhea came quickly to the doorway and listened. And as Mary looked at her face, the plainness of it was transformed into something better than beauty. She had believed that she well knew the girl and her worth; yet this was the first time she had ever glimpsed her own

[96]

servant's soul. "Truly I hear," Rhea glowed. "There is the answer to my mistress' question about my seeing love! Love itself is speaking."

The voice flowed in benediction on the air: "Help those who harm you; help them to see and abjure their mistake; for they that harm are weak, and they that forgive and assist are strong. It is not what men do against you that matters, but how you respond to what is done. If your response be hate, you add your own fault to theirs. But if you forgive and love them that are misled by their darkened minds and unhappy wills, you confirm yourselves in goodness and thereby decrease the amount of evil in life."

"Too great is the evil to be diminished," sighed Mary. "Is the Dead Sea any the less, if a cup of its bitterness be taken away?"

"He would make all the bitterness a sea of sweetness," assured Rhea. "His message is ringing through this slumbering land like a bell."

"A bell? Yes, an interior bell. One hears him less as a speaker without than as a spirit within. Who is he, to invade the privacy of a soul? How is it, child, that you know him?"

Rhea's eyes were circles of shining devotion. "He has walked our streets for days," she explained, "and has even tarried by this house. I first saw him, some mornings ago, when my mistress was yet sleeping. I found him there by the fountain. I brought him bread, for there was hunger in his look; and he blessed the bread but did not eat it. 'There be others hungrier than I,' he said, looking in the direction of my mistress' room. I wanted to go and call you. He read my thoughts and said, 'Not yet. She will come to me in her own time.'"

"Why have you not told me this before?"

"I know not. I felt that he wished me to wait till such an opportunity as the present."

"Did he say more?"

"He merely held his hand over my head. And I was sure, my mistress, that heaven had never been so near to me before. Though it is not the time for flowers, the whole courtyard seemed anointed with the essence of them, and our doves flew round and round him, and the fountain leapt higher and made certain melody as the waters fell. When he went away, my spirit sank. Thrice have I seen him since, in the by-ways with his disciples; and each time my joy was greater."

"I have sensed a change in you, Rhea. A kind of blossoming of nature. Woman as I am, I've been curious. You were always docile, but inclined to be a little impatient and resentful when not pleased. But now — is it that your knowing him has somehow left you gentler — lovelier?"

The girl lowered her head and was silent. There was something in her face that recalled to Mary the aspect of the woman praying by the window in the synagogue of Nazareth.

"Holy must he be, to have such an effect on my little maid!" exclaimed Mary. "Yet, if so, why came he to a place like this?"

"It is his way. He comes where he is needed."

"This house is old in sin."

"Alas, so is the wide world."

"Nevertheless, lilies do grow in mire," reflected Mary. "It is a miracle, child, that no tarnish has touched your soul as you served me. You are good. As good as you were the day your mother left this world and I took you to myself. I wanted you to live in another and better environment, but greedily I kept you by my side."

"My mistress is generous. You shared your house with

me. Would that I could share my happiness with you!
O, lady, let me."

"I am evil."

Once more the night wind brushed the courtyard, and
it was enriched with the voice of the rabbi: "Behold, I
have come to call not the just, but the erring, to repentance. There is more joy in heaven over one sinner that
does penance than over ninety and nine that need it not.
Become like little children, and deliver yourselves to me,
all you who are heavy of heart. My yoke is comforting and
my burden blessed. I will relieve you of this body of
death. I will refresh you."

"Hear, my mistress, hear!" urged Rhea. "Has ever man
spoken like that before?"

Mary's cheek was pale in the moonlight. "Never, child,"
she agreed. "Too well I know! Never has man spoken like
that before." And she strained forward to catch more of
the plea, so singular to a woman of scarlet and so alien
to a dwelling built by one who had followed Rahab's
ancient profession of the flesh.

But the voice ceased. Mary and Rhea could see the
gathering on the roof breaking up. The murmur of many
tongues made a wave of confused sound, while a slave
extinguished the torches.

They went to the edge of the patio and, bending over
the balustrade, waited for the men to exit from the house
into the narrow street below. "You will see him," promised
Rhea. "I shall not have to point him out. His appearance,
even as his speech, surpasses that of any other man."

Soon the company emerged, and Mary's gaze was immediately drawn to a tall figure with a forehead smooth
and large. The hair, touched by the moon, parted shin-
ingly on the crown of the head, flowed in softest strands
below the ears, and rested in ringlets on broad shoulders;

the cheeks had the fine texture of acanthus petals and the color of wheat; the nose and mouth were shaped with exquisite symmetry; the eyes, even at a distance, showed the clear and steady quality of a child's and the lambency of two unbroken tears; the beard emphasized the sheer spirituality of the face. The form was covered with the plainest of white garments falling in graceful folds, and over the shoulders was thrown a blue mantle, exactly like that of the woman who prayed in the synagogue. His carriage held all the simple dignity of a shepherd-king. "It is he," exclaimed Mary. "The boy in the Temple become a man."

A father in the group was holding his sleepy little son in his embrace. One arm of the child lay on the man's neck, but the other dangled as if seeking the touch of someone else.

Jesus extended his hands. The father transferred his burden, and the child nestled his head on the Nazarene's bosom and seized a fold of the white robe with both of his tiny fists.

"See," said Rhea excitedly. "The rabbi presses the little one to his heart."

"I see only him," answered Mary. "So royal, yet meek. So much a man, yet more a god!"

"Look, his holy hand is now stroking the baby's curls, the while his lips are soft with a smile. The child — "

"Like my brother — my brother. Oh, Rhea, this boy could be my own Joas, come to life and receiving the caresses that were his due. How different is the Nazarene from King Herod who, far from fondling children, tortured them! This man indeed has feelings. He would not have permitted the massacre of the innocents, if — if he could have prevented it. Maybe you are right, Rhea. Maybe he was not to blame. But the power of the world

[100]

is not in the hands of the righteous. It belongs to the devil and his legions. I would that the Nazarene were as great as he appears to be good. I cannot believe that he is as good as he appears."

"Does one doubt that the moon is bright when its beams are witnesses?"

"Life, too, is at times beaming, child. But it lies worst when it shines best. This house is covered with marble and plated with gold; yet the crude sun-dried clay of Rebecca's time is still the fabric beneath."

Laughter now sounded at the gate: a bubble, a burst, a peal. The latch sprang up, the portal opened, and three men possessively entered.

"Greetings to Mary of Magdala, rival to Cynthia of the silver bowl!" cried the first, his helmet in the crook of his arm.

"Pearl of Galilee!" complimented the second, his eyes twinkling with the mockery of his meaning. "Or should I say pearls? You are displaying a king's ransom in your hair tonight Mary. But why not? You're a queen — at least to us."

"A queen not of pearls but of opals," frowned the third jovially. "I can never understand why our Mary persists in wearing the wrong kind of jewels. Have I not made my humble contribution toward a more appropriate array?"

Mary moved slightly toward them and put out her hands. Tullus, the first speaker, took one and kissed it. Osias, the second, seized the other and pressed it. Asar, slipping up closer, let his fingers entangle themselves amusedly with a strand of the gems in her tresses.

"Why have you refused to see me?" complained Tullus, drawing himself handsomely erect, and sweeping back his long mantle from his polished breast-plate. "What a

Roman does worst is wait. You have been back in Magdala for many days. The tetrarch keeps asking for you. Even Herodias, who used to impress me as rather desirous of plucking out one of your pretty eyes and wearing it in a locket on her luscious neck, expressed a desire to see you in Tiberias." He laughed. "Only young Salome has not missed you. She ground those sharp little teeth of hers when once I mentioned your name. The whole family, you know, left Macherus shortly after you did, and returned to the capital. Some of the soldiers had gossiped around the place that the headless body of the prophet John was seen parading the battlements in the dead of night; and that was more than noble, sensitive souls like Herod Antipater and his ill-gotten wife could stand."

"Speaking of prophets, Mary," chuckled Asar, "we've just had an experience. That's what delayed us in getting here. Ah yes, there was another attraction besides yourself for us this night."

"Don't look at us like that, lovely one," frivolously begged Osias. "Be not jealous. Asar is speaking not of a woman but of a man. The one out there."

"Out there," half-whispered Mary, returning her interest to the street. The Nazarene, still holding the child, could be seen in the distance.

"Yes," said Asar. "We started forth as soon as we had finished dining and the sun began to set. But nearing here, we noticed an extraordinary-looking person, about whom everybody is talking, wending his way with a score or more of the town's folk, and — well, for a lark and an appetizer to our joining you, Mary — we fell in line with them. They entered the house opposite, and so did we. They listened rapt to everything the lordly one had to say; and so —"

"Didn't we," guffawed Osias, slapping his thigh. "We knew better. But the way the local dim-wits opened their mouths at his words, you'd think he was giving them the honey of Engaddi. Nowadays one has only to be tall, raise the vision, and spout a bit of mystical nonsense — the worse, the better — in order to be acclaimed a prophet."

"But Mary, why do you keep searching the street?" demanded Asar. And turning to his comrades, he waved a foppish wrist and snickered, "Can it be that *our* queen of hearts is smitten with that rabbi? If so, this *is* a night of comedy."

"Supremely so," agreed Osias.

"Of a truth, though," continued Asar, "the rabbi does have charm. I think it must be his eyes. They melt — positively melt. They're not eyes but streamlets. They trickle like clean cool spring water over a brain that's heated with wine. He's the only discourser of his kind, and his is the only doctrine I've even so much as noticed since I started to think for myself. If it equalled his manner of delivery, he'd be perfect. As it is, he's really interesting. Amusing, too."

"Also, a good show-man," approved Osias. "Did you mark, Tullus and Asar, how he won everybody when he took the baby boy in his arms?"

"Shrewd simplicity," appraised Asar. "He's homespun and has the human touch. They say that he does wonders in order to win the masses, who think that anything they don't understand — and they understand nothing — is a miracle. And how he flatters his listeners! He's been known to call them the salt of the earth and the light of the world. Such an outpouring of excess I never heard of before. In a contest for absurdity, this young rabbi would be a king!"

Rhea, unable to control herself any longer, threw all caution aside and trembled from head to toe as she cried, "For shame, to speak thus! You know not whereof you speak."

Mary remained motionless.

"Why, the maid is almost of equal charm with the mistress!" exclaimed Asar. "I hardly knew she was here; and suddenly she becomes the center of things. Anger is a delightful cosmetic. Did you ever see such pinchable cheeks natural-tinted with fresh red, Osias? But I must say that, even in a place like this, servants are usually better trained. Our hostess is evidently over indulgent."

"Speak to me, Mary," begged Tullus who, all the while his comrades were chattering, kept watching the Magdalene. He had known her in many phases but never found her so absorbed in her thoughts before. She seemed a statue ornamenting the room, rather than a personality filling it; as fair a statue as the Galatea that Pygmalion prayed Venus to endow with life. Tullus imagined himself to be the love-sick sculptor of Cyprus, throwing incense on a flame of the great goddess' altar and seeing it shoot up a fiery point into the air in proof that marble would become flesh.

"I would know more about the Nazarene," confessed Mary.

"Oh, spare us," groaned Asar. "Haven't we prated enough about him? The subject is worn thread-bare. Let's have lights, music, festivity, you!"

"I would know more," repeated Mary with spirited insistence.

"What is there to tell?" shrugged Osias. "But if you must have further information, he is a nobody called Jesus. Also Christ. Born in Bethlehem of Juda."

"This I have already learned," said Mary.

[104]

"But have you been informed that his birth was as peculiar as his preachment? A virgin by the name of Mary —"

"The opposite of *our* Mary," interposed Asar, wagging a finger at Osias and winking.

Osias' lip twitched with amused appreciation. "So much the opposite," he continued, "that, if these two Marys should ever meet, it would be indeed a miracle. They dwell in two separate worlds. Well, the virgin, they say, brought forth this godly child. You have nothing comparable to that, Tullus, in your Roman mythology. We Jews are more subtle, if less picturesque, in our theological lore. In the case of Jesus, the story goes that a star streamed down on the spot where he was born and kings came from afar to worship him. And you Romans think that we Jews, who abjure painting and sculpture, have no imagination! Ah yes, there was plenty of excitement in Bethlehem and Jerusalem when the rabbi lay as a babe in his mother's arms. King Herod acted very wisely. What did he do? He whipped out the best of answers to all nonsense — his trusty sword — and ran it smack through the tender little body of every male child under two years of age in Bethlehem and vicinity."

Mary's hand sought her heart and quivered there. Her face was paler than the moonlight and a low moan escaped her. She would have fallen if Tullus and Rhea had not sprung to her side.

"This is strange," puzzled the Roman.

Rhea hastily explained: "My mistress has not been well for the last two weeks, and tonight she is not at all herself. It were best that you depart."

"So," sniffed Osias, "why not? Magdala has many attractions since Romans taught Jews the art of living. It was worth being conquered, Tullus, to learn how to shake off the shackles of boredom. Why waste a healthy night on the sick?"

"Wisdom speaks," chimed in Asar. "I know full many a place where mirth reigns."

Tullus did not withdraw his eyes from Mary. They burned on her beauty. "Yet would I linger here," he breathed, "if only my Cynthia cared. What has come over you, Mary? Has the chatter of these two irresponsible fellows disturbed you? I'll have them go, if you wish, and I'll remain to comfort you. See, I've brought the kind of gift you always liked best." He drew a small box of alabaster from his tunic. "Here is a perfume that Herodias would slay ten prophets to possess. The soul of a Galilean May is distilled into each amber drop. Will you accept it?"

Mary was not even listening.

"Ah well, then!" flushed Tullus, petulant. "After all, my spirit craves not a statue. I'm no Pygmalion. This is not the woman of warmth that I've cherished." He addressed the others: "Let's away, where Bacchus squeezes from grapes their purple blood, and good humor holds sway. The lady of Magdala's mood has driven us."

Hardly had the trio gone as far as the gate of the courtyard, however, when Tullus retraced his steps and begged Mary with fervent glances to invite him to tarry. But her eyes were still given to the night and did not include him in their range of vision at all. Shaking his head, he slipped the alabaster box into Rhea's hand and once more took his departure.

Rhea led her mistress back into the house and tried to have her recline. "I'll lave your brow with the contents of this casket," she suggested.

"No, my child," said Mary feebly. "My mind was meant for pain. Save the perfume for one worthy of it. Now leave me!"

The maid snuffed out the tapers, and darkness filled the room, save for the moonlight that turned the courtyard fountain into living silver and made a carpet of beams to the doorway where Mary forlornly stood.

She sobbed aloud and Rhea, not far away, heard and ached for her. "White doves reddened with their own blood! Innocent babes. Joas, our treasure! How soon, O Israel, have you forgotten and how lightly you can speak the horror that I never forget and that will follow me to the grave! And he — Jesus — so powerless to prevent this crime! Where was his might? What is his mission — his meaning?"

These and other distrait cries fell from Mary's trembling lips, as she blinked away a rush of salty tears. The moments passed. Presently, unobtrusively, a slender figure in a soft blue mantle and a flowing white veil, emerged as if from the shimmering spray of the fountain and walked in the path of the moonbeams, so like a spirit that the feet seemed scarcely to touch the pavement. The air was a velvet hush. "Mary, Mary of Magdala." In tones of celestial sweetness came the call.

Gazing in astonishment, the Magdalene rubbed her eyes with the back of her hand and still beheld a face as luminous as a star released from a cloud and as trustful and loving as a little child's.

"Who are you?" she asked, so low that the trickling murmur of the waters was louder than her words.

"I am Mary, too," the parted lips, with a glistening of pearl between, were saying. "The mother of Jesus. He sent me."

Mary's lips opened in deeper amazement, but no sound came from them. Surely this was not a woman like herself — or like other women — but an apparition.

As if in disproof of the idea, the lady came a step

nearer, and let Mary study her face, and touch her hand, imparting a sensation of utter but gentle reality.

"But your son — he has no reason to care for one who — " Mary faltered, unable to speak of hate in the presence of such a mother's love. "He has never seen me, and knows me not. How could he have heard about one so far from him as I?"

"He sees and knows all that are lost in darkness," the lady assured, smiling a smile of tender assurance. "And often in the deep of the night, he has heard your heart. He called me from Nazareth to come to you. You and I are related in pain. We both knew the agony of King Herod's sword. We each had a dear one."

"My brother died," moaned Mary, her voice trembling under the lash of memory. "Your son lives."

"Your brother lives too, ever happy, every young, ever yours." The lady lifted her hands and eyes to the dome of heaven. "Playing mid the stars."

"His blood was shed."

Now the lady touched Mary's hand, as if to heal her heart. "His innocence," she said, "was saved."

"So many other little ones died too!" breathed Mary, her voice rising to a point of accusation, for she found herself having to fight against the quiet force of the mother's appeal.

"They were angel-borne to paradise," came the answer. "They were the first florets of a new kingdom."

"Of a kingdom that is new, I know not. But too well I know the shame that is as old as man."

"Look up, my sister."

"You call me — sister," said Mary incredulously. "Do you know the life I have led?"

The lady bowed her head.

"And you call me *sister?*"

"God made us such."

Mary shook her head in vigorous denial. "Life has put us worlds apart."

"I am trying to draw near," said the visitant patiently. "Will you not let me?"

Mary recoiled. "Rather, like a leper," she cried, "should I throw a veil over my face and warn, 'Unclean, unclean.'"

"O Mary, look up," pleaded the mother. "In the name of the innocence of the little brother you loved so well, I pray you."

From the lily-like presence, Mary involuntarily raised her eyes. The clean beauty of the skies filled them. "Pure," she murmured. "And I — his sister — in the mire of earth. How much he has escaped!"

"He felt pain but once, and passed from it to blessedness," the mother added, softly pressing her advantage.

"Blessedness? — Yes. — Now I think I know why he smiled at death. To live, to be slain over and over again by the sword of life! — that fate was mine."

"My son would change it. Let him lead you. He has compassion on the multitude of such as you, my sister — lost and lonely."

In a surge of emotion, the sinner fell on her knees.

"O mother — mother of —" She could not finish the phrase.

It was enough. The night wind carried the name, and the whole court-yard resounded with the music of it. Like a note, plucked by David from the harp that soothed the torment of Saul, it vibrated lingeringly.

"Jesus."

9

I TOLD her all, Rhea," confided Mary the following morning as they sat at breakfast in the courtyard. "The memory of her visit would be only a dream, save that I have
proof she was here. See!"

She drew from her bosom a rose with dew asparkle on
its satin petals. "It came from the leafless bush by the
fountain," she explained, "and my lady gave it to me as
a sign. She called my brother 'a rose for heaven's garden.'
No longer can I think of him as aught else. No longer do
I bewail that his young life was culled from this world to
adorn another and a better. Hate fled my heart as I
listened to her, and its opposite entered in. This good
mother brings springtime wherever she steps." She paused
a moment, deep in thought, and then continued, "But
since she is so sacred, Rhea, what of her son? I fear to
face him."

"Fear not. That was what the heavenly choir told the
shepherds the night of his birth. Their message must have
been to us all; for are we not, all of us, shepherds of the
night?"

"Oh, that the night of my wretched life were at last
ending in dawn!"

"This face is the risen sun. We must walk in his light."

"He has already left Magdala," regretted Mary. "His

mother mentioned to me that he set out for Naim where he is needed."

Rhea seized the opportunity and exclaimed, "Let us follow him!"

"I do not dare. And yet — yet I must."

When the mistress and the maid, clad in simplest garments, were opening the gate of the courtyard, Tullus barred the path.

"Mary, I had to come again to see you," he confessed, his brow sullen but his manner subdued. Then, perceiving her simple dress, so unlike his Cynthia's, he asked sarcastically, "Are you on your way to friend or funeral?"

"Perhaps to both." A wisp of a smile sped over Mary's lips. "The life I have known is dead. I go to another."

"Your meaning is mystery. But what does it matter? The important thing is that I missed you last night more than I ever missed anyone before. It still perplexes me why you let me go. I tried to drown my vexation in wine with Osias and Asar, but your face floated in every goblet. I slept only to dream that an unearthly presence stood between us. To lose is to prize. I must have you for my very own. The price? Whatever you wish. A pet leopard with a collar of beaten gold? A span of jet black horses, fleet as an arrow from the bow, for even Pontius Pilate, Herod Antipater and Herodias to envy? Jewels—amethyst, feldspar, emerald and garnet — to dripple their glory over your form? A castle in Tiberias lined with Iberian bronze and Mauritanian lemon-wood? Anything — everything — "

"And what of love?" asked Mary, glancing at the fountain where Christ had lingered and his mother had stood.

The voice of Tullus was hoarse and abrupt. "Could love give more?"

"Or lust less?" said Mary tonelessly.

The Roman stared.

Her left hand held the folds of her mantle to her breast, but the fingers of the right touched the rose that lay near her heart. "The rabbi's face is child-like," she reflected aloud, "as is also his mother's. They both are immaculate."

"The rabbi? I cannot believe that you have succumbed to his high-flown folly. You are too experienced, Mary. A woman of the world."

"I was."

"And still are. Be shrewd. You belong to the kind of life I can offer, and to no other. They say that this man, for all his extravagance of doctrine, has a spirit as unspotted as the leaf of a lily. In all kindness, what would he have to do with a woman of your type? Need I remind you that your name is a by-word in Magdala and Tiberias? If you would really show regard for the rabbi, would it not be better to keep far away from him? Your person could but cast a shadow on a reputation that knows no stain. It would be — selfish — of you to seek him."

"Selfish? Yes, it would be that." Mary's voice broke as she turned from the gate, and, she, speaking to herself, sighed, "What right has shame to look in the eyes of virtue? Dare sin draw nigh to holiness? To what purpose?" Then to Rhea, "Tullus speaks truth."

"Jesus sent his mother to find you," reminded the maid, her face a plea.

"He did, Rhea. But I am much too guilty, too unprepared, to meet the son of such a mother. Perhaps — perhaps I shall never be ready. I am fit only for what Tullus represents and offers. Maybe I dreamed — too beautifully." She sank wearily on a bench near the gate.

"Yes, dreamed," insisted Tullus, glad of this advantage. "But not beautifully enough."

"Remember the rose," begged Rhea, taking her place beside her mistress. "You did not dream."

"Awake," invited Tullus, as he towered over her. "Awake to what is real."

Mary's voice was the far-off murmur of a sea-shell. "*What* is real?"

"My riches. These arms."

The Roman advanced to embrace the Magdalene and, in the act, disarranged her mantle, exposing her hand which held not only the folds of the garment but also an alabaster box. "What have we here?" he exclaimed. "So you have, after all, accepted my gift of last night? But why bear it like this out into the streets?"

"I meant to leave it at your house. This, the last gift received, was to be the first surrendered," said she as she held it toward him. "I had resolved to accept no more the price of shame. Take it."

"More and more nonsense," flushed Tullus, stepping back. "Did you not know that rather than have it back I'd break it, costly as it is, into a thousand pieces? No token of mine has ever been refused." His tone softened. "Keep it. I will come this night to be with you, Cynthia of the moonbeams."

The rose fell from Mary's breast and lay in all its dewy perfection on the pavement. Falling to her knees, Rhea hastily picked it up, kissed the petals, and offered it in her cupped palms to her mistress.

Still holding the box in one hand, Mary received the flower with the other. Her gaze mistily turned from box to flower and from flower to box. Here were two keys to different paths. Which must she choose? The pain of indecision furrowed her brow.

Tullus watched intensely, his passion seeking to envelop and draw her to his side.

The air was still, save for the liquid singing of the fountain; and in the rising spray, Mary seemed to see the dim outline of the mother's face.

Slowly she pressed the rose to her heart.

To reach Naim, the two women walked south, along the shore of the Sea of Galilee, through Tiberias. In the midst of the city, the spirit of the Magdalene faltered, for the splendor of this Roman foundation, reared by the sycophantic tetrarch to the honor of the imperial enslaver of Palestine, and hence sacred to the prostitution of the Jewish race, held everything that could trouble her conscience with reminders of her past. Here in this place, peopled so largely with aliens, the practice of Jewry was miserably adulterated and Zion was reduced to beggary at the gates. Here Herod Antipater and Herodias had smeared the profanation of a pagan culture over the lives of the natives, even as Mary herself had slimed with carnality most of the lives she had touched. Here, as a favorite, she had entered into all manner of festivities and been too much a part of the sensual scenes now to feel free from them. A bend in the road brought the tetrarch's palace vividly into view.

"Invisible hands — seven pairs of them — are clutching at me," she declared to Rhea. "Can they be the grasp of the demons I have served? They will not let me go. With foul breath, they shriek, 'Ours, ours.' This city is their home and I am theirs."

She stopped in her tracks and leaned heavily against an ivied wall.

"No, my mistress," pleaded Rhea. "Jesus drives forth evil spirits from the souls they would afflict. Let us hasten all the faster to Naim."

"Already I have come farther than my strength can

endure. I am footsore and weary. We shall tarry here the night."

"To look back — to linger — will mean again to be lost."

"How can I but look back? Here I had hours and days of release from sorrow."

"Only the false release that the drug of pleasure brings. Did you not always awake, my mistress, to greater distress?"

"But even a few moments of forgetting are to be prized."

"Did not the mother of Jesus grant you this favor?"

"But she has gone."

"And are we not going to her son?"

"This body of mine, child, has been pampered for long years. It is not equal to the pilgrimage. It was unreasonable of me to set out without money or means. And Naim is yet far away."

Grasping Mary's arm, Rhea replied, "This fatigue and weariness, my mistress, are but a portion of atonement for the luxury of the past. Lean on me. I am young and strong."

"O Rhea, you shame me. There are dark circles under your eyes and your cheeks are drawn. You are as out-done as myself. And yet you would have me use your poor youth for a support. You would lead me on."

"You are thinking of the difficulty of the journey; I, of the journey's end," soothed the girl.

"I'll try to share your mind. That will be my strength. But what a weight I drag behind me! If you could see my soul, child, you would run from me in horror."

"His mother saw it, my mistress, and stayed."

"Yes, and she even called me sister."

"A few miles more, and this city of sin will be behind us. Soon we shall be entering the town of Emmaus."

"No, Rhea. Evil is at hand. I feel it. I know it. I rejoiced in the death of John. I wished only harm for Christ."

"Does he not understand? Did he not send his mother to you in proof, and did she not leave you a sign? Touch the rose yet again, my lady. It will renew your spirit."

Obediently Mary thrust her hand into her bosom, and her face smoothed, but trouble tarried in her eyes.

"Do you hear the galloping of horses' hooves in the distance?" she asked. "Look back, Rhea. I dare not — now."

"There is a cloud of dust far down the street. Yes, I see horsemen."

"We are being pursued!"

"Ahead is a grove of thyme trees, mistress. Let us run and take shelter in the shadows till the riders pass."

Moments later, unseen but seeing, the mistress and the maid were dismayed to behold Tullus, Osias and Asar, mounted on horses, dashing by.

"It is easier," whispered Mary, "to leave the past than to be left by it. Tullus has found out where Christ went from Magdala, and knows we are going to him. He must have suddenly decided to take matters into his own hands. His proud Roman nature will not be denied, and he brings his comrades to bear witness. Our journey has ended without the ending we planned."

"Say not so. It is safer to have these ill-wishers ahead than behind," encouraged the girl. "They are out of sight now. We can proceed in peace."

"But, not having found us on the road, they will await our arrival in Naim," hesitated Mary. "They will never let us reach Jesus."

"Is that what the rose in your bosom is saying?" chided Rhea softly.

Mary did not answer, but her veiled head lifted, and

her shoulders straightened, and her feet fell into step with her guide.

Dawn brought them the lordly vision of Mount Thabor, symmetrical as a Grecian sculpture, its flat limestone summit catching the first rays of the sun and plaiting them into a blazing diadem. Mary and Rhea, gazing, were thinking the same thought: that, even as this burst of light was now driving out darkness and ushering in the day, Deborah had once issued from those same heights with ten thousand armed soldiers and conquered Sisara on the banks of the Kishon.

"It is not unlike the mount beyond Macherus," said Mary, "where I saw the spirit of darkness rebuked as if by the son of God."

"There is blood, though, on Thabor," recalled Rhea. "The brothers of Gideon were murdered here by Zebah and Zalmunna."

"Where there is battle, there must be blood," sighed Mary. "I wonder whither the life of Christ is tending. There are others like myself who have resisted him with hate and, unlike myself, have not yet had their blindness opened to the light. Tullus is moved by darkness."

"The Lord has given his angels charge over the gentle Jesus. No harm can fall."

"Off to the west lies Nazareth. Somehow I cannot but associate the peace of that place with the glory of this mount. If Christ should ever have a throne in Israel, would not Thabor well supply the need?"

"He was born to be a king," exulted Rhea.

"A king," echoed Mary. "Israel shall be his realm!"

And as the day was declining and the village of Naim came to view, they paused at a humble house by the side of the road to beg a crust of bread and a cup of water.

There was no response to their knock at the door, so Rhea timidly lifted the latch. On the sand floor of the single room, a woman and a young man were kneeling, their faces etched in a shaft of pink light from the window and their spirits bound up with the unseen.

"Good mother," called Rhea.

The woman stirred, and she and the young man rose up, blinking as if shaking a dream from their eyelids.

"We are strangers," explained Rhea, "on our way to see the rabbi Jesus who is tarrying in Naim. In the name of our father Abraham, would you give my mistress to eat and drink?"

"What we have is yours," replied the woman. "Our poor table is laid. My son Joachim and I were giving thanks to Heaven and Jesus for the greatest favor of our lives. Last night, this house held fear and death. Tonight it knows joy and life."

Mary and Rhea looked at each other in astonishment.

"You are surprised at what I say. Yet more surprising is what I shall tell you. Sit with us and break bread while I speak."

Sitting, Mary and Rhea waited. The working of the woman's face evinced that she was fumbling for words. And Mary, glancing at Joachim, whose eyes were fixed on space, had a conviction that she had somewhere seen this countenance before. Yes, it reflected that of the boy who spoke so long ago to the doctors in the Temple; but even more it suggested the meek and serene visage of the youth in whose throat Herod's dagger had been plunged.

Involuntarily a question sprang to her tongue. "Do you know him who is called the Christ?"

"Know him?" repeated the young man wonderingly. "How could I but know him whom I adore?"

"Adore! Only God can be adored."

"Even so."

"Yesterday," said the woman, "my son lay lifeless. To-day he lives to praise one who, to him and me, is God."

"You mean —"

"As lifeless as the tomb, last night his body slept in this very room and I mourned over it until the dawn. My mind kept turning to Jesus ben Joseph, who has wrought miracles of mercy on the sick in Capharnaum. And I thought: If he can bring health to the diseased, can he not restore life to the dead?" Her voice was almost a whisper, but her eyes were alive with excitement. "All through the bleak hours I called to him. He must have heard. Today, when the small funeral procession was passing to the caves of burial at the western end of Naim, he was waiting. He saw me weeping. Joachim is my only one and I am a widow. So he came forth, placed his arm around my shoulder, told me tenderly, 'My own mother would have me do this,' and touched the bier. Whereupon my son sat up slowly from death as from a great sleep, and Jesus gave him back to me."

Mary left her place at the table and sank to her knees before the youth. "Dead?" she murmured in vibrant awe. "Dead? He heals even death?"

Joachim's answer was a chime from another world. "He who gives life — can he not restore it?"

"I myself have been dead — dead to hope. Dead in blackest sin. Do you not remember the — the things of darkness?"

"What is there to remember of darkness after looking on his face? Now I remember only light."

"Your face, Joachim, reminds me of one I knew, who long ago died for Jesus. Why did not the great power bring him back too?"

"The master's public mission had not yet begun. Besides, one who laid down his life for him was much worthier of rest than I. In fine, my mother needed me, and Christ's own mother knew the need. She passed by here the night before last on her way from Nazareth, as she more than once had done before, and she sat at my bed of illness, stroking my brow and speaking of Jesus. When I closed my eyes in the last cold moment, I was thinking of him; and when the bandages of sepulture were removed by my mother's hand from my head, there he was. I knew him from his own mother's words."

"Happy youth, to have received such a favor! His mother has spoken to me also, and likewise she knows my want. There is little strength left in me, but what I have I will use to drag myself to his holy feet. Perhaps even for me who am a corpse to virtue, there is a renewal of life."

Rising up, she took Rhea's arm. "Come, child."

"Will you not pause and eat?" solicitously urged the mother.

"There is hunger in my soul beyond all bodily demand," said Mary. "This very night, without delay, I must see the Lord or remain forever lost."

"You will find him at the house of Simon the Pharisee. It is the largest dwelling on the main thoroughfare of the town. Too, you will find that his kindness is equal to his power. I can never forget his sheltering arm and his reference to the sainted woman who bore him."

Obeying a sudden impulse, Mary withdrew the rose from her robe. It was as fresh as at the time she first received it. "Please accept this," she begged the mother. "It is all I have. It came from her. I prize it inexpressibly, but require it no longer. This wonder that has happened to your son means confidence to my spirit."

The woman held the bloom in her wrinkled hands and raised it to her lips. "Blessed," she exclaimed, her eyes as bright with tears as the rose with dew, "is the womb that yielded him who has restored the flower of my years!"

10

Simon's reason for inviting the Nazarene to his house was threefold. As a Pharisee, he felt that this man, performing deeds that captured the imagination of the people and prescinding at times from the literal practice of the law, could develop into a menace. The news of his latest exploit of evoking a youth from the dead had spread in a few hours through the country-side like a fire through dry leaves, and tonight everybody was cackling about it as if it were the deed of the ages. Too, a rich Roman with two companions had come to Naim and immediately gotten into touch with Simon as the most influential citizen of the town. Flattered, the man saw no reason for refusing their request that he invite both them and the rabbi to dine with him. Furthermore, there was a custom in Jewish life to welcome all strangers, for the Torah taught that the Lord loved the wayfarer and wished him to be received "as the sons of Jacob were received in Egypt."

When the excitement of the resurrection was at its height that day, a servant had come to tell him of it, and he hurried to the scene. Momentarily fear seized him at the sight of the risen youth, still half-swathed in funeral bandages and trembling in the arms of his mother; but scepticism immediately came to his relief and he made himself marvel at the credulity of those who had gapingly gathered to extol the "miracle." More concerned with the wonder-worker than the wonder, he approached Christ and declared, "I entreat you to sit at my table tonight with my guests and share your message with us in the breaking of bread. I am Simon."

"There was once a Simon of the tribe of Benjamin," said Christ with meek archness, "who, when appointed overseer of the Temple, strove in opposition to the high priest to bring about an unjust thing in Jerusalem."

"You mean him that went to the governor of Celesyria and Phoenicia and excited his cupidity with stories of the rich treasury in the Temple?"

Christ inclined his head.

"But I am not as my namesake," protested Simon. "I would safeguard the sacred funds with my life and never betray them!"

"There is another treasury in Israel," affirmed the rabbi, "that should have protection. Its betrayers will be as many as its defenders few."

"Of what treasury do you speak?"

"The truth."

"It is this that I and my guests would hear. Wherefore I invite you to my house."

"To receive me or to ensnare me?"

Simon's face turned color at the directness of this question that penetrated his thought. "I will try to perform the duties of host in accordance with the commandment of hospitality," he promised hastily and evasively. "Will you come?"

"I shall come."

The exterior of Simon's house was plain, as befitted a people whose ancestors were shepherds and dwellers in tents and originally had no architecture. But the interior gave no hint of the basic simplicity of Jewish life, for it was almost a perfect replica of Roman luxury. The walls were warm with highly tinted Egyptian tapestries. The floors told stories with their polished mosaics. Vessels of valuable metal and ivory gleamed wherever the eye turned, and the number of servants always exceeded that of the guests.

Tonight the dining room, filled with visitors and candle-glow, seemed nearly as formal as that in the palace of Herod Antipater at Tiberias. Simon reclined at one end of the long table with Tullus at his right hand and Osias and Asar at his left, and with certain learned men of Naim — Pharisees — placed according to their rank. The other end was occupied by Christ and his apostles. The servants brought water, and all but the Nazarene and his little company dipped their fingers.

"It is our good custom," observed Simon to his guests, but aiming his words at Christ, "to purify the hands with water before touching food."

"It is a better custom," said Christ, without raising his eyes, "to purify the heart with prayer." And he blessed the bread that was placed before him, breaking it and distributing the pieces to his disciples.

"I perceive, my host," muttered Tullus under his breath, looking askance at the others, "that you have a rebel on your hands."

Taking their cue from Tullus, Osias and Asar mumbled something about a gross disregard of Jewish ceremonial and the peril of tolerating innovators, while each Pharisee in imitation of the host bristled.

"Is it true, rabbi," demanded Simon, "that your doctrine is such as to permit association with tax collectors and sinners?"

Christ lifted his head and gazed straight into Simon's eyes. Slowly his line of vision turned to Tullus, thence to Osias and Asar, and then back to Simon. "Is a tax-collector that takes away the sustenance of Israel any worse than the alien that profits from the tax?" he asked. "And are not all men sinners?"

An angry spot burned in Simon's cheek. "I will not have my guests offended!" he cried.

"Then the purpose of this supper — the truth — must be foregone," answered Christ evenly.

Tullus and his comrades bent toward their host. "This man is a carpenter," recalled Tullus. "He carries his old means of livelihood even to a feast, and would saw off our ears."

"It was at your request," reminded Simon, "that I invited him here. His utterances shall direct our future action. Let us hear him further." And he lifted his voice. "All Naim is ringing this night, rabbi, with praise of the wonder that you are alleged to have performed this day. Was that widow's son really dead?"

It was Peter, the most robust and impressive of the apostles, who responded, and his grizzled beard puffed out from his lips with the vibration of his contempt for the question. "If the boy were not dead before my master touched the bier," he defended, "he would certainly be so by now. Yes, buried."

The Pharisees regarded one another interestedly. Some smiled. Others stroked their chins slowly.

A discussion began, led by Simon, on the subject of Egyptian embalming. "It would be quite impossible to restore a dead man to life in the land of Nilus," he offered. "There a person dies honestly and totally. The relatives see to that. They disembowel the deceased, place the entrails in an urn, and soak the cadaver in a vat of strong and secret fluid. After which, they stuff the remains with spices, enfold them in many bands, and seal them closely in an encasement that matches the contours of the physical form. It would indeed strain your powers, rabbi, to make a mummy sit up and stare, would it not?"

Christ did not deign to answer. His head slightly turned, as if his ear were attending to the sound of voices in the street. There was a look of expectation in his eyes.

"We Jews," accused a Pharisee, "are too remiss in our disposal of the dead. We merely burn incense, anoint the body, wrap the trunk and head separately with strips of cloth, and think that the preparation for the tomb is complete. We could learn much from the caution of the sons of Osiris."

"Only Jehovah," remarked another, "knows how many Jews have been buried alive, through the centuries, by the ignorance of those that cherished them most."

"Death is but a longer sleep than the usual nightly slumber," volunteered yet another of the guests. "I have heard of individuals who slept for days and, to all appearances, no longer breathed; yet they returned, of themselves, to life's tasks. Had the rabbi been present at their awakening, he could have taken much credit unto himself; as could anybody else that cared to do so."

"The theme is too sunless for a happy occasion," objected Tullus impatiently. "Men of Israel, is this not a feast? As a healthy Roman, I am not fond of good food and grim topics at the same time."

Osias and Asar started off a ripple of mirth which lightened the tension at Simon's end of the table.

The sound of many voices at the gates of the house could be heard in the dining hall.

"They are the town's folk calling for the rabbi," explained Simon. "They know he is here and desire entrance so that they can gather up his words. What says the cause to the clamor?"

"Today," answered Christ, "Naim viewed a body coming to life. Tonight, you who are here assembled shall see a soul restored. Simon, there is a woman at the door, accompanied by her maid, who, above all the rest, craves admittance. Will you let her enter?"

"I have given my servants an order to keep all these people out," hesitated Simon.

"Why so?"

"They are poor and ignorant. They know not the laws of purity and impurity."

"Do you? How can the humble who worship the true God defile a home that a worshipper of false gods, two traitors to the faith of Israel, and several hypocrites adorn?"

A flush suffused the face of Simon. "I suggest, rabbi, that you hold your tongue," he said stiffly. "For the third time this night, a taunting insolence has profaned your lips, which should be sealed in the nobility of your calling."

"Is it unseemly, Simon, to utter the truth that should be told? And did you not ask me here to speak it?"

"The man is demented," grumbled Tullus to Osias and Asar just loudly enough for Simon and his fellow Pharisees to hear. "In Rome, we'd make short work of him. Palestine lies conquered because she cannot control even her own mouth-pieces."

"In Magdala, whence we came," remarked Osias, "this rabbi was passably meek. But he grows more arrogant by the hour. The fame of his latest exploit has doubtless heated and expanded his brain. You'd think he was God!"

"Hush!" bade Asar. "Look."

There in the door-way, Mary, with her long hair unbound and dishevelled and her arms extended, stood like a statue astray from a pedestal. One shoulder showed white and bare where the rough hand of a servant had torn the garment away. The fingers of her right hand clutched an object that shone through the spaces of them. Her cheeks were pallid. Her eyes protruded with a nameless hunger, searching out, finding, and riveting themselves on the rabbi.

"Mary!" cried Tullus, springing up.

"The bird has flown right into the net," approved Osias to Asar. "This will be worth watching. What a Roman wants, he already half has."

For a second, Mary looked at Tullus and then, with a moan, hurried to Christ, falling on her knees at his feet.

"For the first time in my life," grieved Simon, wringing his hands, "I am without authority in my own home. Is it that I am as much a nobody as the least of my slaves?" He sat back inert, appealing to his Pharisee colleagues with up-lifted hands and a quick dart of the eye, and his frown rested on the Nazarene.

Tullus had left his place at the table, followed by his two shadows, and was standing close to Mary, unable to believe his senses. Could this be his Cynthia, so shorn of queenliness as to be grovelling before these people — this man? The hair of her bowed head streamed in two red rivulets over the floor, exposing the milkiness of her neck where the strands parted. Her shoulders were writhing in the paroxysm of her sobs. The rabbi's feet were wet with her weeping as she kissed them over and over again. She dried them with what had been her crowning glory.

"Mary!" called Tullus.

She heard not.

"Mary of Magdala!" repeated Osias and Asar.

"Mary of Magdala? — the courtesan?" exclaimed one of the Pharisees, turning his head. "Polluted is your house indeed, Simon, with this visitation!"

For minutes, silence filled the hall, except for the sound of Mary's weeping.

"Her affair with Herod Antipater, right under the nose of the tetrarchess, was worse than shameless," hissed another Pharisee to the man beside him, his hand over his mouth.

" 'Her feet go down into death, and her steps go in as far as hell,' " quoted a third aloud from the Book of Proverbs.

Simon, mortified beyond further endurance, almost screamed to his servants in the door-way, "Cast this creature forth." To his fellow Pharisees, he groaned, "It is written that to touch evil is to be rendered unclean; and into my house has dashed this daughter of the night to curse the whole atmosphere with her presence. All the ashes of a red heifer, sprinkled through my rooms, will not be enough to exorcise them."

"The Nazarene has insulted us for the last time!" cried Tullus, his hand on the hilt of his sword, his face livid. "I have much influence with Pontius Pilate — "

"And we with the Sanhedrin," added Simon. "This — this episode, I promise you, shall have proper effect. I invited the rabbi to break bread with us for sundry reasons, but chiefly to prove him. It is now clear that rumor has not been a liar. The poison of asps is under his tongue. He defies the law of purity. He dipped not his fingers before he touched food. He permits this notorious strumpet to approach his person with her vulgar display of tears —"

In the thrall of his emotion, he stammered and spluttered, finding words only to repeat his command, "Servants, cast her forth!"

Mary, in the midst of her weeping, was not unaware of the storm that her presence had evoked. She glanced up now at the stern and troubled Pharisee, and he appeared small and unimportant. He and his fellows meant nothing to her, with Christ sitting calm, controlled and strong, in a manner that made his simple chair a throne; and she turned her streaming eyes to his face. For an instant their glances met in an exchange of sorrow and mercy. Drawing from the folds of her cloak the alabaster box, Mary opened it and silently poured the contents on Jesus' feet; and the fragrance of a hundred flowered hillsides riffled by a breeze, pervaded the room.

Six menials of the house had surrounded the Nazarene's portion of the table. Agile to Simon's least command and ashamed that a woman had managed to tear her way through their opposition, they would gladly have expelled her forthwith, only that they too had permitted their glances to turn to Jesus and were powerless before his quiet authority which filled both the entire hall with its effect and every man in it with a disturbing sense of what he was. The seconds seemed years in that awesome moment, as they all, guests and servants, waited for the words that they knew would come.

Jesus lowered his lids and let a half smile, much too tender for mirth, wreathe his lips; and then those lips parted, while a tremor of apprehension passed over the room and the woman who had entered without invitation.

"Simon," he spoke unhurriedly, "I entered into your house. You gave me no water for my feet. But she, with tears, has washed my feet, and with her hair has wiped them. My head with oil you did not anoint. But she with ointment has anointed my feet." He paused and let his serene gaze roam over the host and the other Pharisees, who were stricken with chagrin at having a lack of courtesy so openly criticized.

Again he looked directly at Simon and continued: "You

gave me no kiss, but she, since she came in, has not
ceased to kiss my feet." Then in a deeper yet still quiet
tone, he addressed all, "Many sins are forgiven her, because she has loved much." And looking down into Mary's
up-turned face, he whispered, "Your faith has made you
safe. Go in peace."

Wonderment claimed every countenance as Mary let
herself be assisted by Rhea, who had succeeded in de-
taching herself from the spectators in the doorway and
was now enfolding her in her arms.

Outside, the mistress and the maid worked their way
through the curious crowd and, hand in hand, set off
into the night.

In her mind, as they hurried along, Mary's thoughts
tumbled one upon another. Oh, the greatness of the
heart that could manifest so much kindness to one such
as she! Those whispered words of parting, that benedic-
tive smile, that evidence of inner power, that innate
royalty mellowed by a perfect humanhood into the likeness of the sun's very splendor blending with the gentle
blue! — these notes she could never forget. Never had anyone possessed more kingly bearing than the son of the carpenter. The effect of his mere glance was that of a ruler
whose every wish could guarantee instant obedience. So
must Solomon have appeared when Israel was in her
prime. So must he have shown himself to the Queen of
Saba.

Like Saba, Mary at last knew that she had a master
worth serving; and since he could not be pleased in the
way she had pleased other men, she must find other
means. She would — she would. But how?

The night winds, rustling the leaves of the trees,
echoed the question — the most important with which
she had ever been confronted — in her soul.

11

It DID not occur to Mary and Rhea, surcharged with the emotion of the scene in Simon's house, to pick a direction. They merely walked on, lost in recollection of him whom they had found, along a road that flowed like a river of white in the gleaming of the moon; and, to their pleasant surprise, they at length knew that they were again nearing the home of the widow, to which Christ's will had been seemingly leading them.

A lamp burned in the open window and the music of two voices, given to a psalm, was on the breeze.

"Could it be," wondered Rhea, "that the light and the song are for us?"

"Anything could be, this beauteous night," answered Mary. These were her first words since leaving Jesus. "The song is the resonance of his goodness in hearts that are thankful, and the light a reflection of his love."

At the door, the mother and the son were waiting, "Something told us you would return," the woman elated. "He who favored my son this day, would have both me and the boy share the blessing with you this night. Here you must rest for the nonce, and may tarry as long thereafter as you will. My table is still set. Let us sit and speak of him who fills our bosoms."

Speak of him? Ah yes, that would be blessedness. There were so many things to learn, and opportunity had come so late! Oh, the waste of years! But better than converse would it be to tarry not; rather to bear on — to serve his cause. Yet, worn out in body, though never more vibrantly alive in spirit, Mary could not but partake of the hospitality to which he had sent her when he said, "Go in peace." This humble home would be, however briefly, her first school; and here, listening, she could fix her plans for tomorrow's action. Taking a chair at the board, she was relieved that the good woman, with much delicacy, did not ply her with questions.

Her thoughts set her definitely apart and she hardly noticed the cup of wine that Joachim poured for her. He and Rhea exchanged glances, expressive of surprise at Mary's abstraction on the one hand, and of explanation on the other; but, as is always the case with a young man and a maiden, looks lost all their original meaning by lengthening into a gaze. For Joachim surprised a warm glow in the girl, transfiguring her modest countenance into beauty, and his eyes filled with a gently eager interest; while Rhea discovered in him an attractive virtue, which caused her, after a brief hesitation, to let her lashes droop in a way that shaded her inner response as well as her pale cheeks.

Silence possessed the little group and, less awkward than gracious, it drew their dispositions into a unity that was balm. Mary's tensity relaxed and, when the widow at last spoke, she found herself necessarily attentive; for the woman was telling of Bethlehem and the poverty that Jesus, so great and good, had always known. "Though the land had long awaited and sighed for the coming of such a one," she was saying, "there was no place in Israel for him when he was born. Nothing but a cave in which cattle took shelter from storms."

Had the theme been any other, Mary might have continued calm; but here was a challenge to her devotion, and her unstable mood could not resist it. "That," she cried with feeling, "was only the start. But now that his merit is known, ought he not to be properly received? What his infancy lacked, his manhood must have, and must have abundantly, in atonement for that first mistaken night. I changed an ordinary inn in Magdala into a fair residence, as Rhea can tell you. I did it for myself. Would it not now be mete to do something similar for another? Rocks can be turned to marble and a drab interior to gold. He who first saw life in a stable should find it fulfilled in a palace!"

"A palace?" echoed the widow. "I doubt that Christ would ever feel at home in one. His tastes are as simple as his power is sublime."

"Even so, his majesty calls for a sumptuous setting," Mary insisted, emphasizing her belief by tapping her fingers on the table, and gazing at the others with a look that demanded agreement.

"I know," conceded the widow, hesitantly, "that the best is far from being worthy of him. But —"

Then Joachim gave utterance. "When I returned to life this day," he slowly disclosed, "I saw the world in a light that was new and fresh. It was as if I had never really seen it before — its fertile floors from which men draw the means of sustaining life, its blue dome that drips with goodly rain and sparkles with sunshine and quivers with stars, its birdsongs, its moving and breathing ornaments that we call mankind, its keynote of love!" His eyes met those of Rhea, whose gaze once more fell, and then turned to those of his understanding mother. "And when I looked into Jesus' face —"

He paused, unable for a moment to go on, for his voice was choked with feeling.

"His face!" breathed Mary, her own countenance lighting up.

"I bethought myself," continued the boy, "that here was Jesus' home. The whole land. The only estate he would ever wish to have."

"I see otherwise," objected Mary too suddenly and a little harshly. "Nature is far from being fair. It abounds, just as King Herod's body is said to have abounded, in sores. My sight has been troubled with things so terrible and sordid that words can never be found to fit them. You are young, Joachim, and were touched only lightly by the scourge of death; and in the joy of the return which our Master has granted, you behold things brighter than they are. But I tell you that nature is cruel and men copy the cruelty. I know — I know. As a brute, the earth must be subdued, and forced to yield its best. Wealth is a means, and a potent one. Should we let our Jesus be exposed to the sun in the burning heat of the day, and chilled to the bone under the heavens by night? Should we let those that know no love rise up against him? No, Joachim. It is not the world, with its awful commingling of good and evil, that Jesus should have, but only such excellency as nature can be made to supply. Our Lord is by endowment and right the king of men. A palace, a throne, a kingdom — these are his due. The race must grant it!"

"Some of us have only our hearts to give him," sighed the widow, shrunken into herself by the force of Mary's ardent words.

"Then, for such as have only their hearts, hearts are everything. But for me and others like me, who have possessions, more — much more — ought to be surrendered."

"My mistress," reminded Rhea weakly, "has already given her all to the poor."

"Not quite yet," smiled Mary, with a slight toss of her

head. "The steward received my order to dispose of my properties and distribute the proceeds only yesterday. It will take some time to effect the measure. Right now I have changed my mind. The poor are never so impoverished as when an evil sovereign holds sway over them. The best way to help them, I am sure, is to assist a good man, with whatever means at one's disposal, to the highest position. Israel has long groaned under the heel of mismanagement, and the cries of the wretched for fatherly and kingly care are long and loud. I see it all now. I see it sun-clear. Herod Antipater must descend. Jesus must rise."

"Yes," agreed the widow. "But — but are we not, perhaps, mistaking the kind of resurrection that —" Her poor tongue floundered in confusion.

Always impetuous, Mary, with this new-found interest, which was growing more vivid to her and resulting in a fresh access of energy, now felt impatient. "Must our master do everything while we only sit and talk?" she demanded. "He is busy giving his message of goodness to men. It is for men to raise him up, so that his words may reach many and be carried afar. It irks me to rest here — pardon me, good mother—while he is homeless who could and would grace the proudest throne the world has ever known. I want to help as much as I can. I am going to." She stood up, as if ready to dash forth again into the night.

"Stay, my daughter," begged the widow. "At least till dawn. A little pause now will strengthen you for the generous service that is your intent."

Mary locked her fingers together and bit her lip, and paced up and down. For the time being, all calm had left her. She must prove herself. She must start. "The night is long," she complained.

"The way of service is longer," advised the widow. "All our future days can be devoted to it." And she tried to

[136]

calm the Magdalene by speaking softly, slowly, of certain facts about the thirty years which Christ had spent in humble and sequestered preparation for his present mission; facts that had been whispered from Bethlehem to Nazareth and from Nazareth to Naim. She talked on and on, and Mary endeavored to listen; but, with her present vision of the future, the past of Jesus was, like her own, lacking in appeal. She could think only of the devoted duty she would render him and of the illimitable glory he would eventually attain. And so it was little more than wasted music when the woman spoke of him sensing in the blossoms of Nazareth the bloom of souls; and in the grapes ripening in the small orchard near his home, such spirits as would grow to fruitful perfection in the shade of a world that forgets; and in the ascending vines, the design of his kingdom; and in the sigh of the night wind, the reverberation of man's pain; and in the laughter of children, the evidence that sorrow has wings. But there was one thing that she said, of which Mary was fully and gratefully conscious: "He loves little ones. Recently he placed a child in the midst of his apostles and bade them become like him. His mind must have been turning to Bethlehem and his mother at the time."

The thought of the angelic mother of Jesus was just the note that Mary needed. It subdued her mood to a degree of sobriety which enabled her again to plan, reasonably, what she would do.

"I need guidance," she admitted aloud, "and know where to obtain it." But still impulsively, for she was as yet less than a tyro in the long and difficult art of patience, she proceeded, with hardly any consciousness of inconsistency, to formulate certain arrangements of her own.

"Rhea, this very day you must set forth for Magdala, where I myself will never return, and deliver my new wishes to the steward," she declared. "My fortune — ought it not be one of the first donations to the Master's kingdom? And then —"

A lush vista of future service filled her gaze with sparklets.

"Mother, let me accompany Rhea, and guard her on this errand," requested Joachim.

"I was about to suggest that you do so," said the widow. "Indeed, go, my son."

The candles on the table had burned low and were guttering. In a cup of water, the rose that Mary had given the widow lay full-blown and shining, and the light of early dawn made a special halo around it.

All eyes were drawn instinctively to it. And Mary spoke: "Truly, the mother of our Lord has fostered yesterday's and this night's happenings. Joachim lives, and I —"

"We have both been restored," remarked Joachim. "But Christ and his mother, lady, love you more than me, for they have lifted you from a deeper woe."

"My woe was deeper," agreed Mary. "But how could their love for such a wicked one be greater? How could it be at all? It — it could not have been love, but mercy. Love must yet be won, and win it I must. I will."

"My daughter," sympathized the widow, "your battle — hardly begun — already increases. You who would help the master need help yourself. You have said so, if only to forget."

Mary bowed her head. "I thank you, good mother, for your wise counsel and reminder," she murmured humbly, sinking to her knees and folding her hands.

The others watched and listened, but the only words they distinctly heard were these:

"O Lily of Israel, whose root is purity, whose stem is beauty, whose blossom is — Jesus —"

12

MARY remembered Tullus' astute warning about the evil effect of the presence of a woman with a past on a man whose reputation knew no stain, and regretted that she had gone to Simon's house instead of seeking forgiveness in private. She knew that the enmity of the Roman would not rest. She longed to protect Christ, yet chided herself for the thought that one so powerful needed protection. Wealth, yes; patronage, never. Who was a Tullus in comparison with a worker of miracles — a builder of a new kingdom in which the might of Caesar would be less than a blade of grass? Nevertheless, to follow the Master, at least at a distance, was a crying need of her very being. She must set forth.

So, leaving Rhea with the widow and Joachim, for she discovered in the young man's honest mien the beginning of what would be a deep affection for the motherless girl, she returned in the early morning to Naim; only to find that Christ and his apostles had departed to Japhia, two miles south of Nazareth.

In the late afternoon, she arrived at the town, weary in body but burning in soul, and was rewarded by the sight of the Master standing in the midst of a gathering in the marketplace. His noble white-robed figure, blue-mantled and silhouetted against the dark gray stalls, gleamed like a great candle in the light of the parting day. His discourse was drawing to a close. A raw wind swept from the hills and was lending appropriateness to what he was saying, for he always drew his similitudes from circumstances. His theme was the coldness of men to truth.

Mary's experience with truth, up till now, had been meagre enough. But she knew coldness when she felt it; and now she not only felt but also saw it. A woman in rags stood shivering near, a picture of poverty and wretchedness, with dark hollows in her sallow cheeks and with hardly more than a feverish light in her eyes distinguishing her from a corpse. In quick pity, the Magdalene doffed her mantle and wrapped it around the thin shoulders. It was the act of only a moment, but Christ perceived it, and his gaze emitted a brighter lustre in the gloom.

Mary wanted to thrust her way through the gathering and throw herself at his feet. It took all her moral strength to resist this passionate urge; but she was determined never again to run the risk of embarrassing her Lord. Last night's demonstration had been enough — too much. If he now noticed and spoke to her, it would be ecstasy; and if not, it would be fitting.

When the audience was dispersing and she was losing herself in the shadows, he called to her: "Mary."

The sound was to her the essence of a heavenly song. Tingling with thankfulness, she came to him as gladly as a child to a loving parent. "You have left your sins," said he, "but your life must still struggle against the effects of them in your nature. I give you the dearest of assistants, who awaits you in Nazareth."

"I know," answered Mary.

"Our thoughts — yours, hers and mine — are already moving together."

"Be it ever so, O Master, and ever more so."

Taking off his own mantle, he placed it on her shoulders. "The night is cold, and you have given yours away."

"But you, my Lord?"

He beamed upon her and responded, "Your deed is my warmth."

"This mantle is the color of heaven."

"It was woven by my mother," he smiled, the memory adding to the light in his eyes.

"I am a sinner, and she — she — "

"Is grace," he finished. Then he turned to his apostles, and the Magdalene, longing anew to cast herself at his feet, meekly left him, rejoicing that soon her wealth would be at his disposal and drive his poverty away. But when she yielded to an urge to look back, she was startled by what she saw. The poor woman to whom she had given her garment, dyed in the purple of Magdala, was in turn draping it around the shoulders of one — the Master — still poorer than herself; and he was accepting it with a courtesy that gleamed, as if it were a garment royal.

At the entrance to the town of Nazareth, Mary met a boy, in his sixth or seventh year, who carried a little dog in his arms. She inquired of him the way to the home of the mother of the rabbi Jesus.

"I have been waiting for you," he promptly told her. "Mother Mary sent me. I'm to lead you to her."

"The hour is late and the night dark."

"That is why she sent me." And he added, almost with a note of pride in his voice, "I'm used to the dark. There is so much to see in it that I sleep little. And Dodavah — that's my dog's name — keeps me company. I call him that because Mother Mary says it means 'gift of God' and Jesus gave him to me. I can carry Dodavah in one arm. He's lame. Give me your hand."

They had walked a short way down the silent street, when the friendly little fellow saw fit to explain: "I like leading people to Mother Mary, especially at night."

"Why, child?"

"That is when they seem to need her most. And when they cannot come to her, she lets me bring her to them. There's not a sick bed in Nazareth that she doesn't visit. She lets me take her by the hand like you're doing, because she knows how much it pleases me. She's been letting me do it for years — "

"For years? You are so young — "

"It's almost two years ago, though, since my father was put in prison because he couldn't pay all his debts. He lost his spirit when my mother died, and nothing went right with him. I was sent to an uncle in Sidon where there are great big ovens for making glass from sand. And my uncle put me to work, blowing a pipe into the flames. One day the fire got in my eyes. That's why I'm blind."

Overcome with surprise and pity, Mary paused, withdrew her hand from the boy's, and would have pressed him to her side. His head had a cap of curls, and his skin was silken to the touch. But immediately she ceased the caress, smitten with a consciousness of the past. This child was innocence itself.

"Why did you stop?" he asked. "I like to be loved. My uncle used to beat me."

"Poor little soul, hungry for affection!" Mary murmured to herself. "I — I stopped, because I have been a sinner," she explained.

"What is a sinner?"

"One who seeks happiness — or forgetting — where it cannot be found."

"You'll be happy with Mother Mary. I am. She hugs me and makes me forget Sidon. And when I was very little,

Jesus took me in his arms, too, and kissed me. It was Jesus that found me in Sidon and got my uncle to let him bring me back here to live with his mother. I'm very lucky — the way things turn out for me."

"Are you the boy that Jesus once placed in the midst of his Apostles when he bade them become like little children?" asked Mary, suddenly recalling a bit of the reminiscence which the widow of Naim had expressed the night before.

"How did you know?"

"Because, I think, he wanted me to."

"You're like her, and him too."

"Not yet, child," corrected Mary, grateful and regretful. "You must help me to be."

The mother was waiting at the threshold of the small box-like house, with an oil lamp in her hand. She spoke no word when Mary entered, but gave the light to the blind boy, and extended her arms. And as she enfolded the Magdalene to her heart, her eyes rested on the blue mantle that had been her son's. Her lips, shining, emitted a single word: *"Hobab* — beloved."

The months passed, and a perfect arrangement developed between the two Marys whose life was Christ. They took turns — weeks at a time — of following him and, together with other women, administering in the background to the simple wants of him and his apostles; so that neither Naim nor Jesus was without the devoted hand of a Mary.

Tullus sent many messengers to the little town in the hills, and thrice he came himself. But always, as if by Providence, the Magdalene was away; and the quality of the mother, so different from that of any other woman he had ever known, equally disarmed and infuriated him.

"One cannot fight a flower!" he bitterly remarked to Asar and Osias, on his second return. "That's what she is, you know. Frail and beautiful."

"Flowers can be crushed," said Asar.

"This one is too fair for that."

"Why not dispossess her?" suggested Osias. "One word to the authorities of the town would be enough."

"There is nothing to dispossess her of," complained Tullus. "Her house is a small shell, almost empty of furniture. She has given everything but the barest essentials of life away. What she lives on, I know not. Besides, the town's folk would kill anybody that laid a hand on her. She's what you Jews would call an angel; the angel guardian of Nazareth."

"Does she refuse to tell you the whereabouts of the Magdalene?" inquired Osias.

"She merely bows her head when I ask her, and says, 'She is where she is needed.' No more information than that, can I extract from her. I've offered her money, and she looked sad. I've tried threats, and she smiled. Give me any man and I can wrestle him to the broad of his back on the ground; but this mother of the Nazarene leaves me helpless. Worse than that, she makes it necessary for me to struggle against a feeling that I never had before — a feeling of shame. A Roman that ever gets ashamed of himself ceases to be a Roman. I intend to keep on being what I am; and now it's more of a point than ever with me to strike at the Nazarene. If I had my way, he would be in the pit of the fortress of Macherus or beheaded like John the Baptist by now; but Herod Antipater, into whose ear I keep pouring a warning, has never recovered from John's execution. He's even gotten the idea firm lodged in his diseased brain that John lives on in the Nazarene. His fondness for young Salome, who demanded the prophet's head as the price of a dance, has soured into so much hate that Herodias has had to ship her off to Rome on a long visit. The reputation of the Nazarene is increasing by such leaps and bounds with the common people that, for the time being, it is impossible to touch him. But my men are following his every move, just as those of the Sanhedrin are following his every word. At the proper time, the blow shall certainly fall."

"And what of the Magdalene?"

"I want her and I will have her. The change that came over me that night in Magdala after we first noticed her interest in the rabbi, increased in Naim and is now stronger than ever. I suppose I had more than an ordinary passion for her even before, but I never realized it when access to her was easy. Perhaps it is the psychology of a Roman to want and fight only for what is beyond, and to want and fight for it the more when it gets farther away. It may be that this is the explanation of the expansion of a city on the Tiber into an empire encircling the Mediterranean. At any rate, my desire for Mary is a demand that grows and grows like hunger itself."

"It should be easy to find her," said Osias. "Is she not following the Nazarene when she is away from Nazareth?"

"Yes, but she loses herself in whatever service she is rendering him. Repeatedly I've searched the crowds that surround him, and it was as if she were never there. Her glorious form — her copper-colored hair shot with flames — her burnished eyes — her rose-petal skin — all the details we knew so well and admired so much, are covered by the clouds of her new existence. Could anyone recognize even Phryne herself in a thick, enveloping mantle? All the females that follow Christ, hide their faces in what seems to be a frenzy of modesty. It is beneath me to go around lifting veils to find the one and only woman I want. And anyhow, I admit that I am biding my time with her in the hope that her infatuation for the Nazarene will wear itself out, or in the prospect of her coming to me of her own accord for help when the noose is at last beginning to tighten around him."

"And when is that to be?" asked Osias blandly.

"Not far off."

Osias sidled up confidentially to the Roman. "I hear that Mary has gathered all her wealth together and given it to Christ," he baited. "This will strengthen his position and increase his influence."

"Not the way he has been using it. He has been squandering it on those that can least help him." Tullus' lip curled. "The poor."

"But you yourself have conceded that his friends are many," reminded Osias pointedly.

"So," snapped Tullus, "are his enemies."

Amused at seeing his great friend losing self-control, Asar fed a little more fuel to the mood. "You are wrong, Tullus," he warned, "about your Magdalene always moving around in a frenzy of modesty. Rumor has it that of late she has doffed her plain attire and reappeared in all her beauty at the homes of some of our leading citizens. Oh, very quietly, and probably not more than two or three times, but anyhow enough to show that she isn't wholly sanctified as yet, and is using her charms in the same old way. Money, money, money; this time for him — the Nazarene. You see, she wants him to have enough cash to be somebody big, and knows that he must have friends simple enough to supply it. She's won over a few to him already. Strange that she hasn't come to sell herself back to you — for him. Doubtless she will. It's for that I'm waiting."

"Fool!" muttered Tullus, banging his fist into his palm.

"Do you mean Mary or me?"

"I mean everybody, from the rabbi down or — up. Particularly myself."

13

It was true that the Magdalene had approached some of the rich, among them Nicodemus and Joseph of Arimethea. She had found that these two good men were interested in a cause that they deemed to be worthy. They gladly proffered assistance, while the others demanded more for their favor than a mere appeal from a desirable woman and had to be repulsed.

She told nothing about these visits to Mother Mary, and felt wretched at the fact. It was her only secret. How could she unbosom herself to such an earth-angel in this regard? The prerogative of the mother was to foster the heavenly phase of Jesus' future, but the best that Mary could aspire to do was to assist his earthly success. She believed that the Master understood; nevertheless, she could not escape the conviction that the mother, if she knew, would disapprove. So, from the home of a friend beyond Nazareth, and in borrowed finery, which she detested, she had gone to solicit help for her Lord.

It grieved and perplexed her that Christ was not using for himself the money she brought him. Thus far, it had served only to swell the stream of his charities, and it was largely for this reason she had constrained herself to visit men who possessed not only wealth but also influence. The necessity of such a procedure was a constant pain; yet what was pain but privilege, if the final issue would be the enthronement of Jesus in Israel?

It had become the custom of the two Marys to spend a night in Nazareth before the one or the other set forth to watch over their beloved. This was always a time of intimate communion, with Samuel, the blind boy, seated at their feet and eagerly following everything they said. Mary of Magdala had come to love the little fellow with all the ardor of her deep, rich nature, and longed to fondle him, and yet was still too sensitive to her sinful past to touch him. More than once, impatient at herself for denying him the express affection he craved, she almost embraced him; but his innocence was such that it seemed to ward her off even while it invited, and she felt that, if ever it were possible to hold him in her arms and close to her heart, heaven would be testifying to her growth in worthiness. She hungered for such testimony, especially when he raised his eyes, as lustrous as if they had never been robbed of sight, and when the tiny love-ring which his own mother had put in the lobe of his infant ear would twinkle like a teardrop in the motion of his head; and most poignantly when, one day, he came to her heartbroken at the loss of his pet, Dodavah, which had just been crushed to death under a wagon wheel.

There came, too soon, a last night for the little meetings in the town of blossoms. Neither the mother nor the Magdalene nor Samuel was aware of the fact at the time, though a presentiment of sorrow was upon them and they knew not why. They felt even closer than ever before and expectancy possessed them, as the early moonlight played through the vines at the window and spread a pattern of dark lace over the floor, and a nightingale sang from an olive tree in the garden. Christ would presently be with them. Mary had brought the word from Japhia.

[149]

But the blessed mother admitted: "Tonight shadows are falling not only on land and sea but also on my soul. The skies, so serenely blue at the time of my son's birth, now seem sinister and scarlet, no matter how bright the candles that burn on the altar of them; and only roses that are red meet the eye. This spring, not a single white lily has yet opened its lips to breathe to me of his baby flesh. Here, in my corner of Galilee, I foresee so much! The garden sparkles in the dusk, but not with dew — rather as if with blood. I sense the agony that may be his, ere the coming of another springtide."

"O my lady," begged the Magdalene, "see his beauty — not his blood — on the roses. Soon this room will be bright with his face. No harm can come to one so good as he. So powerful." She wanted to speak of Nicodemus and Joseph of Arimethea who were rallying support for his kingship, but a reluctance to betray her own attempts at helpfulness restrained her, and she added, "Only a few days ago, he stilled a storm at sea."

"He did it not for himself, but because his apostles besought him in fear, 'Save us, Lord, we perish!' He never thinks of his own peril. When the tempest raged, he was sleeping."

"Sleeping in a tempest?" marvelled Samuel.

"Life is largely a storm of one kind or another," observed the Magdalene. "Yet the tired body must rest."

"Has he stopped the rain more than once?"

"Only once."

"Why?"

It was Mother Mary who answered. "Because he wants love more than fear. And when he turned the anger of the heavens to calm, his apostles continued to be troubled."

"Why?"

"They feared his might as much as they had feared the menace of death. 'What manner of man is this?' they asked one another. 'For the winds and the waves obey him.' "

"I'd not have been afraid — in the same boat with Jesus."

Mother Mary's hand stroked the boy's head. "I know you would not," she tried to smile. "You are a child. But they — they are men."

Samuel could feel a tremor in her touch.

"Are not his apostles loyal — loyal as we are?" he asked.

"All flesh is weak, my child. Not all of Jesus' chosen ones will have strength, until the Paraclete comes."

"What is the Paraclete?"

"The Spirit of God."

"Isn't that what you have? I think I can see it flying around you like the whitest of doves, while I sit here at your feet."

"And I can hear the whir of its wings in the tone of your voice, my child."

"But why don't the apostles have it, if we do?"

"They do have it — that is, all but one." The mother's voice became a trickle of sound. "Would that that one shared it too! But when it will have come to them as a flame in their very souls rather than as a dove encircling their wishes, then their loyalty, their strength, will know no bounds."

"Even now, is it not large, my lady?" spoke the Magdalene. "I am thinking of the time I heard Simon Peter mention to Jesus, 'Lord, we have left all things for you.' — It was at the shore of Genezareth, the night after he stilled the storm. — Jesus answered him only by gazing down at a broken fish-net in the muddy sands, and then up to the glory of the skies. And it was suddenly open to

[151]

all of us present that what a soul leaves for God is as nothing in comparison with what it gains. In such a knowledge, one cannot but acquire strength and fidelity."

"You have achieved them, my sister," said Mother Mary. "So have the apostles. Yet is there one who has not. One who prefers the broken thing that is near, to the perfect thing that is above — "

"It's hard not to love even a broken thing," confessed Samuel, his young voice unsteady. "I loved my little dog Dodavah and he was lame."

"Jesus knew," soothed the mother. "Remember what he said when others had only words of harshness at the sight of your poor pet: 'Pearls are not whiter than its teeth.'"

The boy then sprang to his feet. "I'm going, Mother Mary."

"Where, dear?"

"To meet Jesus. He is nearing here on the road from Japhia. I want to be near him."

"The sun has set an hour since. A mist is setting on the hills. The road may not be safe at this time for a child."

"I'm not afraid. Do let me go. I want to. I must."

At this juncture, three forms appeared in the door-way, and the two women went to greet the visitors. They were the widow of Naim, Joachim and Rhea. After mutual salutations, warm with affection and simple with sincerity, Rhea announced to Mary Magdalene, "Tullus knows you are here in Nazareth this night, my mistress, and that the Master comes too. Some strangers, passing through Naim, told his spies that you had left Japhia for here; and they in turn hastened on to Tiberias with the news. Before morning, he will have come to drag you away. He is weary of waiting for you and is now making his own course."

"Then before morning," said Mary, "I must be gone."

"It is necessary for you, my lady," warned the widow, addressing the mother of Christ, "to be gone too. We have learned that this Roman, listening to the suggestion of his comrades, has at last determined to draw you from here, after Christ will have departed, apparently to unite you with him but really to wound him by holding you captive."

"I overheard this base scheme," disclosed Joachim, "at the inn at Naim, where I work for our support. The spies had drunk too much wine and were conversing freely among themselves."

"O Mary Mother, I have brought affliction on this house," deplored the Magdalene. "Here you should have peace and rest; and now — "

"Reproach not yourself," said the mother. "All is heaven's will."

"Where shall we go? What shall we do?"

Mother Mary pointed to a snow-white moth which had wandered into the room through the open window and was flying with perfect contentment in the small space that it had bartered for the great outdoors. "Think you that the Providence which cares for even the least of creatures," she asked, "will abandon us?"

"Come, my lady, to live with us at Naim," begged Joachim. "I'll work twice as hard, to supply your needs; and I'll deem it the highest of privileges to do so."

"No, Joachim. Naim is not far from Nazareth, and there our problem would soon be the same as here."

"Long ago," recalled the Magdalene, "I had a house in Jerusalem. I'd almost forgotten it. All my possessions in Galilee have been sold and given away; and my intention was to dispose of this last property in like manner. Can we not journey to the holy city, dear lady, and save a small portion of the estate for our few wants, while we devote the rest to the cause of Jesus?"

"So be it, my sister."

"We shall take Samuel with us. — Where is he?"

"While we were talking, he must have slipped away; going, as he said, to meet my son."

The mother walked to the door-way and peered out into the soft darkness. The nightingale was no longer singing. Not a leaf was stirring. The moon-light lay pale as the cheek of death on the land. Suddenly, from afar, there came a cry.

Huddling close to her, the others waited breathlessly, watching the pure face up-turned to the skies and the meek lips moving as if in prayer.

For long leaden moments they waited. Then, out of the night and between a double row of cypress trees, the tall white-robed figure of Christ, with Mary's own purple mantle draping the shoulders, and with the light of the stars seemingly gathered into the kindliness and royalty of his countenance, approached them. His bare feet moved as noiselessly as if he were treading the surface of the sea. All fell on their knees at the sight of him and of the broken little body in his arms.

"*Hobab* — Samuel!" The mother's lips silently formed the words.

Softly, his limpid eyes treasuries of patience and sympathy, Jesus explained that a Roman chariot had stricken the child down and driven life away.

"O happy child!" wept the Magdalene. "To be called forth in the flower of your innocence! To die in the dearest of embraces! To be held by heaven! To be pillowed on the bosom of divine tenderness! To be sightless to the shame of earth and wide-eyed to the glories above

[154]

it! To be saved from sin and depart in purity! To join Joas and Josue and be their little brother forever!"

"You called back breath to my son Joachim; will you not restore this poor body to life?" pleaded the widow of Naim with Jesus. "Mary of Magdala has loved him so!"

Turning to the Magdalene, he seemed to ask, with his very silence, what was her will. A sudden and terrible struggle arose within her. To have the boy alive again would be happiness. Yes, happiness for her; but what of the child himself? The moments passed, tortuous with indecision. Her heart cried, "Let him, my Master, live again." But her lips would not — could not — speak the words which her reason rejected. In life, Samuel had been deprived of much. In death, should he be recalled to the sufferance that was the law of life? Joachim had been restored to the woman that bore him; and Samuel, by death, had been restored, too, to a mother that had died. Mary had no claims; nothing but the greatness of her yearning. And what was this in comparison with Samuel's joy?

Slowly, mournfully, she shook her head, and the Master lowered his gaze.

"Prepare his resting place, Joachim, in this garden that was his earthly paradise," requested Mother Mary.

"I'll return to it often and heap it with blossoms," promised Rhea, her arm entwined with Joachim's and her cheeks wet.

"It is springtime," said Mary Magdalene, extending her arms and receiving the body from Jesus and wrapping it in her veil, "but no bloom in Galilee is lovelier than his face. At last — at last I can hold him to my breast! See, Mother Mary. Does not his forehead shine like a lily?"

"It does. Like a lily in this garden crimson with sorrow. The first white lily of spring to speak to me of what only such a flower can say."

The widow of Naim and Joachim and Rhea stepped back, as Mary Magdalene, with Christ at one side and his mother at the other, rocked the child in her arms and fancied that he was the little Joas of long ago. "His eyes, wide open, are blue," she was crooning, "like bits of the very heaven they now see. His face is a light that shines in darkness." She touched her lips to the cold cheek. "And — and pearls are not whiter than his teeth."

14

AFTER the burial of the boy, the little group went forth into the night; and when they had reached the hill-crest, Christ looked lovingly down for the last time on the scenes of his boyhood and young manhood. The lights of Nazareth had all gone out, and only the lamps of heaven were burning.

The hour of parting had come.

Joachim could not speak, but his humble silence reached the heart of one who had given him a second life. "Let me follow you along whatever path of pain," it pleaded; and Christ answered aloud, "You, my son, together with your mother and this faithful maiden, to whom I am now joining you in holy wedlock, for I have searched your souls and seen your mutual love, shall be the foundation of my kingdom in Galilee. A year of implicit espousal has passed since first your young lives met. Modesty, Rhea, is your nuptial veil — the fairest a bride can wear. Your head, Joachim, is crowned with heaven's favor — the richest of turbans. Nature wafts its incense around you both. Nightingales are your musicians; the stars, your flambeaux; our affection, your feast. Kneel and be united in the Lord."

The hands of Christ were poised above the boy and girl in the temple of trees, and their souls, together as one, knew heaven. And while they knelt, a chant ascended from the throats of the apostles who had been awaiting their Master on the hillside; the night song of the land of the chosen people, "Hear, O Israel." And Mary the Mother was thinking of her spouse, whose pilgrim staff had long ago sprouted with lilies in evidence of God's election; and the widow of Naim was pondering the inexpressible power that had evoked the life of her son from darkness and was now delivering it to the greatest measure of happiness that can ever be allotted to man in this vale of tears; and Mary Magdalene's thoughts were with the broken blossom of another marriage — little Samuel, sleeping in the garden of Nazareth. "I cannot leave this blessed spot forever," she was telling herself. "I will somehow turn again to it when Jesus is king."

In Jerusalem, Mary's palace, abandoned since the time of the Feast of Fire, when a boy of twelve spoke of the flame of divine love before doctors of the law, rose like a ghost of its former self. With the mother of Christ, she restlessly roamed the rooms and wondered how she could ever have beguiled herself for even a day with a splendor so tarnishable and tawdry. She lifted the lids of jewel cases containing armlets, pearl thorim, rings and amber and gold anklets which used to tinkle when her feet sped along the ways of sin. "Could these ever have been mine?" she asked herself. "They belong, my sister, to the dust that has already taken possession of them," said Mother Mary.

As they were leaving the palace, they encountered a man of spare frame, shifty eyes, and thick sensuous lips. "I am Hebel from Kerioth," said he, addressing them, "and have been sent to you by my friend Judas — one of the twelve that most intimately follow him who is called the Lord."

The mother and the Magdalene looked troubled. Judas? The only apostle whose gaze did not frankly meet and melt into that of the Master! The only one whose countenance, when the Master spoke, did not shine! Yet he had been chosen, and Jesus called him friend —

"I have followed you both on your journey hither," Hebel further mentioned. "For the love of the rabbi Jesus, Judas wishes me to watch over you. My business of a merchant will keep me in Jerusalem all through the summer and the winter till the Passover, and it will be my happiness to be of service to the lady-mother of Jesus and to Mary of Magdala."

"We need no service except one," assured Mary. "We wish to dispose of this property — all save the corner of the garden where stands the small house of the former caretaker."

"It shall be done. There is a purchaser at hand."

"Already?"

"Yes. Myself. That is, if the sum you ask be suitable."

Mary mentioned a figure almost absurdly low, and Hebel clinched the bargain on the spot by withdrawing a bag of gold from the belt beneath his chlamys and handing it to her.

"Here is much relief for the poor," said Mother Mary.

"I would that Jesus might be persuaded to accept it for himself," sighed the Magdalene.

"The poor and my son are the same."

"Let us re-enter the house and draw up the bill of sale," suggested Hebel briskly, bending his head so as to conceal a spark of living fire in his eye as it rested on Mary's graceful and languorous form from which penance had not as yet removed the carnal appeal.

"Will you occupy the place yourself?" she inquired casually.

"Alas, no. I am purchasing it for one who will duly reimburse me."

"Who can he be?"

"He prefers, for the present, to remain unknown."

The women again looked troubled.

"Is it satisfactory that we keep the little house in the corner of the garden?" asked Mary solicitously.

"Quite. I might even say necessary."

The garden was a tangle of brush and weeds from years of neglect, but it still held a richness of cyclamen, and the space around the house of the caretaker, long dead, was thick with anemone, as red as the sacrificial blood that flowed afar from beneath the altar of the Temple and nourished the soil. And with the coming of the two Marys, disorder vanished, opulent beauty returned, and birds found such sanctuary that the cool shadows were gratefully alive with their songs.

To disturb the peace of these lovers of Christ, however, workmen soon took over the estate and were renovating it in every detail. They told them that, when ready, it would be occupied by a great and wealthy man. "He will doubtless object to the stream of poor people that keep coming here for relief since you two ladies arrived," warned the overseer. "What fine person wants to endure faces perforated with leprosy, limbs twisted like the branches of ancient trees, eyes eaten with sores, and a musk of stench from bodies that water seldom touches? How can you yourselves abide them?"

"We see souls," explained Mother Mary patiently.

"And if a decayed building is worthy of restoration," said the Magdalene, with some asperity, "why should our feeble attempts to relieve the wretchedness of lives be taken amiss?"

"The wealthy wish to look only on beauty."

"Then why do they not create it with charity?" demanded Mary.

"If they gave forth their substance in charity, they would not be wealthy."

"Ah," answered the Magdalene, who was learning fast under the mild tutelage of the mother, "much wealthier would they be. Gold is of value only when it is reminted into goodness."

"Nevertheless, you shall not be permitted to make your portion of these grounds a nest of hideousness and disease."

"Then we will go elsewhere to serve God," she defied.

"Neither can that be possible. Hebel, our employer, has told us that here you must remain."

"We are not prisoners."

"It would seem that, in a sense, you are. Hebel has instructed all his men to report to him on your coming and going. His purpose? It is his own secret."

And so the two Marys walked in an atmosphere of apprehension, but their days were so devoted to the service of the needy that they managed to forget themselves in what they were doing; and the summer passed into the long rainy months of winter.

The fame of Christ was mounting. His repute exceeded that of all other rabbis. Even Abba Ghelkian and Chakna-ben-Dossa, whose minds were torches in Israel, acknowledged the carpenter of Nazareth as a man of wonder; and visitors to Jerusalem brought steady reports of words uttered and deeds done. Outside the gates of the Temple, Mother Mary and the Magdalene, heavily veiled, would linger and meet the pilgrims from the north; and always their hunger for news of him whom they loved, was fed, even as the hunger of the prophet to

[161]

whose exile a heaven-sent raven brought bread. And Mother Mary would invite the good messengers to the little house in the garden to eat barley bread and olives and drink camel's milk, for she was mindful of her kinship to them of whom her son had said: "My mother and my brethren are they who hear the word of God and keep it."

"His word is as seed, sown through the land," rejoiced Mary of Magdala. "That was the similitude that I once heard him speak to Joanna, the wife of Chusa, who is Herod Antipater's steward, and to Susanna, and to many others who minister to him of their substance, and to a great multitude. He is the sower sublime, and the field is the world, and his word is love. Already has he sent forth not only his twelve apostles to spread his doctrine, but also seventy disciples. Seventy — the number of Israel's families. Ere another April unfolds its blanket of blossoms over the Plain of Esdraelon, all Palestine will be clothed in moral beauty, and the kingdom of grace, as a bride descending from the clouds, will trail white garments of peace healingly on hearts, and Jerusalem will rise like Joachim from the sleep of death, and the bridegroom will be king."

And the thrill of expectation made Mary feel years younger. She wanted to be fresh, beautiful, for the day when the Lord would be crowned. For would she not stand by his throne where all should be fair in order to be fitting? Though trying to copy the blessed mother's simplicity, she had almost resigned herself to a belief in the impossibility of ever approaching the perfection of such a model. Though they lived together and their hearts were linked, their personalities seemed at times to be utterly divergent. The one cherished silence; the other liked the sounds of life. The one's sense of order and neat-ness was innate; the other's, merely acquired and often faulty. The one was ever calm; the other repeatedly found difficulty in subduing tumultuous emotions. The one preferred to have birds sing in the trees that were their natural home; the other kept a little cage and a tiny prisoner whose chirping at close range somehow made the soul feel freer. The one so cared for flowers as seldom or never to cull them; the other was glad to have bowls of them within the house. When the one bent over a spring to draw water, she saw heaven's blue; the other, not infrequently, only herself. The one never raised her voice; the other was unable at times to bend a strong feeling to mild speech. The one was consistent; the other, a tangle of inconsistencies. Yet both had only one love, one abiding desire, one absorbing purpose: Jesus. His great day would be theirs. The Magdalene pictured the mother enthroned beside him as his perfect queen, and herself, though unworthy, as his adoring handmaid. And while she dreamed, she waited. And while she waited, her soul was more and more fired with the golden prospects of the dream.

Nor did she and the mother always have to seek news of the future king from the pilgrims. It often happened that messages came directly to them. Simon Peter, for instance, sent them a jubilant letter. "The Master brought James and John and myself up onto Mount Thabor," he wrote. "It was eight days after he had said to a crowd, in which we were numbered, 'There are some standing here that shall not taste death till they see the kingdom of God.' And little did we think at the time that ours would be soon the privilege of the vision! Our eyes were heavy with sleep, but, waking, we beheld a wonder that exceeds words. The Master's face, turned to the skies, outshone the sun and his raiment gleamed and glittered. A

[163]

chariot, as dazzling as the lightning that plows the firmament, rolled out of the clouds, and Elias descended; and
Moses, majestic as when he bore the tables of stone from
the summit of Sinai, likewise appeared. But, alas, they
spoke to our Jesus of death — death in Jerusalem; and he
bowed his shining head to their words. The meaning is
not clear to me; for surely, when he leads us to the great
city to celebrate the Pasch, as he intends to do, he will
come not as the rabbi of Nazareth but as the king of men,
and he will enter into his realm and take possession.
Surely his advent will be the death of death and the re-
birth of life. He is royal! I have seen his glory, and it is
the glory of God! Out of the heavens, there came a voice;
the same voice that sounded when John the Baptist
poured the water of Jordan on the sacred brow: 'This is
my beloved son, hear him.' Ah, Jehovah, with all my soul,
I heard and will proclaim. But the day of proclamation is
not yet; for when Elias and Moses disappeared and we
were again alone with Jesus, he bade us: 'Tell the vision
to no man.' I am not betraying his charge in mentioning
these things to you, for well I know that such hearts as
yours are knitted to his own."

It was a night in March when this epistle of Peter
reached the two exiles. They read it together and, going
into the garden, they walked in the dream of the phrases.
A gray mist, blotting out the moon, overhung the foliage
and clung to their garments; a cold finger touched their
spirits and tempered the joy that would otherwise have
run warm within them.

"He has chosen Thabor, and Thabor is his throne!"
spoke the Magdalene. "Deborah had his thousands of soldiers with whom to defeat Sisara; but Christ has his legions
of angels and will lead them against the hordes of Satan.
A new ruler has risen in Israel!"

"O that Israel might rise to such a ruler!" yearned the mother. "But see, my sister. The promise of Simon Peter's letter is prefigured in our garden. Already there are roses, braving the wet winds and shedding their perfume. Count them."

"Ah yes. Twelve red roses. Simon Peter, John, Matthew, Thomas, Philip, Bartholomew, Simon Zelotes, James the Less, James the Greater, Thaddaeus and Andrew. And one other — nothing more than a dark tight bud, eaten by a worm. Could this last, breathing no fragrance, be likened to him of Kerioth whom Hebel calls friend?"

"My son calls him friend, too. Look, the twelfth red rose twines its thorny stem around the single white one that stands at the head of all."

The mother's voice was throaty with a suppressed sob. And Mary Magdalene cupped her elbow in her palm and eased her away.

The following night, the windows of the palace that had once belonged to the Magdalene were flooded with lavender and amber light from lanterns with double-scented wicks, and were opened to the warm breezes blowing from Perea beyond the Dead Sea and awakening Jerusalem from the last of her winter sleep. Hebel's alterations had been completed for days, and again the building stood endued with all the charm of bygone years. And the notes of the ivory halil, the musical instrument that was consecrated to joy, flew from the casements like starlings into the night, circling through the air and reaching the sequestered spot in the garden where the two Marys dwelt.

"The new master has come to take possession of his property," said the Magdalene, "even as the new ruler of Israel will soon come to claim his own."

"Soon," repeated the mother in a tone of mingled relief and sadness. Retiring to a little alcove, she gave herself to meditation; and Mary walked about in the garden, her mind on the roses — the eleven so tall and vigorous, the white one meekly ruling the rest, and the bud drooping in blight.

Lost in her thoughts, she scarcely heard a rustling of leaves behind her and was startled when a voice called, "Cynthia." Turning, she beheld a statuesque form in the starlight, with a prominent forehead, restless eyes forced to steadiness, lips full and hard, a pride-chiselled nose, and muscular arms banded with pale gold that threw off specks of gleam.

"Tullus!"

"You are startled. Yet my appearance is not sudden. Long, long have I waited; and every hour burned with desire. Believe me, I tried to forget you, only to find myself remembering you the more. To remain from you was ceaseless unrest; but I knew that to approach you, while your devotion to this man of Nazareth persisted, was useless. I've given you time, away from him, to be cured of your malady."

"Malady?" repeated Mary. "My devotion has healed a soul that I could have sworn was beyond all help. My labor for him, far from ending, has scarcely begun. Could I begin life all over again, every minute of it would be his. I account as lost all the years before I met him. I — "

"You have been feeding on rose leaves," pitied the Roman. "It was a mistake to leave you here with your thoughts to idealize this unimportant meteor. It would have been much wiser of me, I now see, to let you follow him along the mean ways of Galilee and daily see his increase of follies. After almost three years of service to the poor, he is as poor as any of them. His imprudent and gratuitous insults have alienated almost everyone who could or would sustain him. He has surrounded himself mostly with social scum — fishermen and wretches of every kind. You considered him a personality — a rising star. His soft words moved your heart and lulled your mind to repose. But I tell you, Mary, what almost everybody knows: this wonder-worker with the melting eyes has no more future than a criminal nailed to a cross."

"How little you know him, Tullus!"

"How much you overestimate him! O Mary, let the masquerade end. You have miserably denied yourself, pinning your faith to sheer fancy. You have grown frail. Your cheeks are pale. Is that a streak of silver I see in your hair? I admit that your beauty is deeper since you met him. It used to be a light that played on your face, but now it is rather a glow from within. More than ever it holds me, and so I am here to claim not only this property, which means nothing to me, but your heart, which means all. Take back everything. Here is the proper setting for the discontented opal that sought to be a pearl." He indicated the bright jewel-box of a palace. "Be no longer a slave to illusion but a princess to fact."

He slipped his arm around her waist and tried to draw her to him. She wrested herself away, leaving her mantle in his hands.

At the threshold of the little house, Mother Mary, aroused by the voices, stood waiting. Her hand sought the Magdalene's, and together the women defied the strong Roman presence.

Tullus smiled. "Two sparrows confronting an eagle," he commented, flipping the mantle to the bushes. "It is as easy to hold you here, you know, as it was to find you. The man of Kerioth, called Judas, has kept me informed.

Neither the mother, the admirer, nor the rabbi of Nazareth has any friend that the love of money or the fear of
might cannot turn to faithlessness. You are virtually my
prisoners; and he — the miracle worker who, with all his
power, is powerless to do anything for himself — will
presently be no more than another lamb ready for the
slaughter. He has crossed the Jordan and the borders of
Judah. His rag-tag followers think that here, in the center
of Israel, he will strip the rich and adorn the wretched.
The fools gabble of a kingdom and envisage the greatest
fool of all as their king. Yet, in that I know you both have
set your all on this man, I offer you his safety, if you but
listen to the dictates of reason."

"What may such dictates be?" asked the mother, her
manner detached, as though she were listening merely to
the ramblings of a child.

"That you warn your son and deter him from his
course."

"My son's will is to do the will of Him who sent him."

"Who sent him?"

For answer, the mother turned her eyes to the heavens,
silver-spread with the lustre of the *hodesh* or new moon,
around which delicate little cirrus clouds, messengers of a
fair tomorrow, made a circle as if of cherubs.

Tullus could not but note the harmony between her
face and the beauty above. Was it that the one reflected
the other? Ashamed of this concession to sentiment, he
hastened to say, "All mothers, I suppose, think their sons
are more or less divine. Every male child is a god to at
least one woman, just as every woman to at least one man
is a goddess."

His gaze again fastened on Mary Magdalene. "As for
you," he said, "it is certainly the part of prudence to
forget this meaningless man of Nazareth before he drags

you further down the scale of life. Concede the distance you have already descended. Yesterday you proudly owned this palace — this estate. Today you crouch in a corner. Yesterday you commanded; today you cringe. What of tomorrow?"

"My tomorrow," answered Mary, whose indignation was mounting, "is in eternal hands; and so long as it remains there, it is safe."

"We shall see. Having waited so long, I can afford to wait yet a little longer. I will retrieve my mistake of not having let you trail the Nazarene through his errors of last winter. I will let you know the final effects of his mission, as they unfold here in Jerusalem during the coming week. You shall see for yourself that your god is not even a man! — O Mary, I do not seek to hurt you. I want only to enfold your life with care and comfort. I want to take nothing from you but your self-deception as to this rabbi's worth, and to give you everything in return. Won't you heed me? You'll be doing yourself, and him, the greatest of favors. Keep him for a friend, if you must; but let me be more. Then will you be assuring him, whose enemies are increasing like a locust plague, of yet another friend — one powerful enough to save him from degradation and possible death."

"Such can never be," cried Mary, "for one so good and mighty! The king cannot but attain his throne. Have you forgotten his miracles?"

"No," confessed Tullus. "I keep hearing the reports of them. They puzzle me; but I'm astonished also at the magic that fakirs from the east and the west are ever performing. What I do comprehend is the fate to which his deeds, coupled with his defiance of the leading men of the land, are hurling him. It is all right to attract Israel, but all wrong to offend its rulers. What is magic without intelligence? What is an art that saves others and cannot save itself?"

"The art of sacrificing self for others is supreme," asserted Mary.

"If you really believe this, then why hesitate any longer to give yourself to me? If Christ means much to you, surely you must abhor the prospect of having him needlessly suffer. With me, you can throw a safeguard around his person and his purpose."

Mother Mary's fingers tightened their hold on the Magdalene's hand, for she felt the wavering that the sudden force of this argument necessarily caused. "Leave us, O Roman," she begged.

"Leave you I shall — for a while. You, lady, as a mother, ought hold your son's interest high. Speak to Mary and show her the way of wisdom. I offer her and him much and ask little."

"You are asking for souls and offer dross," said the mother slowly and sadly.

"Is it dross, woman, that the fruit of your womb be saved? What madness in you has dried up the springs of natural affection for your own flesh and blood?"

"The springs are flowing — "

"Yet you would see your son in peril! Is this motherhood? Is this mind?"

"It is love, O Roman, of which your present blindness cannot conceive," cried the Magdalene. "You suggest that we save Jesus at the price of slaying everything for which he stands. This is as unsubtle as it is outrageous. There are other ways."

"You misread me. What part of a man lives on, if his body lies dead?"

"His dream lives on, when he dies for it," replied the mother. "It receives his life."

"So soft a face — so hard a heart! And yet you think that it is we Edomites, as you would call us, who are cruel — "

"Tullus," cried Mary Magdalene, "your tongue should wither in your mouth with such speech. Was it cruel of the mother of the Maccabees to enspirit her sons for the law of Israel? Did she love them the less when she assisted them to the summit of nobility? Is not love proven and perfected by sacrifice?"

"Sacrifice, sacrifice." The Roman disgustedly pounded his fist into his palm. "I have heard from Asar and Osias many a story out of the chronicles of this land, and they all irk me with their constant harping on the theme. Abraham ready to stab his son Isaac; Jephte doing with his daughter according to his insane vow; Ruth surrendering everything for Naomi. According to your queer religion, may not an individual ever think of his own welfare and ordinary impulses? Is not personal happiness at all important?" Summoning anger to his aid, he took a deep breath and continued: "I have done with you both for the present. You can have a breathing spell to consider my position, before I act. But I am in no mood for much further delay." He swung on his heel and took a few steps. Then he turned back and his manner changed. "All through the lonely winter, Mary," he pleaded, "I have analyzed my feelings for you. They are not just passion. There is something in you, richer now than ever before, that makes me not only want but also need you. There is a depth to you, caused by experience or pain, I know not which, that is filled with a gift of sympathy and understanding; virtues that you have been lavishing on this rabbi of Nazareth but that I have required much the more. He has his mother — a peerlessly gracious lady. I do know how much she loves him, despite what I've said." His eyes rested for a moment on the blessed virgin's face, and then returned to Mary. "Will you not let me, who have nobody, have you? You can do with me whatever you will; even mold my mind, I daresay, to your own estimate of the Nazarene. I offer you a relationship wholly different from our former one. I ask you to share my all."

His gaze was keen and alert to the change in Mary's expression at the sincerity of his words and the vista that he was opening up to her.

"Do not answer me now," he finished. "Sleep on what I have said. And come to me tomorrow, Cynthia. Surely you will."

The following morning, Mother Mary noticed the Magdalene standing at the cottage window and looking in the direction of the palace.

"Are you thinking of him, my sister?" she asked.

"Rather of the good I might do him," confessed Mary of Magdala, "and others through him."

"Let us go forth into the streets of the city."

"To what purpose?" hesitated Mary.

"To find an answer."

The morning was clear but, overnight, a vagrant wind from the north had left the air cool.

They passed many people — the rich smug in their mantles of felt, the poor pathetic in their sackcloth and rags. "There are many wealthy folk — like Tullus — in Jerusalem," observed the mother; "but the poor abound. Think you that such as keep fostering their riches can bring themselves to much concern for their brethren?"

Mary was silent, for she knew where the question tended, and recalled that the Roman's philosophy contained no idea of self-denial or relinquishment. But would it not be possible to change him?

Their route wound through the sheep market. The larger animals huddled together with their lambs in the tight pens, awaiting their only deliverer — death. Their blood would spout in the Temple; their bodies would be burned; the rams' skin, dyed red, would be used as a covering for the tabernacle. "My son," recounted the mother, "has always loved these creatures. In Nazareth, he knew the name of everyone of the flock that grazed on the hill nearest our home, and he had but to call it to have a furry head nozzling his knee. To him they were a type of the innocent poor, destined to be the victims of man and to bear in their flesh his sins. John the Baptist referred to Jesus as the lamb of God, and Jesus has described himself as the good shepherd who, far from leading his sheep to death, would lay down his life for them. Are you thinking of him or of another, my sister?"

"Of both, my lady," answered Mary, her voice tremulous with the strain of dilemma. Would it not be kind to the unfortunate of the city to secure a rich friend for them? Another leader to supplement with material blessings the spiritual solicitude of the good shepherd? Would it not profit the good shepherd himself? Had not Tullus declared that, if she surrendered herself, he would be pliable to her suggestions? Could she not do what she would with him? He could marshal more influence and possessed more wealth than anyone else she knew.

Beyond the sheep market lay a wretched quarter hard by the pool of Bethesda, emptying its liberal quota of the deformed and the diseased, despite the chill of the day, into the waters; human sewage, the off-scouring of society, the halt, the blind, the ulcer-eaten, the hideous. Bethesda — *house of mercy*. Beyond the help of men, these poor children of Adam, still bearing beneath their unsightliness the image of God, splashed in the liquid dirt, believing that at least the Lord had not forgotten them and that he would send an angel to stir the spot with holy medicament.

"Today," said the mother, "another angel has visited the house of mercy. Behold, my sister."

The Magdalene, lifting her head, uttered a cry of joy, for there, on the farther side of Bethesda, in the midst of a sea of upstretched hands and surrounded by the twelve, stood the tall white-robed, purple-mantled person of Jesus.

A breeze brought to her the tones of his voice, as on that last and memorable night in Magdala. He was speaking to a sick and wasted man who lay on a couch at the rim of the pool. "Arise," he commanded. "Take up your bed and walk." And obedient to a power greater than the consciousness of his infirmity, the man immediately stood on his feet, and the flush of health seeped into his cheeks, and his limbs took on the evidence of strength and vigor. A shout, exultant, frenzied, went up from the united throats of the people.

"Is not this the answer?" asked Mother Mary quietly. "Think you that my son needs the aid of such as Tullus, or rather that such as Tullus — sick in soul — need the aid of my son?"

She slipped her hand into the palm of the Magdalene, who pressed it and raised it to her lips.

There were other Marys who loved Christ and reflected the spirit of his mother. The name Mary signified to Israel a tear, and well expressed the tenderness of these women who devoted themselves to him who would be known as the man of sorrows. There was Mary of Cleophas with her four sons, two of whom had become apostles. There was Mary, the mother of Mark, whose home

on the upper slope of Zion teemed with simple hospitality.
There was Mary, the sister of Martha and Lazarus — him
who, the Magdalene and Mother Mary would soon learn,
had been restored like Joachim to life, though his body
had lain four days in the tomb. Cherishing his mother's
name, Christ seemed to have special regard for those who
bore it, even as those who bore it seemed to have special
regard for him.

Less than two miles from Jerusalem, the peaceful little
village of Bethany — the Nazareth of Judea — tucked itself
on the eastern slope of the Mount of Olives near the
point where the road to Jericho abruptly descended
toward the Jordan Valley. Thus was the place a link between Christ's baptism and Gethsemane. Its name meant
"house of misery," as if the shadow of pain were upon it;
but the next few days were to include such placid hours
for the Lord in Bethany as would appear to dispel the
meaning. There stood the home of three most sincere
friends — Mary, Martha and Lazarus; and there his other
dear ones, together with the dearest of all, would
foregather.

Mary the Mother and Mary Magdalene fully understood that it would not be well to receive him in their
cottage near the palace of Tullus, and, therefore, they
followed him to the village. Meekly they walked at the
end of the procession with the other Marys, not even
making their presence as yet known to him; and still they
knew that every step of the way, his heart was throbbing
in unison with theirs and that, in due time, they would
be focal to his attention. The claims of the unreclaimed
were prior to theirs. Souls that had not yet heard his
message must first be fed. Bodies ravaged with disease
must be permitted to press themselves to his immaculate
person. Those that needed him most must be nearest.

He discoursed to the people as he slowly walked along; and at the wisdom of his words, hard faces fell into the soft contours of childhood, dull eyes emitted gleams, despair became hope, and a sense of comfort and understanding possessed the heavy-laden. And the Magdalene, who thought she already loved him so much, felt an increase of devotion at the utterance of his every word. She innerly castigated herself for having, thus far, only begun to serve him. Her limitations chafed her like chains on her wrists. She must do more to have him acclaimed. The land must be aroused. Why, oh why, was it still sleeping? The divine vision that he was giving to the few should be the joy of many. It must shine from the summit of every mountain in the land — Gerazim, Ebal, Zion, Thabor, Olivet. What could a mere woman do toward such a sublime end? Perhaps little; perhaps much. Had not Judith, with nothing but the appeal of her sex and the love of Israel, been strong enough to overcome Holofernes? Had not Esther won the favor of Assuerus and thus saved her people? Had not she — Mary — cast aside the things that once separated her from the sight of God? And now that she was privileged to look on deity in the face of Jesus, was she not strong enough to fight, like a lioness, any enemy of the sight? Forgetting herself, could she not do all things in him and for him who strengthened her? Should she not lose herself in active gratitude for one who had probed and cleansed the recesses of her being and enspirited her to the heights? Her humble dependence on him ought not exclude but confirm a determination to serve him worthily, and worthily she would! But how? He seemed to desire that she remain prayerfully with his mother rather than that she be fervently abroad in his interest. Would he still have her wait, who longed to hurl her energy at the inertia of Israel?

Though the distance from Jerusalem to Bethany was so slight, it was late afternoon by the time Christ reached the home of the two sisters and their brother. As he stood at the threshold, he turned, and his eyes, filled with love, sought out his mother and the Magdalene; the woman who had never known the acid touch of a single sin, and her whose soul had been seared with so many; the one, the flower of grace — the other, a triumph of the power of it; the one, beautiful from birth — the other, renewed in the birth of inner beauty. Their feet were swift to his glance; as for their spirits, they did not need to come to him, for they had never for an instant left him.

While the other Marys busied themselves in the yard outside the house, gathering dry twigs and grass for a fire in the jar-shaped oven of clay, and kneading bread for the evening meal, Christ communed with his favorites.

"Winter has passed, the rain is over and gone," he addressed his mother, using the words of the Psalmist. "Arise, and come. Come, my dove, my innocent one. Come from Libanus and be crowned. The hour is at hand. The kingdom is ready."

"But will it be delivered in pain, my son?" trembled her lips.

"The pain will pass. The glory will remain."

"You were born to me, son," she recounted, "without any of the anguish that is common to childbirth. You came like the breath of spring, and my soul abounded in gladness. As I pressed you to my bosom, I knew not whether to nourish you as my infant or adore you as my God; and the voices of angels told me what to do — to adore you even while I fed you. O my son, peace marked your coming into the world! Must your going be in pain? Cannot the kingdom be born in as much sweetness as the king?"

"The pain that atones for sin, my mother, is sweetness."

"Then give me the pain, O my beloved, and save the sweetness for yourself."

"No," cried Mary of Magdala. "Only the guilty should suffer. Ought not I, who have so much joy in standing near you, be sorrow's bride?"

"You have already suffered, Mary," said Jesus gently.

Dusk had entered the room and, in the orange glow of the oil lamp that Mary Cleophas had ignited, the Magdalene's face was transfigured, as if an angel sculptor had remodelled it to a new type of charm. The lips drooped with sadness for the past; the pale oval cheeks glistened in their softness with tears; the eyes, dim to self, were vivid with the light of her new allegiance. And Mary Cleophas remarked to Mary, the sister of Lazarus, "How much, in such a brief time, she has come to resemble the lady mother of our Lord!"

15

LEAVING Mother Mary with Christ in Bethany, the Magdalene stole away by night. Though the Master had revealed that tragedy was part of his life's prospect, she could not accept that the hand of man be raised against one so blameless and that the greatest sacrilege of all time be committed — if it could be prevented. Surely it was the office of a friend to safeguard this friend of friends, this heaven-sent son of God, this hope of the world!

The highest Jewish authority in the land was Herod Antipater. Mary could not but think of him in this crisis. Perhaps he still remembered and esteemed her. True, Christ needed neither him nor any other man; but Israel needed Christ, and should be stirred to action for him. He was meekly bending to human conditions even at the very entrance to his kingdom. Though he awaited trial for himself, ought not his lovers effect the absence of it for him? She had intended never to look on the tetrarch's face again; but now, in her distress, she decided to go to him and open his eyes and ears, if possible, to the enormity of a crime in the making.

For information about his arrival in Jerusalem to celebrate the Passover, she set forth for the K'far Jonah — the house to which, long ago, the body of the martyred youth Josue had been taken, the morning after King Herod's massacre, to await sepulture. Jonah had been a friend of

Mary's parents and often, in her childhood days, had taken her on his knee. When she first returned to Jerusalem from Magdala, in the early heyday of her sinning, she yearned to visit this kindly person and speak to him about her dear ones, but did not dare. He would have had a right and a duty to drive her from his door. She had learned, during one of her recent visits to the Temple, that Jonah's son, Obediah, was a priest; and so she now felt that, through the son, the father would be aware of the time of the tetrarch's coming. Too, she at last had no hesitancy about interviewing the good man. She was ready.

In the dawn, as she passed by the Gate of the Essenes, she noticed an elderly person standing, with a water jar on his shoulder, by the community fountain. It almost seemed as if he was waiting for her; and as she came closer, she recognized Jonah. He had not changed a great deal. His beard was white and flowing, and his shoulders were stooped, but his countenance, untouched by evil, still held much of the freshness of younger years.

"Do you remember me?" she asked, and immediately smiled at herself for the idea that his mind could possibly go back so far. But she was pleasantly surprised when, after scrutinizing her for a moment or two, he replied, "Zora's little child, grown to the exact semblance of Zora herself! Surely you are she."

"I am; the unworthy daughter of so excellent a mother. It amazes me that the sins of my life have not obliterated all likeness."

"There is that in your eyes, my daughter," spoke Jonah, "which tells of much inward change which takes away the ravages of wrong. I can see that you, like our father David, have said: 'I have labored in my groanings, every night I will wash my bed: I will water my couch with my tears.'"

"Christ called to my soul and, coming to him, it received the gift of tears, but likewise the joy that goes with it."

"You have hearkened to the Lord? You know Jesus?"

"I both know and love him. And you, Jonah?"

"I both love and know him. He came to my house to visit me when he was only twelve years of age. He met my son Obediah, then a boy like himself and now a priest of the Most High; and Obediah brought him to me. They both sat at my feet as I told them of Herod's night of blood when your little brother Joas lay on the funeral bier beside the youth Josue. I told them of the fate of Joas and your mother. I told them that, in the very room where we three — Jesus, Obediah and I — were gathered, the body of Josue, slain by Herod because he would not betray the child of Bethlehem and the monarchs of the east that had come to adore him, lay in waiting for burial. Only later did I learn that Jesus was this child; so, at the time, naturally I was astonished when he insisted on being shown the exact spot in the room where Josue had lain in death. And when I indicated it to him, he rose, went to it, knelt, and kissed the place thrice. 'Here on this very spot, consecrated by the noble dead, a great sacrament of the living shall one day be instituted,' he promised. What he meant, I know not; but his words have lingered and echoed in that room through the years and, for the last few days, the atmosphere of it has seemed filled with gracious spirits preparing for some extraordinary event. I can feel them going to and fro, sprinkling the air with peace and prayer and the suggestion of another world. That room, daughter, is the vestibule of heaven. I spoke to Jesus of you, Mary. I told him that you had tried to save your little brother, only to lose all. I told him how I had searched in vain for you and feared that, in an anguish too bitter for a young heart to bear, your life would be worse than death. His eyes filled with tears, as I spoke; tears for you, Mary; and again he made a promise. The promise was this — 'She shall be found. She shall be more than saved.' "

The Magdalene clutched to her throat her mantle — Christ's garment, which she had worn ever since he gave it to her on that bleak night in Japhia; cloth of purest wool, woven by his mother's hands in the calm of Nazareth; symbol of innocence and grace.

"He was thinking of me — even then?" she asked, almost incredulously, her voice trembling with awe and vibrant with thankfulness.

"He was indeed. Jesus ever looks ahead. To do good is his passion. Lent to earth, he belongs to heaven. I followed his career, unfolding in spiritual power and beauty. I took Obediah to visit him and his Mother and holy Joseph in Nazareth. I grieved as for a brother when Joseph was gathered to his fathers, and begged Jesus with his mother to bless my house by coming to live with me here in Jerusalem; but he said, 'The time is not yet.' At last, though, my plea is about to be granted. At last, I shall have him, however briefly, with me; for two of his apostles appeared at my gate last night and assured me that, ere the Pasch has been finished, here the Lord shall have entered in. All through the night, gladness has filled my heart and home. Here the Lord with his apostles will celebrate the feast. Here will be such a night of blessedness as can erase from memory the night of blood in which Zora, Joas and Josue wafted out their souls."

"But unless action is quick, Jonah, that night may be marred. A storm is gathering around the Lord in Jerusalem. Has Herod Antipater yet arrived?"

"He has. His banners and trophies adorn the tower of

the Hasmonean palace; and Obediah says he took residence there yesterday."

"To him I must go to speak for Jesus. I know him well."

"Would you not be endangering yourself, my daughter?"

"I am thinking only of the peril of my Lord."

"You say well. All of us should forget ourselves in the Master's need. But first come with me to my home and be refreshed. You have plenty of time. The tetrarch, fatigued from his journey from Tiberias, will doubtless be sleeping late this day."

And as Jonah and Mary walked along, he spoke to her about his visitors of the night before, Simon Peter and John. "They, too, found me at the well," he mentioned. "They said the Lord Jesus had bidden them make ready the Passover and to arrange that the lamb be eaten in the special room of my house. The house is not really mine, but my master has left me in possession of it through the years, out of appreciation for my service. He also has known Jesus from boyhood days and believes him to be the elect of God. Like myself, he is thrice honored that the Lord comes, and is helping me to have all things in readiness."

Jonah led Mary into a walled garden and up onto a terrace over-hanging Jerusalem. "Behold the city of the king of kings," he invited. "Instead of a palace of spotless marble gleaming up out of a lordly grove of orange trees, pistachio trees and cypresses, he chooses my humble abode. Through the retrospect of years, he remembers the youth who died for love of him, and will fill with his living presence the room where Josue lay ready for the tomb."

Mary gazed down from the terrace on the streets of splendor and sorrow and sin, and could see, in her mind's eye, the crime of crimes that was being readied against the meekest and kindest and truest of men. Disloyalty to the Lord! It wound in and out of the crooked ways like the monstrous reptile it was, through a maze of rocks and burnt brick and lime-stone. It coiled around the Hippicus Tower, the Phasael Tower, the Mariamne Tower, the Fortress of Antonia, and even the walls of the Temple itself, causing the whole city to tremble to its very foundation. Blind, blind Jerusalem! — unable to see the woe that she was drawing on herself, if she persisted in an attitude against one who had demonstrated his sonship to God. Must not the divine wrath smite a land that opposed him of whom Jehovah himself had twice testified, "This is my beloved son"? Who — what — could forfend the fate? Oh why had the miracles of Jesus touched only individuals and not the nation itself? Christ had said that, raised up, he would draw all hearts to him. But had not his works of mercy already raised him up? Were not Galilee and Judea ringing with his name? He was a king, and his kingdom was at hand. He must not be thwarted!

Taking her by the hand, Jonah now guided her into his house and to a small hall. "Here," said he, "is where Josue slept and a great sacrament will be born." And he pointed to three couches and a table covered with spotless linen. Mary's quick eye took in every detail: the canopy, the cloth, the ablution-basin, the two-handled chalice for libations, the copper jars and vessels, and the beaker of ruby wine; the hearthstone, or *kiraim*, where the bitter almonds would be kneaded with lemons, vinegar, cinnamon, dates and figs and baked into the form and color of a brick, in memory of the labors of the Egyptian captivity.

"Be you the first to sit at the table — the only one — before the Lord's coming," urged Jonah. "I shall bring you bread and fruit."

"No," demurred Mary. "My food is to serve the Master. Let me have a hand in preparing the feast. Let me grind the wheat for the unleavened bread. Let me strew the house with fermented grain. If it is not too soon, let me wash the coriander, succory, endive, thistles and lettuce; even though, later, your worthier hands repeat the task."

"The daughter of Zora shall do whatsoever she pleases in my house," agreed Jonah.

And as Mary plied her tasks, she noted that, in front of the chief place at the table, the morning sun was making a little pool of sheer brilliance on the polished floor. "It seems," she remarked to Jonah, "that heaven itself is kissing that spot."

"The brilliance is often there," said Jonah, his eyes swimming in reverence. "There is where Jesus, as a boy, knelt. There is where Josue lay."

The Hasmonean palace had a guard at the gate, and Mary waited while a soldier carried in her request for an audience. Presently she was being led through the royal garden and she could not but contrast the prevailing luxury with the poverty of one who charged his followers to take neither scrip nor purse nor change of raiment on their journeyings. The carefully laid pathways, amber-colored in the sun, wound through a sea of close-clipped grass interspersed with little colorful islands of spring's earliest blooms. A mirror of a pond brought a piece of the blue sky down to earth, and a pair of swans, queening themselves on the surface, appeared to be floating in air. A peacock of Ophir, not to be out-done in grandeur, raised its opalescent fountain of tail and strutted as showily as an oriental prince. Marble statues, forbidden to Jewish orthodoxy but fostered by the Roman influence that had become a part of Herod Antipater's career, gleamed from the cool green depths of arbors.

Mary stepped back at the sight of a familiar form approaching her. There under the budding branches of lemon trees, walked Herodias, a thin smile on her lips, full as if with a scarlet poison, and cruel.

Suddenly the tetrarchess paused, and let Mary come the rest of the way to her. She stood erect in her jewel-fretted sandals, revealing her ruby-tinted toes; her graceful long limbs were scarcely concealed by a clinging robe of turquoise silk, cinctured with a band of silver; her slender throat, which her admirers likened to a tower of ivory, fittingly raised the eye to what many sincerely considered the most attractive face in Israel. But Mary, whose standard of beauty had changed, recoiled from the eyes, sea-green and enlarged with antipathy.

"I intercepted your message to the tetrarch," announced Herodias, her voice juicy with bitter-sweetness. "Not that I am averse to your seeing him; but I wish first to have speech with you myself. We all know of your strange new love for the rabbi of Galilee, and my personal interest has been aroused; the more so, now that I see the effect that this devotion has had on your appearance. Any man who can turn Mary of Magdala from an orchid to a comparative blade of grass — for you do know how you now look, my dear, do you not? — is a miracle-worker of the first rank. I approve of him."

"Would you help him, my lady?" eagerly asked Mary. "Peril stalks him. That is why I am here."

Herodias inclined her head.

"Oh, how can I thank —"

"Do not try — yet," said the tetrarchess, each word a drop of acid. "Do you remember John the Baptist?"

"Remember? At first, I thought that the memory would

drive me mad. John was as innocent as a child in the womb. Had I known in Macherus what I know now, I'd gladly have delivered my body to be cut to pieces rather than have a hair of his head touched."

Herodias' brow darkened. "More than once," she disclosed, "his gory head has floated in the black stream of night through my room, and his open eyes are always afire with accusation. His dead tongue, which I pierced with a golden needle, berates me. I don't mind telling you that I have taken to the custom which my husband's father practised: I keep a light burning beside my bed and have a servant sleep near. It is the same with the tetrarch — only worse. He believes that not only he but all Israel is haunted by the prophet. He swears that John has returned to spurious life in the person of this man called Christ."

"Christ is no mere man."

"That is what Herod maintains. And I'm inclined to think so too. Of course, I discount most of the stories I hear. Passing through ignorant minds, the most ordinary events come from mouths as marvels. But the tales are so persistent that, at length, I'm inclined to accept that the Nazarene is at least an unusual and powerful person."

"That he is — and more. He exercises his might only for good. If mercy were personified and walked in our midst, it could be no different from him. But what would you have me do in order to enlist your aid?"

"I would have you induce him to visit both this palace and the one in Tiberias and expel the visions that disturb me and my consort alike. Only last night — awake or dreaming, I know not which — I again saw the trunkless head of John. I would have you prevail on Christ to bless our troubled lives with peace."

"Gladly would he do this for you and for Herod Antipater. But the price of peace is repentance. Are you grieved, as I am grieved, for the death of John? Have you wept, as I have wept?"

"Not a single tear has fallen, or shall ever fall, from my eye at the just desert that overtook the evil-mouthed prophet." The jaw of Herodias so hardened that the outline of it was steely in the rays of the sun. "He spat toads on my name."

"Not on your name, my lady. Not toads."

"Have a care! If you offend me as he did, what is to prevent a similar fate for you?"

Mary looked down but her spirit rose. She was not afraid. "Would you have me ask Jesus to bring a blessing to guilt?" she asked. "Philip Boethus — your husband — is exiled in Rome."

The eyes of the tetrarchess narrowed beneath her heavy dark lashes into menacing slits. Her bosom was agitated under its covering of silk which threw off ripples of light. For a moment, she could not speak. But when her voice returned, it came in a measured tone. "I see. You would have me gone, so that in freedom you might worm yourself back into the graces of the tetrarch. The blade of grass, at last weary of its low estate, would again become an orchid. It is necessary to have me well out of the way —"

Mary winced.

"You are a crafty woman, siren of Magdala. But I, too, am wise in a knowledge of my sex and the weaknesses of men. You know that Herod Antipater still wants you and that you have only whetted his desire by your long absence from court. You know that, with me stepping aside, you could aspire even to be tetrarchess yourself. Carefully have you laid your plans and taken your time. Now, under the guise of good, you seek to effect your deepest wrong."

"My lady," begged Mary, extending hands which slightly trembled.

"You think my union with Herod Antipater unhallowed, just as the prophet John thought," went on Herodias ruthlessly.

Mary did not answer.

"This from you, not one of whose many affairs has ever had a sanction!" laughed the woman mockingly. "Besides, do you not know that divorce is permitted by both the Shammaite and the Hillelite school? The latter justifies it even when a husband is not satisfied with his wife's cookery."

"Christ does not teach that."

"*Him*," scorned Herodias. But she could not keep from spoiling her fine scene by adding, in a note of wistfulness, "Him — too."

For a moment the silence was strained. It snapped when she went on to mention, with an irrelevance intended to be arch, "In this palace, even as under the fortress eyrie of Macherus, there is a dungeon. You used to visit the one there, I recall. Such places can be so interesting — and convenient. Would you like to see this one?"

Mary closed her eyes.

"Your Nazarene, I hear, is on the decline," the woman remarked, her threat wrapping itself in a show of pity. "Alas, you thought He would be the most authoritative man in the land. Now you must regret that you linked your fortune to a falling star."

"My fortune is nothing," disclaimed Mary. "His star is firm."

The woman's eyes flickered as she asked, "Then why are you here?"

Mary sought for words and, finding none suitable, lapsed into a quietude that piqued both herself and

[189]

Herodias. How could she impart her wild fears that, though Christ was all-powerful and his kingship certain, the delays and the anguish that men's ignorance and inertia ever cause were stretching between him and his crown? It was even more to assist Israel to sanity than Christ to glory that she was here. She knew that he needed no human hand, but was keenly aware of his habit of acceptance and deference. Only against hypocrites did he ever raise his voice. His frank antagonists always passed unscathed. Courtesy and patience were a vital part of his majesty.

"Your muteness is a mask," came the charge. "I have worn many myself — pretty ones, too. So I'm not deceived. You are more subtle than ever before. Tullus, the rich Roman, has a fancy for you, and I have a fancy for Tullus. You shall not lure either him or my husband from me. I've been informed that a gorgeous nest is ready for a bird of paradise here in Jerusalem; and what my Roman sees in you, now, is sheer mystery to me. Those ridiculous clothes, that shapeless purple robe and plain blue cloak!"

With a helpless gesture, Mary disowned all blame for Tullus.

"Evidently you can be true to no one," went on the tirade. "You must have numbers."

"There is but one," cried the Magdalene, stung with the injustice of the remark.

"The fact of your coming proclaims you have doubts about the power of this one. If he were as mighty as you hoped, I'd not be needed by you. No, woman of Magdala, I am not impressed. I should work up a specious charge and rid myself of your annoyance forever. But I've had my surfeit of blood and the needless torment it brings." Her brows knitted. "I have long suspected that there was something in the back of your mind the day you talked with me in Macherus, and that its poison distilled itself into my purpose against John, quickening me. You beset me in my weakest moment, and I yielded; but the guilt was not wholly mine. May John's decayed lips curse you to the grave! May his eyes burn through your soul in the deep of night! May the teeth of the dead bite into your living flesh and leave the mark of damnation on you! May —"

Mary gasped in horror and shrank away. Could it have been that Herodias' words were true? She had wanted the Baptist removed. She had, though only momentarily, knelt to gloat over his severed head. But no — not *that!*

"The sweat of revelation is on your brow," cried Herodias triumphantly, almost hysterical with her desire to share the burden of her intolerable guilt. "Once you came to me with murder in your heart, and now you come with guile on your lips. But this time I am proof against you. The ghost of John could be appeased — at least partly." Her lids almost closed on a stare that was calculating and bold.

"I deserve only the worst for my past," said Mary. "But the Master's future —"

"The Master, as you call him, was John's rival. Did not the people follow the Baptist until the Nazarene drew them to himself?"

"John but prepared the way for Jesus."

"So?" the woman's teeth clicked. "John knew he was being ousted from the affection of the people by the wonder-man of Galilee. You never told me why you were against the Baptist. I see the reason now. You didn't object to his being sped out of this world, did you? Oh, no! A favorite has to have a clear field."

Mary could stand little more, but breathing hard, she

gripped herself. "I had never met Jesus," she insisted, "before I saw John."

"Whether you had met him or not, your mind was full of him. You let a remark drop, which I've always remembered. You said: 'With the Baptist gone, I shall be nearer to Jesus.' "

"I meant nearer to revenge."

"Never met the Nazarene and yet seeking vengeance on him?"

The woman took in a deep breath which would have been followed by an explosion of contempt, only that Mary was protesting; "The story is long and goes back to my childhood days."

"And now you are all agog with whims to help him and to get others to do the same?"

Herodias threw up her hands. "Well," she muttered, "this is good. It pleases me. Now I know how to placate the spirit of John doubly. Jesus and you. Two are better tortured than one."

Mary shuddered. "Not Jesus!"

"Once avenged, John will haunt neither me nor my husband anymore."

"But Christ — the king of men —"

"If he can be taken, he is as weak as any man. They say that he claims divinity. Jehovah will bless my household for putting down a public blasphemer. Peace shall be ours."

"Bloody hands — can they bring peace to your heart? Did you not say —"

"I will not kill you, Mary of Magdala. Well I know what your malignity would spew at me from the grave. When you die, it must be at the hand of nature or — yourself. If you live," Herodias paused grimly, "beware of me. And your Christ —"

"No power can slay Him!" the Magdalene ringingly affirmed, her spirit exultant with conviction. "He holds the keys of life. He is the son of God."

With the dart of a cobra's head, the tetrarchess demanded: "Would divinity permit a strumpet to plead its cause?"

Mary drew her veil over her eyes, torn between two desires: the one to accept this insult for the Lord's sake, and the other to scratch out the victory-bright eyes of the insulter. Blindly her hands stretched forth. It was only a sense of contrast that saved her; a sudden flash of memory that, though one woman hissed, "Strumpet," another — the purest in all Israel! — said, "Sister."

Ashamed at being ashamed of shame, and now all regretful that she had exposed the judgment of her king to an evil woman's tongue, she murmured: "I should not have come. I should have known."

"Yes, you should have known that one like you can do only harm." Herodias drew from her bosom a small phial. "I have here a distillation of snake venom. It is so potent that, if applied to the smallest cut in the finger, it sends death leaping through the veins. What is life without happiness but a yawning grave? In Rome, the end of joy is the end of living. We here in Palestine should learn the Edomite lesson of not letting wretchedness run its course. You were never happy, Mary of Magdala. Often have I read it in your eyes; and your new love is but new misery. Relief for you lies in this phial."

She pressed the tiny bottle into Mary's hand. "Just abrade your skin a little and pour this liquid into a warm bath," she directed. "Lying down in the grateful waters, you can dream away what remains of your life."

The picture pleased the Magdalene's tired mind. But had not Christ spoken of the weary taking up their load and following him? Following him to his day of glory when all that Herodias represented in Israel would be no more. That day, that day! To live for it would be sweet. To die for it —

"If I were to use this poison," she found herself saying, "would you promise to devote all your ability, and Herod Antipater's too, to clearing the path for my Master? — to speeding his day?"

Herodias let the restless little tip of her tongue glide over her lips. "Do you doubt me?" she reproved, with woman's immemorial art of evasion.

Hope withered in Mary's breast. Without another word, she turned her back on the silken weaver of deceits and retraced her steps from the luxurious garden in which birds were flying but somehow had forgotten to sing.

Herodias, her cheeks hot and her eyes glinting dangerously, beckoned to two soldiers standing a short distance away; and when they were at her side she pointed a determined finger at the retreating figure.

She talked rapidly.

As Mary wended her way toward the Temple, craving the guidance of prayer, the confusion that she had so often suffered in the years that preceded her conversion, and many times after, was again upon her. To experience the stabbing thoughts and reasonless emotions of Herodias was like falling wounded into a turbid depth. She felt soiled by a chilly kind of uncleanliness that reached to the bones. She could see herself — her past self — so graphically in the base psychology of the tetrarchess, that she was assailed with a fear that the graces of the past two years had been nothing more than an illusion and that yesterday's sins were the sole reality of today. Beelzebub must be regarding her with glee. She did not dare to look

around, for she was almost certain that the arch-fiend
was following her closer, closer, clutching at her veil.
Though the air was cool, and her skin was marble-cold,
her brow dripped with sweat. She pressed the vial of
poison to her heart and, cold as it was, it imparted a comparative warmth to her flesh.

Almost mechanically, she mounted the steps of the
Temple and reached the Court of the Gentiles, still conscious of a hellish presence behind her, fancying that
sardonic faces were peering from the rows of columned
arcades, unable to raise her eyes to the roof of cedar wood.
Presently there were murmurous sounds that grew loud.
Then a rough hand fell on her shoulder and sent a trickle
of arctic fear from her throat to the soles of her feet. A
man bellowed, "You, are you not the harlot of Magdala?"

Her tongue clove to the roof of her mouth. "You see —
she does not deny it!" ventured another to the by-standers.
"Nor does she let us hear her voice, for it would reveal
her profession. The lips of a harlot are like a honeycomb
dripping, and her throat is smoother than oil; but her end
is bitter as wormwood and sharp as a two-edged sword."

Women craned their necks. Men smirked and nudged
one another.

"She has vaunted her sinning from one end of the land
to the other," a third accoster dramatically swept on.
"She stands shameless in this place of sanctity. The forni-
cation of a woman shall be known by the haughtiness of
her eyes, and by her eyelids. This woman has drunk of
every water near her and sat down by every hedge. Her
gaze has burned with the sparks of hell. Gems have
tinkled on her neck and fingers and ankles. Cosmetics
have painted her cheeks. Her breast is a scorpion nest;
her beauty, Lucifer's lamp; her embrace, the coil of a
snake."

Like the wounded thing she was, Mary turned every which way, seeking to escape the intolerable voices hurling accusations around her. The crowd closed in.

A counter-murmur arose. "The Rabbi of Galilee." "The Nazarene." "Jesus ben Joseph." And all eyes turned to the calm and unearthly figure approaching. But Mary's reviler still clawed her shoulder.

"Rabbi," he called out, "the adulteress of Babylon has come to the house of the Lord. To cast her forth is not enough. According to our father Moses, such should be stoned."

And as Christ began to speak, silence fell. "Moses referred to the sinner that still sins. Our Father in heaven forgives the repentant."

"This creature is still a sinner. She has invaded the holy place to seek new victims for her unholy traffic. Her eyes have been soliciting the men that are gathered here for the Pasch."

"Raise your veil, Mary," commanded Jesus.

Her trembling fingers, pale with the dead paleness of ivory, complied. And as the veil slowly lifted, the spectators, awaiting the vision of a siren's bold and beauteous face, receded in surprise. This was the countenance of no fleshly charmer, but of a weary and frightened woman. Beauty still gleamed there, but far less from the soft oval surface than from an interior light, like a piece of alabaster held against a flame, or as a pillar of Tyre lit from within by a lamp. Her eyes were deep in their violet sockets and covered by their azure lids through which tears, quivering, made a sparkling and blinding blur.

Jesus, dropping on one knee, trailed with his finger the dust that many feet had left on the polished floor of the Temple; touched it as if to say, "Thus has the soil of her life been touched by grace to spiritual bloom. The mire of earth, nourished by rain and warmed by the sun, becomes a lily. A soul, bedewed with tears and fostered by heaven, becomes a shrine."

Lifting himself up, he proclaimed: "He that is without sin among you, let him cast the first stone at her."

The men shifted their glances and edged back farther. Without sin? Who was sinless, save the rabbi himself whose floral purity filled the Temple like a breath of the hills of Nazareth from which he came! Would his shining hand cast the first stone?

Again he bent down and his finger moved through the dust in indication that his mission was to seek and raise the lowly, while the pride and deceit of Israel towered in self-righteousness. And the men seemed to see their sins written in the traceries he made. One by one, and all but one, they moved away; but the women remained, their eyes moist with a realization that at last, in Christ Jesus, their sex had a champion — one who stooped to help even the most fallen and disprized among them, one who unmasked the part of man in the errors of woman, one whose goodness made the very stones, trodden under foot, flower with moral lesson.

The only man that remained, came forward and knelt before the Master and the Magdalene. Under his turban, his gray hair in ringlets framed a thin withered face. He raised a trembling hand to Christ, as his ashen mouth formed a single sentence: "I thank you, Lord." And then, stooping, he raised the hem of Mary's garment to his lips.

"Who are you?" she asked in wonder.

"One who once started you, Mary of Magdala, on the path of darkness with a false string of pearls. Long have I prayed that you would find the truth. Today my plea to heaven is answered. Today have I glimpsed your soul.

[197]

— Do you not remember me in Rebecca's house and on the hill-crest of Nazareth?"

"Can you be — " Mary's eyes were still brimming with tears, and she could hardly see.

"Yes, my lady. I am Phares."

Like a rush of spring into the sway of winter, hope returned to the Magdalene's heart. It came less from the Master's kindness, great as that was, than from his authority — the evidence of his kingship and his effectiveness, both near and far, present and past, over the lives of men. Even Phares — Phares! — had been completely won.

Nothing — nobody — could succeed in opposing the king.

His day was near. Perhaps, as near as tomorrow.

16

Mary tarried when Christ and Phares left her in the Temple. The Master had breathed only one word to her, "Bethany," after her male tormentors dispersed; but His eyes had expressed so much! She was certain that he knew everything she had done and said since her withdrawal in the night from the house that sheltered him and his mother. He understood even the crazed impulse to end her own life, in order to hasten his future, which Herodias had aroused. She sensed his appreciation but read his forbiddance. The phial slipped from her hand, just as the dagger had fallen from it in the wilderness; and its contents spattered like blood on the floor. With a sigh, she turned away. It would have been solace to die, even in vain, for him —

When she was in the street again, a man sidled up to her. "You did not come to me, Cynthia," he charged bitterly and yet with the tired mellowness of a too great desire, too long denied. "I could have taken you, but truly I wanted your good will. O Mary, don't you see that your love for Christ is mistaken? If you truly loved him, you would have given yourself to me and thus protected him."

"He is at last ready to transcend all aid and take his throne, Tullus," said Mary, her soft throat arching in pride. "Now I know."

Tullus bit his lip in vexation. But he tried faintly to humor her. "Granted that he will be king," he reasoned, "think you that he will need you in his day of ascendency, who now needs you not at all?"

"He regarded me as necessary enough to be defended against those that demeaned me in the Temple," declared Mary, tossing her head.

"Can you not see that he was simply using you to gain the sympathy of your sex?" belittled Tullus. "Besides, that affair in the Temple was staged, exaggerated. The old reputation of Mary of Magdala in Jerusalem has been dead for years. You are really little known here today. I have just spoken with two soldiers from the Hasmonean palace, and they revealed to me that Herodias had hired them to stir up a scene against you. You would never have been noticed, with your face covered by that heavy veil, if the malignity of the tetrarchess had not pursued you. It follows you still. You need me, Mary. Yes, and the rabbi does too. Won't you let me help? I warn you that trouble is near for him and his. Last night the Sanhedrin met in solemn session to deliberate his case, and they are to meet again. Though blameless in your eyes, he has woefully offended the religious leaders of the land by trampling on the law, tinkering with the rites, twisting the truth, consorting with tax-collectors and such as you, and eating the bread of strangers and Gentiles. His egotism is enormous. He calls the Temple his father's house. Even now a throng is gathering, with his approval, a few streets away — I saw them as I came hither — to escort him like a king through the high-ways and by-ways. Such arrogance cannot but be his undoing." Tullus frowned to see that he was making neither headway nor impression.

"He violates no law, but fulfills them all," refuted Mary.

"Devotion has robbed you of judgment," stated Tullus surlily. "But I care not what he does or doesn't do. I am thinking solely of you, Mary, and how his downfall will effect you. He can run all the risks he will, but I am resolved that you shall not share them. You are coming with me."

She drew her mantle around her, ready to flee.

"A Roman's will has its way, even in Jerusalem," asserted Tullus, seizing her arm.

Beckoning to two slaves ready with a litter, he tightened his grasp. "It is useless for you to cry out or figure in another scene," he warned, taking her other arm. "A woman's complaint is nothing against a man's, especially a Roman's."

He dragged her, struggling against him with all her depleted strength, dominating her spirit with his muscular physique and making it clear that, this time, she was assuredly his captive. Her voice failed her; it came like the half-mute bleating of a lamb. At last, thoroughly exhausted, she sank back on a mass of pillows and suffered herself to be taken. The slaves closed the curtains swiftly, buttoning them firmly to the sides of the conveyance. With a heavy heart, she could feel them lifting and carrying the burden of her wretchedness.

At the palace of Tullus, once her own, she was too weak to rise. Some maid-servants came to help her, and they studied her quizzically as they lifted her like a child and brought her to a room especially prepared for her reception. They laid her on a divan, removed her simple garments, and anointed her body from head to toe with rarest oils until it shed a honey-sweet fragrance. They combed her long flame-red hair into the ripples of its former glory and fastened its fine-textured folds with gemmed clips. They blended a pink tint into the paleness of her cheeks. Over her form they slipped a lavender tunic of sheerest Ionian material, scented with stacte and cassia, which fitted like a caress to her beauty, and adorned her wrists with bracelets and her feet with instep bells and ankle chains. Around her neck they placed a glittering chain from which a vial of perfume depended. Lastly they poured a reviving wine through her unwilling lips.

"Our mistress is radiant," enviously said one. "See for yourself." And kneeling, she held up an oval mirror framed in onyx.

"Bring me the clothes in which I came," was Mary's only comment on her reflection.

The woman took up the penitential robe of purple and the home-spun mantle from the table and placed them in her hands. Mary stroked the robe longingly, and held the cloak to her breast. Her tears fell on the blueness of it. His day was so near, and would she not be privileged to see his entry to it?

"Our mistress is given to grief," noted another servant wonderingly. "Is it a hardship to exchange these poor things for a glowing tunic?"

"The bitterest I have ever known," exhaled Mary, "since — "

"Since you first met Christ?" interrupted and finished a third, so low that the others, moving about the room, did not hear.

"Do you know him?" asked Mary quickly, with bated breath.

"He cured my father at the Pool of Bethesda," whispered the maid, a slight and modest girl who resembled Rhea.

And the words of Jesus, "Arise and walk," came back to the Magdalene with all the force of a personal command. He had been speaking to her and to all people in

trial and trouble, when his healing speech fell on the
sick man. He was speaking now, for everything he said
transcended the moment of utterance and echoed afar
in lives. One must not languish, but be up and about the
Father's business of goodness. Did it matter what happened so long as his voice and the heavenly reassurance
of it were near, as they could not but be near in the
living memory of his words? There was — there must be
— a way of doing his will. It was not his will that she
should be back here in the realm of paganism that had
been foresworn. Might not this grateful servant girl be
a means of deliverance? Might it not yet be possible to
see the day?

"Stay close to me — closer than the rest," she begged
intensely. "It is essential that I go to him. You shall
help me."

"I, mistress?" The maid looked affrighted. "How?"

Mary recalled the night of long ago when her young
mind was able to contrive a means of releasing her little
brother Joas from King Herod's castle, and she felt con-
fident that somehow she would now be able to free herself from the present situation. "I'll tell you later," she
promised. "Place these garments where I can get them
readily."

A bell tinkled at the door and Tullus, stately and fes-
tive in an amaranthine robe and a crown of olive leaves,
entered. "You are Cynthia again, my Mary," he approved,
his gaze alight. "Here is where you belong — an opal in
its proper setting. All the plainness and ugliness of the
nightmare of an existence that you have been enduring,
have passed. The Nazarene is not the only one that raises
the dead. I myself have evoked you from something worse
than a grave. Henceforth nothing coarser than silk shall
touch your skin, and nothing harsher than music shall

fill your ears." And taking both her hands in his, he drew her to a banquet hall.

The large room was centred with a long table upraised on the wings of metallic swans and heaped with viands. The reclining couch, covered with scarlet halicore skins such as were used for the roofing of the tabernacle in the Temple, and supplied with softest cushions of African partridge down, seemed fitted for a god and a goddess. From four braziers, placed in the corners, rose the mingled odors of sandalwood, cistus, Indian saffron, mastich and myrrh, sweet and exciting as the notes that were vibrating from the strings of concealed instruments.

"Is your mind filled with flowers and jewels?" smiled Tullus as he assisted her to the couch.

She did not answer. There was nothing to say, for all this wealth and display were to her as if they were not. Her mind was filled with a picture of Jonah's supper room where a modest table awaited the coming of the Lord; and of a plain little home in Nazareth; and of Bethany; and most of all, the day when all the splendor which men ever conceived would be ashes before the glory of her king.

A clamor rolled into the street below and uplifted itself in billowy waves to the banquet hall. Tullus left the table and went to the terrace, looking down. His lips worked strangely. "Come," he invited Mary. "This spectacle is for you rather than me. The orgies of Tyre and Sidon have more sense."

And Mary, her eyes straining, held her hand against a quick wild throb in her throat. Throngs of people from every direction were pouring from the streets into a mighty stream, and the air was shaken with their shouting. The noises grew louder and louder, coming not only from the throats but the very souls of the people, as if the long sad story of Jerusalem had come to a chapter that atoned for every sigh and dried away the memory of every tear; as if at last the heavy stone of the years had rolled away and hope, like a new-born light, had risen to expel dark grief with a thousand golden spears.

Up from the torrent of emotion, the brisk and rhythmic waving of palm and olive branches and willow withes, the snatches of psalms, the sea of outflung garments, the shower of blossoms that were dotting the scene with all the tints of the rainbow, the discordant and yet strangely harmonious babble of voices, there rose and burst, like silver bubbles, special sounds that were the rarest music the Magdalene had ever heard. "Hosannah!" "Jesus!" "Son of David!" "King!"

The day. The day!

It was here.

"Tullus, Tullus, why stand we idle?" she cried. "Comes the king! Dare we not go to greet him in his glory?"

Suddenly she was glad of her rich raiment, of her beauty, of the privilege of being alive. She folded her arms over the ecstasy in her heart at the prospect of soon standing by the Lord's throne and sharing in the birth of the new Jerusalem. She tingled in every cell. Her feet, winged, moved of their own accord to the street. Tullus, astonished at the degree of her feeling, did nothing to stop her. He had dominated her will with his body. She was now dominating his with her spirit. Dazedly, he followed her.

When she reached the door of the palace, Jesus was passing by. A sense of anticlimax, as sudden as it was real, fell on her mood like a smothering pall. On a mean little gray animal, with a sagging head and a stringy mane, and with tired feet patiently plodding the stony road, he sat. She trembled, now not with joy, but fear.

The words of the prophet Zacharias, which she had read with Mother Mary, tolled in her memory: "Fear not, daughter of Zion; behold, your king comes sitting on an ass's colt." But they were not enough. Where was the great fire-breathing charger of her fancies? Where the glittering silver-spun robe which the very seraphim were to have woven? Where the sceptre? The crown?

True, his sacred head, well above the concourse of the people, ruled the spectacle, and there was kingly testimony in his profile which, against the slanting rays of the sun, seemed etched in purest gold. But the glory, which should have brought Jerusalem to her knees, was wanting. The insensate breezes assumed to fling back his soft brown hair and swell the sleeves of his tunic, as if they were his master instead of him being theirs. His whole aspect was that of a personified prayer, rather than that of a man of infinite power. He appeared as detached from all the excitement as a star from a storm. His cheek was as blanched as the linen that his mother's hand had woven for him in Nazareth, and not flushed with the pride of a royal estate.

"Your king!" mocked Tullus, recovering from awe and finding voice. "The same today as yesterday, only more ridiculous."

Mary could only say, "Let us follow him and see. His course is the Temple. There — there —"

They mingled with the crowd, rubbing elbows with cripples that hobbled along on their staves or the arms of relatives; the blind, groping in darkness; bodies that could have been refugees from tombs; fragments of life to which the Master's words to his apostles, after the miracle of the multiplication of loaves and fishes, might have been aptly applied: "Gather them up, lest they be lost."

The Roman looked his nausea.

There were women in the throng. Mary of Cleophas, surrounded by her four sons; Mary and Martha, the sisters of Lazarus; Mary, the mother of Mark; a tall Samaritan with her jet black hair exposed, and rings twinkling from her ears; Joanna; Susanna; and others whom the Magdalene could not recognize. She strained her eyes. Where was the Master's mother. In Bethany — alone? Mary was faint with longing to go to her, or rather to have her here. What would the coronation be without the queen?

The procession was nearing the Temple. "Now," palpitated the Magdalene, "now he will manifest himself. The heavens will open. We shall see."

Tullus' jaw set firmly. "Enough!" he cried. "Never before has earth witnessed so sorry a demonstration of the lack of majesty in a man that would be king." And taking Mary's arm in a grip of iron, he dragged her through and away from the milling throng.

Back in the palace, at the very spot from which they started, the Magdalene and the Roman again stood. The street was deserted and quiet, though far-off voices from the Temple made a living background for the silence. Of a sudden, the sky was shedding so much splendor that all the flashing swords of all the great armies of all time would have been relative waves of night. Tullus stared. As far as his gaze could go, it was dazzled with such a celestial brightness as his memory could not recall. He contemplated Jerusalem. The walls, the box-like houses, the towers, all were turned by the magic of the moment from brick and stone and mortar into blazing light; and the Temple, as if receiving Jehovah himself, was a mass of jubilant flames, with its gates like so many vivid pearls and its heights like sheets of transparent glass. Sardonyx,

[207]

sardius, chrysolite, beryl, topaz, chrysoprasus, jacinth, jasper, sapphire, chalcedony, amethyst and emerald seemed to pool their lustres in the astonishing structure.

"Behold," cried Mary, startled from her despondency. "My king is being anointed! This is the reflection of his glory!" But suddenly a moan welled up in her cry. "And I am not there — "

"My head aches," complained Tullus. "All this brilliancy is annoying. Only the fortress of Antonia and the hill of Calvary look real to me in the landscape. Let us go inside and be sensible."

That night, when the Roman lay sleeping the deep sleep of flagons of wine, Mary exchanged clothes with the sympathetic maid, covered her face, and slipped into the servant quarters where all was dark and still. Thence she stole through the garden to the cottage where, with Mother Mary, she had worked and prayed and dreamed away the long days of winter, spinning and winding yarn, grinding meal, kneading dough and tending the oven for the needs of the poor, and conning the words of the prophets and the doctrine of Jesus. There she doffed the hand-maiden's dress and put on her own purple robe and blue cloak. Something told her the king would have it so. Concealing in her bosom — she knew not why — the vial of nard which had that day been given her by her adorners, she groped her way to a hidden gate in the garden which she knew well. Happily it was unguarded.

Soon her feet were speeding through the streets, and the star-lit route of her choosing led to Bethany.

17

THE sun was rising over the Mount of Olives when Mary met Simon Peter at the gates of Bethany.

"Heaven be praised!" he exclaimed, with his hands extending and the glow of his earnest face accentuated by his black, gray-flecked beard. "We have all worried and prayed, for we heard of what happened to you in the Temple yesterday and realized that, like the Master, you have enemies."

"What of my Lord? Where is he? Did he take possession of his Father's house? Has he been acknowledged by the priests as well as the people? Were the heavens rent and did hosts of angels descend?"

Peter shook his head slowly at the swift flow of questions. "No," he answered ruefully. "He entered the Temple like the humblest of Jews, and most of the people soon left him. But had they remained, they would have seen a transfiguration somewhat like that which I witnessed on Thabor. When he went into the portico of the Basilica of Herod, majesty possessed him and he seemed taller than ever before and his eyes were swords of flame. He towered with wrath at what he beheld. He seized a rope from a crate and swung it with one hand while he overturned tables and cages with the other. The birds flew forth from their confinement, and circled higher and higher, like hosts of souls freed from the ties of earth.

No, Mary of Magdala; angels did not descend, but the doves were as spirits ascending. The face of the heavens was not rent, but the commerce of the earth was shattered. The Master looked as divine as when he was on the mount, while he purged the holy place. 'My house,' he cried to the money-changers, 'is a house of prayer and you have made it a den of thieves.' They cowered and fled at his rage. They seemed to know him for a king. Why, I've kept asking myself, did he reveal his royalty to the profiteers of Israel and withhold it from the pious who had acclaimed and accompanied him?"

Mary's face was lined, almost haggard, with perplexity. "Perhaps," she offered measuredly, "his might was the only language that the money-changers could understand."

"It could well have been," approved Peter, relieved. "I had not thought of that. All through the night, I've been walking, and mulling over many things. I am spent with restlessness and fear. The Lord is safe now in the house of Mary and Martha. I left him sleeping in a booth on the roof, and I tell you that, in the rays of a night-lamp of a star above him, his face had the smoothness of childhood. He was no longer the man of wrath who spread terror in the Temple; he was rather the boy of Nazareth or the little one of Bethlehem. Or so he appeared through the tears in my eyes. O Mary, his might is the might of God, but his meekness holds it in abeyance. For his Father, he is all zeal; for himself, he is utterly lacking in concern. How can we shield him? The sun of this season is marked with blood. While I have been sleepless with care, his enemies have been awake with design."

"Fear not," bade Mary, in the language of Rhea and the angels. But her quotation was empty, for the day of which she dreamed had not been, after all, quite the day at all. The king had not conquered Jerusalem, and Jerusalem had failed the king. Turning, she gazed on the city and paused to consider the irony of its attitudes. Yesterday it might have had everything for which it ever sighed. Today —

And a great pity for Jerusalem, still so much like what she herself had been, took hold of her. There the ancient metropolis stood, sheathed in the pink light of morning, yet sprawling like a tomb, tall and vast. With life and beauty all around, it chose death and ugliness. Just as here in gentle Bethany, the buds of fig-trees were opening there in the valleys of Kedron and Hinnon; oleanders were spreading their branches over the sweet and abundant waters of Siloam; poppies were striking their vivid red flames in numberless gardens; lavender, sweet peas and jasmine were scenting the shadow of David's wall. The breath of a fresh season was purling around the old sores and sadness, even as the warm invitation of the Master to newness of life; but Jerusalem, despite yesterday's demonstration, preferred her past and the pain of her accustomed ways. She took no hint from nature and the passage of winter into spring. She lay in her self-made sepulchre like a living corpse, dreaming a dream of death, rejecting the author of life, mouldering with memories rather than rising with vision.

And Mary shared the sorrow of him who, as Peter, breaking in on her preoccupation, was saying, had wept for the city that had not accepted the grace of weeping for itself. The city that wanted a true king and would not have him.

When she entered the house of Mary and Martha, Christ and his mother and his apostles were seated at a table, waiting. Jesus' eyes met hers with welcome and he motioned her to a place. And close to the woman who bore him. Mary felt that a light was shining on the wave of her emotion, bespeaking peace and patience. The wild beating in her breast subsided. Her hand sought the clasp of the mother's, and her head fell on the soft responsive shoulder.

Then the doorway darkened with many people, and shadows stretched their length across the floor.

"See," breathed the Magdalene to Mother Mary, her eyes brightening. "His friends far outnumber his enemies. These folk have come to form a living wall of protection around their Lord. The soul of Israel has at last awakened."

"Where is he?" the leader of the throng of visitors demanded, striding forth. "Our eyes would behold for themselves a sight that is unique. The wonder that Bethany and Jerusalem proclaim has trickled to our ears, and we have come from the Valley of the Jordan, journeying through the night, to see what we have heard."

"The witch of Endor conjured up the shade of the prophet Samuel," declared another, "but only divine power could evoke a body livingly from the grave."

"We know of the raising of the daughter of Jairus and the son of Naim's widow," said a third, "but those were cases of unburial. Lazarus is reported to have lain corrupting for days in the tomb. It is he that we have come to see."

The brother of Mary and Martha, who had been helping his sisters to serve Christ and the apostles, now stood forth. Thin and vague in his gray tunic, he seemed to be a presence emerging from the air. The aura of another life clung to him and he gave the impression of being poised between two spheres, belonging to the one by right and to the other by sufferance. There was no mark of decay on his skin, but its paleness was the gleamless paleness of the dead. His pupils were sparked pin-points in the rounded mildness of his eyes, and his white lips vibrated with a soft-spoken but earnest rebuke: "You have come so far to see so little! Is the wonder of the life that has been given to everyone of you, any less than the wonder of my returning to life? You should have more amazement at the throb in your own bosoms than at the fact that my heart beats again. Cannot God who creates life, renew it at will? Think of him and not of me. He called: I but obeyed. It is he that you should be seeking. Gaze not on me — a shade that lives again — but on him, the Lord of life and the conqueror of the tomb!" And he pointed his long slim finger at Jesus.

The visitors fell on their knees and touched the floor with their foreheads. Time stood still. The room was wrapped in the light and the soundlessness of eternity. The Magdalene could feel the beating of her heart. A fresh sense of the power of Jesus was upon her.

It was Judas who broke the spell. Rising, he spoke nervously to the prostrate visitors: "The morn has advanced, and only a few hours divide us from night. Our Master should have this brief time with his own."

The men lifted themselves up and slowly left the house — their gaze lingering not on Lazarus this time, but on Jesus.

But Mother Mary's glance was turned to Judas, and the Magdalene followed it. To her consternation, she saw a darkness in his face, as if the death that had passed from the body of Lazarus were finding an abode in his soul. He returned her stare and crooked a finger in indication that he would speak privately with her. Rising, she bowed to Christ and his mother and followed the man of Kerioth out of the room.

"I can talk freely with you," said he, when they were

[213]

beyond the threshold, "because you know from experience the strange labyrinths of life. There are snake-pits in my soul. Therein temptations writhe and hiss. At least they appear to me to be temptations one moment; but the next, I interpret them as worthy whisperings and stirrings. Lost in doubt am I. How can I find the peace that you have attained?"

"My peace," confessed Mary, "is as yet imperfect. If only our Master had yesterday been crowned!"

"You share my disappointment," said Judas, toying nervously with his beard. "We do understand each other. But the Master! There, O woman, is mystery. From it, I recoil."

"Life," uttered Mary, "is mystery. Yet we cling to it."

"I know, I know," irritably cried the man. "But we must have something more than mystery to live for —"

She noted the twitch that kept coming to his sallow cheek. He was not well.

"I have a dream," she reminded him. "I found it at Jesus' feet and his mother's side. But I, too, fear. It seems to me at times that I have mistaken, marred, it. Yet is my vision too fair to be revised or relinquished. I see my king clothed in a shining that makes the noon-day sun grow pale. Israel rising in the light like the dead from the tomb — all the land a Lazarus! The present poverty of our Lord, which it is our joy to share, a plain flower-stem that is destined one day to break into such a bloom as eyes have never yet seen!" Her upraised hands fell helplessly. "Words are too weak."

"I have a dream too," countered Judas. "It is twin to yours, only that clouds keep passing over it. Sometimes they are all I see."

Mary searched his drawn face for his meaning. "I began aright," he further unbosomed himself, "with a passion to have Jesus loved and accepted as the king of Israel. But as his works grew mightier, culminating in the resurrection of Lazarus' decomposed body — " His finger-tips pressed deep into the hollows in his cheeks and his shoulders quivered.

"Why be appalled at the very proof of glory to come?" she tried to rally him. "It is true that the sight of one who was dead, serving at table, cannot but shock our earthiness. And yet, is there not a soothing — a calm — to the brother of Mary and Martha? Does not his meekness invite us to be unafraid?"

"You follow me not," gloomed Judas. "I do not fear Lazarus so much as the fact that even such a powerful deed as our Master's has had so little effect. Lazarus himself minimizes it. Those men who, even now, were bowing to the floor, have departed but to forget."

"Whither turns your mind, O Judas?"

"I cannot say. But this I believe: The Lord must prove himself not only with miracles."

"You would have him — "

"Yes — rise up and strike down the enemies that his humility has multiplied!"

"He overturned the tables in the Temple and drove out the money-changers," defended the Magdalene, alert to the opportunity of doing this for one who had defended her.

"That was not enough. The money changers are little people. He must beard and shatter both the Sanhedrin and Rome."

Unable to resist the sweep of this argument, Mary could not but admit, "It would be glory indeed! It must come. But who can speed the Lord's action?"

"Now you catch my meaning," nodded Judas, rubbing his hands and eyeing her furtively. "If he were thrust before the court of Israel or Edom, he would have to show, beyond the shadow of a doubt, who he is; and the day of our people's deliverance from the sons of Hanan and the hordes of Rome would be at hand. That day has too long been delayed. We can wait no longer."

How could the Magdalene oppose a fever of longing that matched her own? She wanted Judas to go on, nor did she have to wait.

"Either Christ must confront his enemies," he offered emphatically, "or the good he has done for the people will have gone for naught. They are fickle. Tomorrow they will be following yet another Messiah."

"What would you do?"

"I would I really knew," faltered Judas, concealing and yet insinuating that he had sighted a course. "Oh, how quickly the scene would change, and with what gold and splendor the kingdom would begin, if — "

"Words curdle in your throat," observed Mary, troubled. "What are you trying to say?"

Still, with studied hesitancy, he fingered his thin red beard. "If Tullus were here!" he at length murmured, leaving his idea and all its implication to be finished in Mary's mind.

"Judas!"

"I mean it, woman. Tullus is an intimate friend of Pontius Pilate, a favorite of Herodias, and the chief pagan enemy of the Master." And he wheedled: "You can bring him."

The Magdalene's lips were white, and the look in her eyes made Judas cringe. "I would only have you hasten the establishment of the kingdom," he hurried to assuage. "Not until the pride of Rome locks horns with the power of Jesus will all the people know that a new ruler has truly risen in Israel. The moment your Roman comes to lay a hand on him — well, cannot you see it all? Our Master, with his authority over life and death and the elements, will show himself splendid against the foreign tyranny that has enslaved our people. He will drive the devils from the land, just as my namesake Judas, the son of Shaphan, once rid the Temple of the profane golden eagle that King Herod had permitted to be foisted there. That he can — and will — do all this, you doubt not. He is greater than a dozen Caesars."

"Yet has he said: 'Render to Caesar the things that are Caesar's,'" Mary parried against the obnoxious allure of what Iscariot was saying.

"Caesar's things are blood and tears. These has he spread over our innocent land, and these shall be turned back on his head. Our Master will call down fire and brimstone on the affronters of our nation even as Jehovah poured destruction on the cities of the plain. The time for vengeance has come. An eye for an eye — a tooth for a tooth — "

Mary was torn deep within. "Judas, I cannot do this thing, though the purpose be great," she had to cry out. "I have pleaded with both Herodias and Tullus for the Master, but must not betray him to either of them. His day is his own. We want it with all our souls, but have we a right to choose it for him? When he is ready — "

The face of the apostle grew thinner, and lightning plowed his eye.

"Must the groaning of Israel go on, when at last we have a leader who can bestow gladness?" he demanded. "Have not our unhappy people suffered more than enough? Edom is sucking our substance away. At this moment, the procurator is planning an aqueduct as an excuse to get his hands on the treasury of the Temple. With the tithes that the priests demand and the taxes that the Romans take, life is worthless for the poor whom Christ loves. Ah, he will thank us for bringing the agony to a turning point."

"Us?"

That one word, in a baleful flash, revealed to Mary the worst flaws of all Iscariot's scheming. He was placing his accent less on the interest of Israel than on himself, while inviting her to do the same; and he was presuming that the Master needed him more than he needed the Master. In horror and pity, she made no comment but walked hurriedly away, leaving him to his clouds, though still — in her own different way — sharing his dream.

His plea followed her: "Would you have me — one of the chosen twelve — go to the Sanhedrin against him?"

She did not even hear, in the intensity of her eagerness to be back at Mother Mary's side and to look directly into the eyes of Jesus.

Shortly after Mary returned to the company at table, a knock sounded at the door and she went with Philip to answer it. Certain Gentiles, standing there, requested, "We would see Christ."

Her quick spirit, depressed by the conversation with Judas, leapt at the realization that, even beyond the circle of Israel, the fame of the Master had spread. If he had friends without, how many more he must have within! And surely some of them — a great many — would prove firm. Yesterday's demonstration could not have been meaningless.

The Gentiles — a motley that included stalwart legionnaires from Jericho and bronzed Askelonites — entered, but huddled near the threshold, evidently ill at ease in so humble a dwelling that sheltered so celebrated a man, and taken back by the quiet and disarming presence of one

[218]

whom rumor had made more magnificent than Caesar. But his very first words surcharged them with a feeling that their eyes were about to witness great things.

"The hour is come," he announced, "that the son of man should be glorified."

What? Here — how — now? The Magdalene was stunned. Had yesterday's procession been only a prelude? Was this really the day? But Bethany was almost as lowly as Bethlehem! Could this humble house be selected for the royal ceremony, and the temple of Herod ignored? Could any people but the chosen few recognize Christ as the new king, in such a setting? Was Israel not even to know? Mary's dream, even in its very hour of reality, was worse than bedimmed; lost in wonderment which would never end. All the joy of Jesus' announcement mingled with utter confusion in her heart; a tumult in which the further words of her Lord were only murmurous and indistinct to her ears, though a strange note of sadness and a suggestion even of death, so inharmonious with cherished ideas of the day, tolled like a bell in a rising storm.

Then a rumble of thunder reverberated through the room. The walls shook, and a shadow, as of a pair of great golden wings, passed over all those present. The humbleness of Bethany seemed instantly changed to a grandeur exceeding the acme of Solomon's reign, and the plain chair of the Master sparkled and gleamed like mother-of-pearl.

"It is the majesty of my Father," explained Jesus, his face as lustrous as the star that illumined his birth.

The two Marys, with one accord, lifted up their gaze, for it appeared to their utterly alive fancy that the roof had been thrown open to the skies, and that hosts of angels were descending through the pearly blueness of air, and that the very thunder was mellowed into music with the rhythmic motion of lesser wings. Nearer and nearer, the heavenly hosts seemed to move; and all the refulgence of the sky, where a great break in the clouds had left a sheer avenue of glory, was trained, for Mary and the mother, on the room of Bethany, as once on the stable in Bethlehem. The Magdalene felt certain that, entering, the beings of another world circled the holy virgin as a queen and swathed her in reverence, just as a little child had years ago been enfolded in a long white veil.

Guided, as it were, by cherubim, and without the least command over her own action, yesterday's sinner left her place and stood beside Jesus. Taking the vial of nard from her bosom she — the woman of Magdala who had had many lovers and now loved one — raised the ointment with pale hands and let the shining drops fall slowly, solemnly, on the head of her king of kings.

18

In TULLUS' mansion, Mary lay listless. Against her fervent protest, the servant maids would let her do nothing for herself but went through the former ritual of bathing her body, combing her hair and confining its unruliness in a circlet of gems, draping her form in a silken tunic, and easing her weary feet into silver sandals. She refused the wine that they urged upon her. She yearned for the sympathetic girl who had quietly fostered her previous escape, and was further disheartened to learn that she was gone — suspected and dismissed to another establishment. She prayed that Tullus would soon appear, for every moment meant much and she longed for the meeting to be at an end. What she would or could do after it, she did not have strength enough to let herself think. Only by keeping the memory of Christ's mother in her consciousness, was she able to maintain a grasp on reason. "Mother, mother of Jesus," her soul was calling.

With an effort, she raised herself on an elbow, letting her feet dangle from the couch, and her sandals sparkled back to her forlorn gaze. It was five days since Christ had ridden triumphantly into Jerusalem, though it now seemed years ago. It was hard to make her befuddled mind realize that so lately she had annointed her king in the home at Bethany. How exultant she had been, as she walked down the road to Jerusalem! Something had flowed into her spirit while the nard flowed over his head. Never had her heart felt lighter or throbbed more gratefully and her feet barely touched the ground as she sped along with the joy of her determination to recruit an army — yes, an army — of friends in the city for Jesus. Ah, those were treasured moments on the way from Bethany; but now everything was changed. Already she had been a prisoner for three days and hence missed the significant unfolding of the life of the Master, every detail of which was precious and vital to her.

Tullus had kept her informed, but only to taunt her. He told her of the Nazarene celebrating the Passover with his apostles last evening, for his spies were everywhere, and of the plot to capture him. She shuddered as she recalled her own agony in those hours when the Roman, overwhelming in his uniform, paced up and down the room, pelting her reeling mind with words — words, first burning with passion, then blame, then blandishment, and at last threat. How she withstood him, she could not explain. Everything was against her resistance; even the soft clothes and the scent of the ointments that covered her, tormented her tired body to yield. All she could remember was her continual utterance, beneath her breath, of the names of the Master and his mother. Then the added torment of the Roman's insinuation that it was she who was sending Christ to his doom, exchanging his life for an instant of her own! She had seen the power of the Lord, and knew infallibly that he controlled life and death; but also she had seen how he refused to exercise that power to save himself, and the idea now possessed her that his was a kingdom that exceeded understanding even as much as it invited belief. Now, as she reviewed these days, it occurred to her that perhaps it had been his will that she thus be withdrawn from the rapid flow of events in order to be given time to gather together all the confused notions that had sprung from her love and zeal for the king and the kingdom. She remembered that one time, months ago, he had said to his apostles, in the midst of a busy day, "Let us go apart and rest awhile." In retrospect, her act of anointing him seemed to be, instead of the end, a mere beginning of the consecration that would be required of her. In a flash, all her life during the past year swept before her, and she felt a deep humility — a consciousness that her extraordinary privileges in the friendship of Jesus and his mother still left her the least of the lowly.

But into her inert form was creeping the impetuosity that had marked her entire career, and her listlessness departed. Rising to her feet, she strode across the room in a sudden access of realization, mingled with pride, that she had been privileged to see two phases of the Master's career accomplished. He had been honored and acclaimed in the streets of Jerusalem, as a king should be. He had been anointed by her own hand — moved by his will, as if an erstwhile sinner's repentance were heaven's most cherished balm. Now there remained a third stage which, truly, was the most necessary and essential of all. The king must ascend his throne. But where were his sceptre, his crown, and his royal raiment?

A shadow fell across the floor, spreading its length like a great dark hand. It caught Mary's eye, and she whirled about, her silken robe flowing away from her like an angry gesture and her gems glistening in the sun.

Tullus had noiselessly entered. His grim look gave way to admiration at the sight of the Magdalene, as queenly and desirable as ever before. His gaze trailed her from the crown of her head to the silver sandals, and he said softly: "Today my Cynthia is herself."

These words brought her back to the world of immediacy, and her spirit wilted as she murmured, "There is little left of me." Shaking her head, she glanced almost pleadingly at him. "No, Tullus, this is not I that you see. This is what your imagination would have me be. You make me wear these clothes, and keep me captive in this house, but my true home is at the feet of the Nazarene, and my richest garment is the mantle he gave me."

The Roman's jaw clamped shut and he brushed past her to gaze for a moment out the window. Then, turning around, he hurled at her the accusative question, "Are you still thinking of him?"

With some of her old fire, Mary flung back, "And why not? Of whom else should I think? Of you who waylaid me on the road from Bethany? — with your hirelings and your political power and all the other trappings by which you tried to turn your puny self into the semblance of a man."

Tullus winced under her lash and Mary, as if speaking to herself, muttered incredulously, "And he asks why I still think of the Master!" Limply she sank on the divan and buried her hands in her face.

Tullus, recovering from the first shock of the unexpected attack, stood before her with his feet spread apart and his arms folded over his breast. Once more he was the self-possessed Roman in his rich attire, and with a satisfaction he did not feel, he warned, "If you are still thinking of him, your thoughts are given to the dead." There was coldness in his voice as he continued, "This very day — yes, even this very hour — your infatuation shall cease on Calvary, unless — " He smiled sardonically. "Unless you can continue to love a corpse."

Mary was on her feet in an instant. But all the fight had left her, and anguish appeared in every line of her countenance "You mean — " She choked as she pressed out the words.

Irony fled Tullus, and his tone lowered at the sight of the woe in the face that he loved as much as he was capable of loving. He nodded. "Pilate has passed the sentence," he announced; then, as if waving away a meaningless incident, "Oh, he hedged and temporized; but your priests were arousing the people, and when someone shouted that he was no friend of Caesar's, the procurator washed his hands and gave in."

Mary's mind was reeling in a black and red void. "The people!" she scoffed. "Empty vessels into which the malignant few pour their hate."

She paced the room nervously, wringing her hands. "A few days ago, Jesus was acclaimed, and, if he willed, he could have taken his rightful place in Israel." She drew a hand over her face, reluctant to put a bitter fact into speech. "Now, just five sun-sets later, they abandon him." She could say no more and, once again, in a paroxysm of grief, she sank on the divan and wept bitterly.

Tullus gazed on her with mixed emotion. As a man of many affairs, he still believed that he knew how to handle her. In fact, it had always added zest to his association with women if they had spirit. He could persuade them when they were pouting, but now he was amazed, even as once before in Simon's house in Naim, to find himself helpless at the sight of a woman bent in sincere sorrow. A spark of his better nature — or was it something that seemed to pervade the very air these last few days and seared the soul with suggestion? — moved him to extend his arms to the Magdalene. As he leaned over and placed his hands upon her shoulders, she started. Looking up into his eyes, she begged through her tears, "What will they do — with him?"

Even before the Roman could answer, a sound came rolling into the room. It quickly grew louder and revealed itself as the clamor of a mob. It galvanized them both, and instinctively he raised her to her feet, and they walked quickly to the portal that opened onto the balcony. The volume of voices rose still higher, but, as yet, they could see only a surging mass of humanity. As Mary stared in apprehension, a spectacle suddenly drew her eyes to itself with taut strings of horror. Jesus, covered with blood and grime, bleeding from innumerable wounds, crowned with a crown of thorns, mocked with a reed in his roped hands, led by a halter around his neck, and staggering under a grewsome weight! *Crucifixion.*

The knowledge of his fate broke upon her like a tidal wave, and she felt herself going down into a sea of night. She held onto the balcony railing with a grip of steel until her finger-nails began to crack as they tried to bite into the stone. The sight of her was almost as tragic as that of Christ himself, and Tullus' face went pale as he held her up. Through the pounding of the forces engulfing her senses, the points of her recent meditation pushed their way. He was anointed king — he needed a crown, a sceptre, and royal raiment. The crown of thorns? The reed? The bloody garment adhering to his flesh? Mystery — mystery! But the veil was being rent. What was it that he once said? "I, if I be lifted up, will draw all things to me." She must go — she must go to him.

Arousing herself, she turned to the Roman with all the appeal she could command. "Oh, Tullus, I am beginning to see. He knew all this was to happen. There is something — something mystical — here." Clutching his arm with her right hand, she pressed her other against her heart and cried, "And I know that I must be with him." Then with a burst of feeling, "Tullus, if there is any goodness in you, let me go — let me go to him. It means everything to me."

The Roman regarded her silently, but persuasion continued to flow from her lips. "You were always more decent to me than the others. Sometimes I even felt you had an unselfish affection for me. Grant me this one wish, I beg of you!"

Never in all his travels throughout the world had he experienced anything like this. No one but Mary had ever belittled his wealth and preferred poverty. No one had ever repulsed his advances, much less his entreaties, for he had never entreated anyone but her before. Was he losing his manhood — or gaining it? Was it this mystical note she mentioned, that had put such foreign ideas in his mind these last few days? Certainly there was a baffling element in the whole affair, and the impression was being heightened for him by a sensation that the sunny balcony was growing suddenly dark.

He recalled his Mary of other days, and her appreciation of the finery which now she spurned. Now, a captive, she loathed what she welcomed then, and was willing to throw herself at the feet of one whose status was the lowest and who had never shown the slightest carnal desire for her. Perhaps there was more, much more, to life than the flesh. Perhaps —

The problem was too great for a psychology unused to speculation on a moral plane. He must have time to think things through.

He studied the honesty of her eyes and, for the first time in his life, there was a tone of selfless tenderness in his voice, muting his words almost to a whisper. "Go, Cynthia," he breathed. And as he turned her toward the door, he added, "Ask your king to uncover to me the riddle of his kingdom."

Without another word and with a gleam of gratitude, she dashed toward the stairway, picking up the Master's blue cloak as she sped through the room, tearing the gems from her hair, and leaving them ascatter on the thick-carpeted floor.

Back on the balcony, the Roman took one last look at that strange procession milling its way. He shook his head and re-entered his empty domain. Carefully he closed the Phoenician glass portal behind him, causing the room to become even gloomier than before. He noticed the massed shadows, but they suited his mood, for there was deep thinking to be done. He had to meet someone here, and the darkness would lessen the shock when they came face to face. It was that dire hour in which a man must confront himself and — perhaps — his God.

19

As in a dream, not of glory but dismay, Mary found herself with the mother in the procession marching to the hillock, bald and bleak, beyond the northeast corner of the city walls; the dread place of skulls — Calvary to the Romans and Golgotha to the Jews — where death wore no mask and the birds of the air stripped flesh from bones.

The very breath of hell assailed the nostrils as the crowd neared the site. A bluish miasma floated through the air from the swollen and bursting entrails of hideous, half-devoured corpses that had been hanging on crosses, insect-swarming and gore-encrusted, for days and nights. A vision as startling as that of Ezechial smote the sight. Gaunt and rotted skeletons; sockets draining on torn and leathern cheeks a green fluid that had once been eyes; tongues protruding at awful lengths out of ghastly clenched teeth from which the lips had curled back and withered away; shredded limbs twisted and frozen in all the distortions of final moments of despair; avid circles of vultures wheeling overhead, ravenous for the unspeakable, waiting; everything to outrage the gift of life and the gaze of the living! Satan's mind laid bare.

Mary and the mother endeavored to bar out this replica of the abyss by looking only on Jesus; but all the tragedy of the body-sown hill, drenched and sodden with the evidence of man's worst inhumanity, was concentrated in his torment and reflected from it. Their every nerve was plucked and twisted.

Most of the Jews held back from ascending the hill; less from squeamishness, however, for they had grown all too used to Roman barbarity, than from the fact that to touch the bones of the dead would mean defilement. They let the blood and sweat-drenched figure crawl on between the shining spears of soldiers to the awful summit, while they stood and watched from the base. Only the mother and the Magdalene, together with Mary of Cleophas and the apostle John, who had espied and hastened to them, followed close behind.

The sun, in shame, had hidden itself behind a fulvous bank of clouds; and the air was as cold and heavy as death itself; and the women struggled for breath but scarcely dared to breathe. Here was the last outpost of human horror. And the Magdalene pondered: Just as in Bethlehem Christ had descended from the heights of heaven to the direst poverty of man, now on Calvary he was ascending to the peak of man's pain. What more could he do to prove the sincerity of his love and his love of sincerity? Mary slowly began to see. Poverty and pain, far less of the body than of the soul, were the wounds not only of Israel but the world; and by gathering all this deeper affliction unto himself and offering it to the Father, perhaps he was satisfying the divine justice, for the sins of the race, to the last farthing. Only God could repair the offenses of man against him; and the infinitude of the Master's suffering now seemed to the Magdalene a testament, even greater than his miracles, to his divinity. To have succeeded in saving him from all this — would it have been to thwart him? Was he bent on drinking his cup to the dregs? What else could he do for his kingdom, who would do his utmost, but give it his blood? Was he literally feeding the hunger of mankind with his very self, dying for the love of men even as he had lived for their enlightenment? Surely, if so, into the dullness of their minds and the sluggishness of their hearts would come, at least in time, the conviction that no love for them could ever be or ever have been greater than his! Here was a supreme sacrifice that afforded them a new bread, a new wine, to sate the famine and thirst that underlay existence. Here were merits that could clothe the nudity of their souls. Here the grace that could ornament the shabby innerness of their lives. Here the answer to the sigh of the ages. But here, too, a woe that Mary could not endure, however exalted the issues.

The soldiers removed the cross from his shoulder and from that of the man who had been forced to help him carry it. They placed it to one side, while they jostled Christ to his feet and ripped off his single garment, almost one with his wounds, which his mother had woven in another world — the little realm of Nazareth — and into which she had spun her dreams. Dreams of her son's happiness and success and acceptance. Dreams such as mothers have ever dreamed since the race began. And now this nightmare of stark reality!

The rude act had opened the weals in his skin anew and taken away bits of his flesh. Tottering there, clothed only in agony and outrage, he wrung the hearts of the faithful few. Mary Magdalene pleaded with the nearest Roman to have the tattered robe returned to the Master's nakedness, and he was not too insensate to refuse, but only indifferently did he wrap it around the loins.

Then, like carrion, Jesus was flung backward on the cross. A kneeling soldier seized the head in his two hairy paws, lifted it slightly, and bashed it down on the harsh wood with a sound of crackling bone and fibre. It always facilitated an execution, if the victim were stunned and thus prevented from writhing. The Magdalene clung to the mother, her throat taut with the shriek that was too terrible to come.

Dull blows resounded; blows of the hammer on the heads of spikes and on the hearts of the loving. A hole had been dug in the evil soil, and now the cross, with both hands of the living victim nailed to it, was tilted up by means of knotted ropes. It teetered for a moment and almost crashed before the men succeeded in affixing it. On the *sedile* or rest, which projected from the lower part of the instrument, Christ's feet were placed, the one over the other, and prised with a special iron piece to keep the trunk from ripping away from the upper limbs. The broken tissues of the palms and feet were three fountains. The teeth were buried in the underlip. The eyes half rolled from their sockets like great garnet marbles.

Mary Magdalene looked from the face of the Master to that of the mother, and found every line repeated in her anguish. *They were crucifying not only the son but the woman that bore him.*

Two thieves were crucified with Jesus.

A Pharisee, coming close to the central cross, threw up his hands and voice in such an extreme of derision at the victim that one could see that he had had to swallow his true emotion in order to express the false. "Between two thieves!" he gloated. "Thus is the Nazarene duly dishonored!"

Mary turned her eyes and glared at him, contemptuous and unafraid of his person but angered by his words. "See you not," she almost shrilled, with ringing asperity, "that, in thus dishonoring Christ, the Sanhedrin and Pontius Pilate have signally honored two thieves?"

She would have said more, but the mother's hand, pressing her arm, withheld her.

The Pharisee moved away.

Tenebrous gloom spread over Golgotha, as if the Prince of Darkness, poised between the sky and the earth, were flinging his pinions wide in a sweep of triumph. The chill of a strange vapor beaded the foreheads of the spectators, while the density of it oppressed their breathing and coated their eyes with its dull gray milk. The coarse jeers and gibes of the soldiers and the murmuring of the chief priests and Pharisees, utterly forced, had died away. A silence, louder than sound for the mother and the Magdalene, fell on the hill; and in it they could hear the dripping of blood and feel the wild beating and straining of the greatest of hearts.

Hate, darker than in the days of her reprobation, assaulted the soul of the Magdalene. Hate for those who had nailed love to a cross. Hate for the guilt that was throttling guiltlessness. Hate for a humanity that could be so inhumane. Hate for the perversity that had chosen darkness and rejected the light. Hate for herself as a member of the race that had received the blessings of God only to crush the God of blessings. Hate for the monstrous crime of Israel, for whose restoration she had often prayed. All the faith and the charity that she had acquired in the period of her finding and knowing the Master, and in the company of the mother, were yielding to the siege of this most fatal of hours. A curse was springing to her lips. A moment more and it would have been uttered.

But a voice was coming from the cross; mournful, deep, meek, and soulful. The same voice that had expelled demons, and was doing so yet again. The assailants of Mary's spirit fled at the sound and left no hate, but the beginning of an endless pity, in her breast. "Father, forgive them," the dying Jesus was saying. And not only was he pleading with heaven for his murderers, but offering an excuse for them: "They know not what they do."

"If you are Christ," snarled one of the thieves, mad with pain, "pray not to God to forgive these two-legged beasts. They know what they are doing. They are making us die a hundred deaths. Save yourself and us."

"We die justly," groaned the other, looking down at the pale, upturned face of the mother who stood beside the central cross, and knowing that the off-spring of such beauty must have been goodness. "But this man has done no wrong."

Moved to sympathy for the criminal, Mary Magdalene begged Mother Mary: "Pray for him."

"I am praying for him," was the almost inaudible reply.

Once more the man spoke, his gasping breath dwindling to a stammer. "Lord, remember me when you come into your kingdom."

And Jesus promised: "This day you shall be with me in paradise."

This day of wrath — was it to end in heaven? Was its darkness to dissolve in light, its misery in joy, its shame in glory? Was the extreme of suffering thus near to the supremacy of hope? Was Calvary not a mound of death but a threshold to life? Would this be heaven's victory over Satan?

The soul of the Magdalene stirred.

A tear, the first, sparkled in the mother's eye.

And over the troubled countenance of the repentant thief, a peace was stealing. "In paradise?" he cried, twisting his head and fixing his blood-shot eyes with all the

ardor of his being on the personification of love itself.
"Lord, am I not already there?"

Mary Magdalene, envying the man the privilege of
dying with Jesus and entering with him into happiness,
found herself silently supplicating the Master for a share
in this favor. What purpose in life could she have, with
the beloved gone? The road ahead wound empty and
appalling.

Again the Saviour was speaking. He had forgiven all
his enemies and besought the Father likewise to forgive
them. He had pledged blessedness to a poor comrade in
wretchedness. He must now address his dearest one whom
he was leaving behind, here on earth, to mother the kingdom even as she had mothered the king.

"Mother," he called from his throne of affliction, "behold your son." And to the apostle John, whom he cherished above the rest, he gave the command, "Son, behold
your mother."

His faint breath ended in a long low sigh. A sigh
which, in its lingering, seemed to Mary to have a special
meaning.

The face of Jesus had shrunken. Contracted with suffering, his whole body, spare and delicate as ivory, with its
streaks of red mercifully subdued in the mist, was almost
childlike. And Mary Magdalene thought of young Josue
whom King Herod had martyred, and then of her own
little Joas. Joas on whom she had lavished her first affection
and without whom her life had so long been an aching
void. Joas, the innocent victim, was like Jesus; Jesus, like
Joas. And the silence of the Crucified spoke to Mary's
soul: "Sister, behold your brother."

One of the chief pangs of crucifixion was the extreme

thirst. The Psalmist, foretelling the passion of the Messias, had written: "My strength is dried up like a potsherd and my tongue has cleaved to my jaws." Mary conned the dour words, as she watched the working of the Master's chest and the drooping of his chin. It was not in her nature to stand by helplessly when anything could possibly be done; so, tearing off her mantle which had been his, she offered it to a soldier in exchange for a little water with which to relieve the discolored lips. He shook his head. "There is no water to be had," he gruffly told her.

"I thirst!" gasped the dying.

"Give what you have," Mary almost screamed in her desperation. "Anything — anything to lessen the burning."

A vessel of grape-must mingled with myrrh — the brew which the Sanhedrin permitted to be administered to the condemned for the purpose of stupefying the senses — was at hand. The soldier dipped a sponge in the bitterness and raised it to Jesus. It was fire added to fire. It was the fulfillment of the prophetic lament: "In my thirst they gave me vinegar to drink."

Mary would have dashed the sponge from the soldier's hand, save that the mother's touch was again on her wrist, conveying a worldless restraint. The Master was yearning not for liquid to slake his bodily thirst. His love was calling for love. He was panting for the living waters of the spirit.

And Mary lifted the brimming chalice of her heart to him.

He seemed to quaff it. The heavy breathing grew calmer. The cracked and foaming lips tried to smile. The head fell once more on the breast as if in acknowledgment, and a ray of light struggled through the clotted eyes as if in thanks.

The darkness thickened. Two lictors ignited some torches and spaced them around the three crosses; but the tawny tongues of flame could not leap high in the viscous air and their light was but a lesser dinginess. All nature, bereft, lay under a pall. Not a breeze was stirring, and the odor of death encompassed the hill in suggestion that every grave in Jerusalem was belching forth its secrets. Lower and lower the vultures swung. Tighter and tighter the arms of the Evil One encircled Golgotha.

The soldier to whom the Magdalene had offered a bribe, seized the robe that girded the Master's loins and tossed it to his comrades for a diversion against the weirdness of this most unusual of executions. They could distract themselves a little by casting lots for it. Mary tried to reach and grasp it away but a blow on her shoulder sent her reeling back.

"My God, my God," cried out Jesus in his utter nakedness and desecration, "why have you forsaken me?"

The agony of the ages pulsed in the question; the sacred humanity had come to the last door of endurance; pain could go no farther. Mary Magdalene sank to the earth, clutching the soil of Calvary with her bare fists, tearing her hair, trying to gather some small part of the Master's desolation into her flesh, calling on the mound to cover her, bedewing the foot of the cross with her tears even as she had once bedewed the feet of him who was now dying.

The mother's hands could not reach Jesus' head. So, kneeling, she lifted that of the Magdalene and pressed it, in lieu of his, to her breast.

Once the Romans had crucified ten thousand Jews in Jerusalem and thus reared a forest of crosses and turned the city into one tremendous wail. Yet had they slain only men. Now were men killing more than the race — the Master.

There was night over all the earth, for the eyes of nature had dimmed.

There was sadness over all the earth, for the heart of nature was breaking.

The earth quaked, and the rocks of Golgotha were rent, for the heart of nature had broken.

"It is finished."

The mother's cheek, whiter than the asphodels of Nazareth, touched the holy tree. A warm breeze, redolent of gardens, penetrated the icy air. Mary Magdalene was minded of a little grave in Galilee, alive with flowers, where the child Samuel, who had breathed his last in Jesus' arms, lay sleeping; and she prayed that the Lord himself might now rest in the embrace of his Father.

A rift through the clouds made a deep cleft in the sky. The last door had opened. "Father," throbbed his voice, as meagre as that of a tired child, and then suddenly loud with longing, "into your hands, I commend my spirit."

Mary raised her tear-stained face in the light. At last her understanding was complete. The evidence seemed as clear as the waters of Cana which had once reddened into wine; and she blushed that it had taken her so long to see the crystal truth. His kingdom was not greatness but goodness; not exterior pomp but interior perfection; not the restoration of an earthly Israel but the foundation of a ghostly one. Earth had had and would have its Herods, proud, selfish, cruel, decadent; and multitudes had writhed and would writhe under their sway; but here was the kind of king, the only kind, that could rule hearts and, with his very wounds, heal them. She had once believed that his birth brought death, but now knew that his death meant life; the only life worth living; the life of the spirit. And the living spirit was love.

Her mind reverted, over the long stretch of years, to the hill-side of Bethlehem where shepherds still watched their flocks, and angels had linked two worlds, and a child was born. "He will be re-born over and over again," she told herself, "in the lives of the lowly, the contrite, the humble."

Another thought brought balm of Gilead to her soul: In the night of his nativity, a star had shone down from heaven to earth; and now, in the day of his deliverance, his perfect sacrifice, starlike, was shining up from earth to heaven.

Holding the hand of the mother, she rubbed her eyes. The unutterable horror of Calvary had melted away like a mist, even as all blood had drained from the snowy body, frail as a flake, that lay glimmering on the cross.

The king had entered his kingdom.

*   *   *

Two lilies — the one white, the other scarlet; the one straight in the sun, the other bending its head but curling its petals upward — reared their beauty in the wake of his glory. A pledge of an undying spring.

Finis